KEEPER

A BRITISH SPORTS ROMANCE NOVEL

AMY DAWS

Published by: Stars Hollow Publishing
ISBN: 978-1-944565-47-3

Editing: Stephanie Rose
Formatting: Champagne Book Design
Cover Design: Amy Daws

Dedicated to my author friend, Nana Malone.
Thank you for your endless guidance in this crazy world of books.
I'm "Keepering You" forever.

Homecoming

My Dearest Booker Harris,

I'm emailing to inform you that I'm moving back to London in a couple of weeks. Germany has been lovely, but I miss my home country.

I thought you might like to know. ;)

-Poppy

Miss Surprising Poppy McAdams,

Wait...wait...What? You're coming back? Where are you living? Why are you coming back? Did you get a new job? It's been six years since I laid eyes on you, and you inform me you're coming back via email? Call me sensitive, but is your mobile broken?

-Booker

Mr. Detail Manwhore,

You would have been able to lay eyes on me if you had that thing called Facebook. Or Instagram. Or Twitter. What kind of twenty-five-year-old bloke doesn't have social media?

p.s. I would have called, but I'm more pithy via email and that annoys you, so just enjoy it. ;)

-Poppy

Miss Pithy,

Social media is annoying. And let's face it, once you've seen one dick pic, you've seen them all.

-Booker

Mr. Dick Pic?

Funny, I would have thought as a famous footy player, you'd get more tit pics than dick pics. Maybe some dirty knickers…That sort of thing. My mind could go wild with possibilities.

-Poppy

Miss Active Imagination,

It's those possibilities that keep me off social media for good. Plus, I enjoy being mysterious. ;)

So, where are you staying? New job?

-Booker

Mr. Persistent Detail Manwhore,

It pains me to say this, but I'm going to stay with the parental units for a couple of months. And you guessed it. I got a job teaching German to Year 7's at a private school in Hoxton. I start in September.

However, the school also offered me a night class position teaching English as a foreign language in their learning annex in Shoreditch. Another teacher backed out last minute and the money is too good to pass up, so I'm coming home early. I'll be a proper Chigwell commuter bee from May until my flat opens up in July.

-Poppy

Miss Commuter Bee,

You're going to commute from Chigwell? You'll have to take a train or bus and then transfer to the Tube. That'll probably take at least an hour. You'll have to get a car.

-Booker

Mr. Read Between the Lines,

Money is tight. That's why I'm coming back early for the great-paying secondary job. Travelling the world and higher education is hard on a savings account. ;)

-Poppy

Miss Low Funds,

Taking the train or bus at night doesn't sound very safe. Haven't you heard any of those human trafficking horror stories? I recently attended a charity event about it, and I couldn't sleep for weeks. You'll stay with me.

-Booker

Mr. Confusing,

How would staying IN CHIGWELL at your dad's be any better than my parents'? Have you forgotten we're neighbours? I've been gone a while, but my memory is apparently far superior to yours.

-Poppy

Miss Destiny,

I'm moving, literally in two weeks. Vi found a flat for me in Shoreditch of all places. This couldn't be more perfect and you know it.

-Booker

Mr. Newsworthy,

You're finally moving out of your dad's! Go you! Congratulations! Maybe now you'll have a bit of a life outside of football.

-Poppy

Miss Flatmate,

Don't avoid the offer. You're staying with me and that's all there is to it.

-Booker

Mr. Bossy Booker,

I know we've known each other forever, but two months is a long time to stay with someone you haven't seen in SIX YEARS!

-Poppy

Miss FLATMATE,

You're still my best friend. You may have buggered off to Germany for far too long, but nothing changes that fact. You staying with me until your flat opens up is destiny's way of giving us an opportunity to rekindle our friendship. Also, rent will be highly competitive. I accept payment in the form of hugs.

-Booker

Mr. Cheesy,

Who are you and what have you done with my best mate, Booker Harris? I thought you only hugged me when I cried. Where's the brooding little boy who used sticks to pick the dirt out from under his fingernails?

-Poppy

Miss Denial,

You'll be pleased to know that my personal hygiene has improved immensely since primary school, which should make paying rent more enjoyable. Plus, I'll say whatever is necessary to keep you from commuting night after night. Poppy. I'm not kidding. This is East London. You're staying with me and I don't want to hear any more argument.

-Booker

Mr. Practical,

I hope you know what you're offering. You do remember what I'm like, right?

-Poppy

Miss Poppy,

I fully expect to hear you singing in the shower.

-Booker a.k.a. Your Future Flatmate, even though you won't admit it yet

Flatmates

Booker

"**A**RE YOU TWO GOING TO HELP ME UNPACK, OR ARE YOU JUST here for wanker-colour commentary?" I drop a huge box of pots and pans on the French oak flooring in the kitchen of my new flat. It's not the biggest flat in the neighbourhood, but it's situated in the heart of Shoreditch Triangle, London, which is a great spot to be. Plus, it's been completely renovated and updated with modern finishings, so I really like it.

My brother Camden drops down off the counter he was perched upon. "Booker! Did you see your kitchen has two ovens?"

"Not that the prat can actually cook." My other brother, Tanner, adds as he opens and closes the oven doors like they're objects from outer space. "Living with Dad for twenty-five years has spoiled the child."

"You guys lived with him just as long as I did!" I argue.

Camden ignores my completely valid point as he hitches his voice to do his imitation of the Queen that he thinks is so hilarious. "My Baby Booker gets a cook and a housekeeper for as long as he likes."

"And Baby Book will never touch a dirty laundry item. We have people for that!" Tanner chirps, mimicking the same pitch.

Camden shakes his finger. "Baby Book shan't drive himself to practice."

"Or wipe his own arse after a code brown round." Tanner's last jab sends Cam into a fit of laughter, and the two high five like the tossers they are.

I roll my eyes and ignore them like I have for most of my life. There's no use fighting with these two. Firstly, they are twins, so they will *always* gang up on me. Secondly, my brothers and I know that living at home with Dad had major perks.

Our family home is on the outskirts of London in Chigwell. It's a large, brown brick mansion that was quite sparse most of our lives. But when our dad, Vaughn Harris, took the managing job with Bethnal Green F.C. and my three brothers and I started playing for him, he did some renovations. Now it's kitted out like a footballer's dream come true, complete with an in-home gym and stationary goals outside. Our sister had no interest in playing, so she got her restaurant-quality kitchen, where she was happy to work her way through our mum's old cookbooks and support all our football endeavours.

Growing up was all about hat-tricks, penalties, and the full-time whistle. We were a football family. End of.

As adults, we're more the same. Camden plays for Arsenal while Tanner and I continue to bleed green and white for our dad's team. Our older brother, Gareth, is a defender for Man U, and Vi is currently enjoying the life of being a new mummy to her six-month-old surprise baby she had last year.

However, being surrounded by footy fanatics isn't easy. I have to work harder than all of them to keep from embarrassing the Harris name. My whole life, my brothers have seemed bigger and stronger than me, drilling balls at me between the posts at superhuman speeds. But, despite my meek size as a child, I learned to appear larger than life in front of the net. It was survival.

Over the last few years, my body has finally caught up with my mind. At six-foot-one, I may still sit an inch or two shorter than my twin brothers, but I'm more than equipped for the position of goal-keeper now that I'm nearing thirteen stone.

"All right, where do you want me?" Camden groans amongst the sea of boxes.

I do a rapid survey of the space. Vi found me a fully furnished flat, which is nice because we didn't have to haul a ton of items up two floors. It also meant I didn't have to go shopping. "If we can get the kitchen sorted, that would be grand."

Tanner rips into a box and starts dropping spoons into a cutlery sorter. "I'll gladly get your kitchen sorted, broseph. Anything to get you to stop sofa-surfing at my place."

"I hardly sofa-surf," I argue half-heartedly. "I merely crash there on nights I don't feel like driving twenty minutes back to Dad's. And excuse me for wanting to spend some time with you guys."

"You cock-block, baby bro," Tanner retorts. "Morning sex with Belle is a lot harder when I can hear you through the walls taking a leak."

Camden flings a kitchen towel at my scowling face, but I catch it easily before it hits me. "Specs and I are actually trying to work our way through every room in the new house, and you are hindering that epic goal."

I shake my head. "It's still mind-boggling that you two managed to land girlfriends at all. The fact that they are both doctors makes me feel like at any minute, someone is going to come out and tell me I've been punk'd."

"Specs is *very* real." The lewd smirk on Camden's face forces me to look away.

Indie—or "Specs" as Cam calls her because of her love for funky eyewear—was a surgical resident at the Royal London Hospital when Camden tore his ACL last year. They fell hard and fast. Then somehow, Tanner ended up with Indie's best friend, whom is also a surgeon. Now, Indie is the Bethnal Green assistant team doctor, and

Belle is working under some famous feotal surgeon and preparing to wed herself to Tanner Sleazeball Harris. How these two knobheads ended up dating best friends who are as close as sisters is disturbing. These days, so much is changing in our family.

So yeah, I guess the sofa-surfing is a bit intentional. I don't want the fact that they're all starting families to change what makes the Harris family, the Harris family. We're Harrises. We're close. End of. I refuse to lose them.

Tanner drops a box by Camden and adds, "He'll stop inserting himself in our love lives now that he's going to be living with his girlfriend."

"Poppy is not my girlfriend," I deny as anxiety creeps up my shoulders over his words. "She's just…Poppy."

Getting her to agree to stay with me took some major convincing, but I'm nothing if not persistent. And selfishly, her living with me will help me worry about her a lot less.

"Your childhood best friend whom you've slept in the same bed with, created a secret love shack in the woods with, and still claim to have never shagged?" Tanner pins me with a look that says he wasn't born yesterday.

"It was a fort," I defend. "And she's only staying here until her lease opens up."

"Famous last words, baby bro," Tanner says. "Things can change quickly with girls. Look at me and Belle. I wanted to marry her after one month of being with her. She's the one who made us wait." He crosses his arms and leans back against the counter. "You'd be surprised how much fun sex with the right person can be."

I roll my eyes. "Just because you prats don't know how to have platonic relationships with women doesn't mean I don't." I get back to work on the remaining boxes.

Poppy has always just been Poppy. Despite what Camden and Tanner think, we never crossed that line of friendship and that has a lot to do with them. When I was little, I watched them break countless girls' hearts. Every time I started to get used to one of their girlfriends, they disappeared, never to be seen again. Then of course, I watched our dad mourn the death of our mum for years. It was brutal. So I learned that caring for someone romantically eventually meant losing them. And fuck me, I want to avoid that like the plague.

Poppy is too good of a friend for me to ever risk losing her. Truthfully, she's the only real friend I have who isn't family or teammates. When she up and moved away to Germany, I was gutted. We were best friends with plans to live in London and take the city by storm. Her with her infectious personality, me with my footy skills. It killed me when she said she was leaving, and I wasn't even in love with her. Imagine how bad it would have been if I had loved her.

After she left, I threw myself into football and did everything I could to shift my position from reserve keeper to first. I was consumed with ending that inferiority I felt in my life. It worked, too. Not long after her departure, my football career started taking off.

But all those experiences are why I keep the circle of people whom I truly care about small. Caring about too many people increases the chance of suffering that gut-aching loss.

Now, Poppy is back. Sure it's been six years since I've laid eyes on her. We also didn't part on the best of terms, but we've gradually started emailing and texting more over the years. Phone calls occasionally. We've been slowly getting back to Booker and Poppy, which is good because it's always felt completely mental that we haven't seen each other in all this time. I suppose I could have visited her in Germany, but she was so closed off about her life over there, I could tell she didn't want me to. Even her timing when she came home for Christmas seemed intentional because I always happened to be playing elsewhere. It felt like the Great Wall of China was separating us instead of a two-hour plane ride. I hated it.

I'm practically vibrating from the anticipation of wrapping my arms around her again. In the flesh. My best mate. She's coming back at the perfect time, too. My family is rapidly changing all around me, making me feel unsteady. I've never been good with change, so I'm chuffed to bits to have my best friend by my side again.

I still remember the exact day I met her. It was such a tense time for my family. Dad was emotionally AWOL after Mum died. Vi was merely a kid herself and trying to take care of everyone. Gareth was a moody sod. We were all so alone in that house and, being the youngest, I felt like no one ever heard me.

When I look back, I realise it was Poppy that helped me find my voice, even if it was because she asked me to sing with her every single day.

Booker

7 Years Old

"I hate you, Tanner! I hate you!" I scream as I run out the back gate of our garden and into the woods behind our house. My big sister, Vi, is screaming for me to come back. The way her voice sounds makes my chest hurt, but I don't stop. I can't stop. I want to run until I disappear from the whole world.

After I run for a long time, the pain from my bloody nose starts to make me cough, so I stop and rest. I sit on a large tree I find that's tipped over. I wipe my nose off with my sleeve. It hurts so much that my eyes water, but I'm not crying. I'm too mad to cry.

Tanner always makes me be the goalie. Then he waits until Vi's not looking to kick the ball at me as hard as he can. I hate him! One day, I'm going to be as big as Tanner and Camden, and I'm going to stop all their stupid balls from getting in the net so they never score a goal ever again. Then they won't be able to cheer like stupid monkeys.

"Stupid bloody Tanner," I grind through my teeth.

"Bloody better describes that crud on your face."

I jump up to my feet when I see a girl I know from school standing in front of me with a black dog next to her.

"What are you doing here?" I moan, out of breath from my run. I look all around to make sure no one else is here with her. If there are more girls from my class here, I'm going to kill Tanner.

"I could ask you the same thing." She crosses her bony arms and wrinkles her nose at me. She's dressed in a bright yellow sundress that's covered in mud, and her long blonde hair is dirty and full of sticks and tangles. "You're sitting on my stage." She points to the tipped over tree.

"I'm not sitting anywhere." I look behind me.

"Well, you were sitting on my singing stage." She reaches down to pet her dog. "Me and Pink were getting ready to perform our third act of the day, but I had to take a piddle break."

"What are you talking about? Who's Pink?"

She rolls her eyes. "My dog. Duh."

I look down at the black dog. "Your dog is black."

Her eyes pop out of her head. Then she kneels down to cover the dog's ears. He licks her cheek when she whispers loud enough for me to hear, "He doesn't need to know that!"

I frown and start to walk away because this girl is weird.

"You're in my class," she says with a scratchy voice. I roll my eyes and keep walking. "We're also neighbours," she adds, and I stop to look at her again. "My house is on the other side of this park. Your house is right there."

"Why are you telling me this?"

She shrugs. "We could be mates."

"But you're a girl."

She squeals and quickly covers her own ears. "You're spoiling all the best secrets today!"

Her funny face makes me laugh. It feels good to laugh. Tanner and Camden only make me mad. They always play too rough, and they are so fast that I can never catch them. Why do they always run from me?

This girl's not running from me. She's standing really still. I think I like her. I feel different around her, that's for sure. She looks at me like she likes me, too. Not like I'm an annoying little brother.

"We could sing together," she says, letting go of her ears and petting her dog with one hand.

"I don't sing," I grumble.

Her lips pucker like a fish. "Well, what do you like to do?"

I kick at a stick. "I like to build things sometimes."

"Want to build a fort? I've been wanting to build a backstage, and you look like you'd be a very strong stagehand!"

I shrug my shoulders because she's so annoying. "I am pretty strong."

She smiles really big. "It shows. But first, do you mind if I sing while we build? I find singing soothes Pink's troubled soul."

"Erm…sure, fine."

She hands me a stick. "I'm Poppy McAdams. It's nice to meet you, Booker Harris."

Just as I finish unloading the dishes into the cupboard, a loud crash rips me out of my walk down memory lane.

"Oh, cockwomble! What have I smashed?" A husky female voice comes from the hallway on the other side of my flat door. Camden, Tanner, and I stare at each other for a brief second before rushing toward the door to see what all the commotion is about.

My brothers get there first, blocking my view with their giant frames. I see a couple boxes tipped over on the landing—one open with the contents spilled out all over the place, including marbles that are rolling our way.

"Nobody move!" She sings the last word on a high note. "We have marbles on the floor and professional athletes at bay. Save yourselves. I can handle—" Her scream echoes off the brick walls as another crash happens, followed by a small yelp of pain. I can't take another second of this, so I shove Camden and Tanner aside and walk out to see the mess.

Poppy McAdams is sprawled out on the tiled hallway floor, her legs at an angle that makes me cringe and her arms clutching a tackle box of some sort. My eyes move up her body because I haven't seen her in so long. I have to do a double take to make sure it's actually her.

"Help her up, Book," Camden urges.

I quickly shake the stupor off my face and reach out to give her a hand. She stands slowly, avoiding my eyes as she surveys the mess and brushes the dirt off her cropped trousers.

Finally, with an exasperated sigh, she looks at me.

And even though I'm looking at her and I know she's Poppy, she seems completely different.

Gone is her long, stringy blonde hair. Her silky, platinum blonde locks are now short on the back and sides but still have length on the top that sweeps stunningly across her forehead. Never have I seen a short haircut make a girl look more feminine, but that's exactly what this haircut has done. Her cropped hair highlights her full lips and the arch of her cheekbones perfectly. She looks like a model.

My gaze drops to her body—once skinny and gangly and usually covered in dirt—and finds curves and angles where they'd never been before. And her eyes…Even her eyes are different. They've always been pretty, but somehow they grew into huge doe eyes. They're framed by impossibly long lashes, accentuating the green of them so much that they look almost inhuman.

"Booker!" She sings my name and reaches for me, nearly slipping again on a loose marble. I catch her in my arms and try to ignore the fact that she smells different as her hands wrap tightly behind my neck. "I can't believe it's been six years!"

My throat feels tight as I huff out an incredulous laugh. "Hiya, Poppy. I erm…hardly recognise you."

"Oh, Book, it's only a haircut." She pulls back much too soon and whacks me on the chest like we see each other every day and the earth isn't spinning off its axis right now. "I'm the same old blundering mess I've always been." She looks past me, still gripping my arms for balance as she skates her way to the doorway. "Well knock me over with a feather, look at the Harris Twins! All grown up and STD-free I assume since I hear you're both off the market?"

Cam and Tan chortle like morons. When she exchanges hugs with them, I take the opportunity to check out her backside because, well, I can't help it, I'm still floored. She never had an arse like that in secondary school.

"You've come a long way from singing show tunes in the park, Pop," Tanner says playfully as he ruffles her hair.

She beams. "Well, as you can see from the mess I've made, *some* things never change." She looks Tanner up and down and gives his beard a tug. "I'd say you've come a long way from shagging girls that snuck in through the conservatory."

"Camden did that, too!" Tanner defends, his hand against his chest in mock insult.

Camden's got his flirty voice on thick when he adds, "Had we known you'd grow up to be such a fox, we would have kept a closer watch on you."

He winks and Poppy's throaty laugh pierces through my chest. Annoyance creeps over me as I watch my two brothers blatantly flirt with her. It reminds me of all the other times in my life when they took the spotlight and left me in the shadows.

My voice is gruff when I interrupt. "If you two are done sexually harassing Poppy, maybe you could grab me a broom to clean up this mess."

Poppy's big round eyes slant in sympathy. "Sorry about all this, Booker. I guess it's good I leave the fancy footwork to you guys."

Camden returns and hands a broom over to me. "No worries, Pop. It's the strikers who have the golden feet, not the keeper. We'll let Booker clean this up while Tan and I help you with the rest of your stuff."

Poppy tries to argue, but the two idiots are already ushering her carefully over the marbles and down the stairs before I have a chance to catch a second glance of her.

That reunion did not go at all as I expected.

Like Brother and Sister

Poppy

I'M MOVING IN WITH BOOKER HARRIS. I'M MOVING IN WITH *Booker Harris! I'm…moving in with Booker Harris.* I sing the last bit in my head because then the statement seems to resonate a bit longer.

It still sounds peculiar, even in a B-flat.

I was prepared to take my time moving back to London when my lease started in July. But one good job offer later and here I am. In Booker's building. With his brothers. Like nothing's changed.

Booker's offer was awfully sweet and incredibly unexpected, especially considering the last time we saw each other was six years ago and it wasn't the best of goodbyes. But commuting would have been a nightmare, and his flat is very close to the school I'll be working at. It was silly of me to try and refuse.

Right?

Right.

That's totally it. Booker's my best friend and I haven't seen him since I was nineteen. What better way to reconnect with an old friend than to move in with him for an extended period of time when there's nowhere to run and hide?

Never mind that I'll have to share a bathroom with him. So what if I find bonk juice on the shower wall because he has to tug one out after a stressful match. It's no biggie if he catches me arse over tit as I'm attempting to shave my poop chute. Speaking of which, what happens when I have to poo? Or when he has to poo? We're mates, right? Totally cool! I won't mind a bit if he can hear the *ploop, ploop* of me backing a couple out.

Good God, how do couples do this?

How do they decide to cohabitate with each other? Booker and I aren't even in a relationship! But here we are, blazing right into this without a care in the world like it's a normal Sunday. Don't mind me. I'm only moving in with my best mate from childhood who happens to swing a penis between his thighs.

I'm going to have to hide my tampons.

This is easily the maddest thing I've done since I left London for University in Frankfurt for reasons I don't care to revisit. But there is a silver lining: I became fluent in German and earned my Master's in education. Now I'm able to help mould young minds and teach them the language of the country that birthed the Brothers Grimm, Beethoven, Mercedes-Benz, and Oktoberfest! Those reasons alone were totally worth flying across the English Channel.

I digress.

I'm back in London! This is what I've needed. Germany—while lovely and perfect for broadening my horizons—never felt like home. The French have a word for that feeling: Dépayser. To feel displaced from one's native land or familiar routine. I missed my home country.

And, despite myself, I missed Booker. He is still my best friend and losing him was really hard. So I'm going to take this time with him to reconnect. To help feel right again. He's convinced that living together will be like old times.

After one brief hug where I wrapped my arms around a large, twenty-five-year-old version of Booker—where I could feel the warmth of him, the firmness of his muscles, remember his scent and how he always hugged me whenever I was sad—I'm convinced that I can do this.

I'm no longer in love with Booker. We're best friends and nothing more, which is a relief because my eighteen-year-old self was a deluded cow. I almost ruined everything by sharing those silly feelings I thought I had. It was all so foolish. I was such an imaginative child that I had warped basic acts of friendship into acts of true love. Thank goodness I now know the difference.

Poppy
12 Years Old

"You there." I turn when a voice from somewhere in the night nearly scares the piss out of me. I see a tall, beautiful brunette with legs up to her armpits striding through the garden right for me. "What are you doing here?"

I quickly swipe away my tears and wipe my nose on my sleeve as she steps out of the darkness and under the motion light streaming over me. I've been standing at the backside of the grand Harris house for the past ten minutes, waiting for the painful ache in my chest to stop. Then I was going to climb the twenty-foot trellis into my best mate, Booker's room. Easy peasy, lemon squeezy. What's she doing here?

She peers down at me like I'm a hobbit and she's Gandalf the Grey. Her eyes follow the paths my residual tears left on my cheeks. I'm still rendered speechless. God, her hair is cool. It's cut into a short bob at her chin and makes her big boobs stand out like round dough balls.

Okay, that's a lie. Her hair has nothing to do with her boobies. But those are two very nice qualities she has, along with those spider legs of hers.

She laughs and it sounds like Christmas. "Do you speak?"

I push my blonde hair out of my face. I've been telling Mum for ages that I want to cut it. "Sometimes," I mutter, trying to sound cool. I think she buys it.

"Well, can you tell me why you're out here?" Her eye-lined eyes pierce me with judgement. Mum won't let me wear makeup either.

I point up to the window. "Erm…Booker is…erm…my mate."

She laughs again—that glorious peal of church bells. "Why didn't he tell you where the key is hidden?"

She bends over and lifts the rug in front of the door. Why didn't I think to look there? When she stands, she shows it to me with a grin, like we're sharing a special secret. I move over, and she inserts the key and turns the knob. She pauses on the threshold and looks back over her shoulder with her gaze narrowed. "How old are you?"

I consider lying and telling her I'm sixteen because that seems like the age when cool things start to happen to people. Instead, I blurt out the truth. "Twelve." I'm such an amateur.

She shakes her head. "A little young to be sneaking into a boy's room in the middle of the night, don't you think?"

Well, this would be a first. I consider telling her the real reason I'm here, but then the pain comes back in my throat and I think I might cry. So I change directions and ask, "Who are you here to see?"

"Tanner, though I'd happily visit Gareth or Camden if they were an option. Booker's a bit too young for me." She winks and giggles, so I giggle back. It seems like the polite thing to do.

"What about Vi?" Booker's sister is so nice. If I were older, I'd want to be her mate.

The girl smirks and whispers, "I'm not here for girl talk."

I whisper back, "Then what are you here for?"

She puckers her mouth and licks her lips like a serpent. "Never mind that. After you." She gestures for me to walk in and follows close behind me.

We pass through the dark conservatory and into the long

marble-floored hallway that leads to the front door. I've been in this house a million times, but it feels a bit different in the middle of the night. The Harris house isn't known for its warmth and comfort. Really, Booker comes to my house more than I come to his. But things have been different lately. Booker and his brothers are all practicing with the football club their dad manages, so I've been seeing less and less of him. I miss him.

I take a sharp left to climb the grand staircase. There's a dim lamp at the top of the stairs illuminating our path.

The girl whispers in my ear, "Stay to the right side on the steps. The rest of it creaks like Granny's rocking chair."

"Booker doesn't have a grandma." At least not one that I've ever seen.

The girl begins laughing in hushed tones, so I do as she says, only tripping twice because I activate my perfected James Bond MI6 stealth walk. I've tested it out with Booker in the park many times, and I know I look cool doing it.

When the girl and I complete the long climb, I watch her as she passes me, stopping at the first door on the right. "Toodles," she says with a wink and opens the door. I catch a peek of a shirtless Tanner laying on his bed with a lamp on. He looks up with a grin, obviously expecting her.

I shrug and tiptoe to the end of the hallway to Booker's room. I've been in his before, but for some reason, this plan seems so much scarier than it did a moment ago. But then the pain in my chest returns and all I want is my best friend.

Quietly, I open the door and catch a faint outline of Booker's bed as my eyes adjust to the lack of lighting in his room. "Booker," I whisper. He shoots up like a gun went off. He's always been a light sleeper.

"What is it? Who's there?" He ruffles the top of his dark mess of hair and shakes his head to wake himself up.

"Shhh! It's me, Poppy."

"Poppy?" he asks and swings his legs off the bed. "What are you *doing here? How did you get in?"*

"I was going to climb up to your window like a brave white knight, but a girl was here to see Tanner. She showed me where you guys hide the key, so I…walked in with her." Man that seems so much less dramatic than my original plan.

"Oh, okay," he states with little feeling. "What's up?"

He says the same welcoming phrase he says to me on any regular day, but after the night I've had, that simple question brings a quiver to my chin. "Book…" My voice cracks. "Pink died."

"Oh no, Poppy! How?" He rises up out of the bed and pads barefoot over to me in the dark. My arms are hugging myself as tightly around my middle as I can stand, but he manages to wrap me up even tighter. "What happened to him?"

I sniffle into his shirt. "I came home from piano lessons and Pink was going crazy, growling and nipping at me and my sister…It was like he didn't know us!" I stop talking to let out a few soft cries, and Booker begins rubbing my back in slow circles. I bury my face in his smooth, soft chest and have a proper cry before I tell him the rest. "Dad took him into his clinic and did some tests. He says it was a brain tumor and that Pink didn't know what he was doing. We had to put him to sleep, Booker. I watched the entire thing."

"You watched him put Pink to sleep?"

"Yes," I croak.

"But, why? That sounds awful."

I sniffle and wipe my nose on my shoulder before answering. "Gran always said that when you love someone enough, your sole purpose in life is to make sure they are good enough to get to Heaven. Pink always made sure I was good enough, so I had to be there to make sure God knew Pink was good enough, too." My voice trembles and a sob bubbles in my throat. When do I run out of tears? When I do, will I make more tears if I drink more water? I hate tears.

"Oh, Poppy," Booker soothes as he shuffles me over to his bed to sit down. I rest my head on his shoulder and he tucks me under his arm.

"He was a good dog and he definitely made it to Heaven."

"I don't know how Dad does that to dogs every day. Puts them to sleep. It's nothing like when they really sleep. His eyes stayed open. It's the grossest thing I've ever seen. I thought I wanted to be a veterinarian like Dad, but never again. I hate everything about that place."

Booker shushes me, and I stop sniffling for a moment so I can yawn. "Do you want to sleep over?" he asks.

I nod even though I know I shouldn't. Mum said a couple years ago that Booker and I couldn't have sleepovers anymore because we were getting too old. Yet she doesn't mind when I stay over at Emma's house. It's not fair.

I lie down on the edge of Booker's small bed and we face each other. Suddenly, he sits up and turns his bedside lamp on, casting the room in dim yellow light. I squint at his dark eyes as they pin me with sadness. "Sorry, I know you hate to sleep in the dark."

I smile and attempt to close my eyes, now comforted by the light shining on my lids and the warmth of him next to me. But Pink's eyes appear behind my lids. "I can't stop seeing Pink's sad little eyes, Booker. Who will make sure I make it to Heaven now?"

He exhales and wipes a tear running down my nose. "You have me for that, silly."

I follow the Harris Twins up the four flights of stairs to the second floor, watching them balance three boxes each to my one. They razz each other the entire way up, and I smile as memories of our childhood trickle in. Booker and I used to hide from Camden and Tanner all through the park, making up scenarios where we were chasing down bank robbers in a high-speed chase. We loved playing MI6, mostly because it let Booker be boyish and it let me use my imagination. He didn't even mind when I said that I had to sing in order to open up all the secret passages. It was fabulous.

I wonder if I can get Booker to sing now?

When we reenter the flat, Booker's standing in the middle of the living room. My eyes are instantly drawn to him, drinking in every square inch and noting all the subtle changes about him.

After tripping and spilling my shit all over, I never got a chance to really take in the sight of him. Of how much he's changed. How much he's matured. Now that I can, I notice how different he looks. True he still has that dark, tousled hair that curls at the ends when it needs a cut. And those smooth, curved facial features with dimple creases that will forever make him look more like a boy than a man. Even that tenderness he gets in his dark eyes lurks within.

It's all still there.

But now there's something else. Something more powerful. Maybe it's the way he stands with his arms bowed away from his sides as if he's ready to catch something. Or the thick muscles that line his shoulders to his neck. Or the satiny olive skin covering the veins down his forearms. He has a *presence* about him now. He feels larger than the room.

I swallow hard and barely hear Camden tell Booker they're going to leave because Cam has a team meeting. The boys wave their goodbyes to us, and the audible *click* of the door closing makes my mouth turn to cotton.

Not ready to meet Booker's dark eyes head-on, I twirl on my heel and begin rummaging through a couple boxes in the kitchen to find the gadgets I have to contribute. I didn't bring much because Booker informed me the flat came fully furnished. So my boxes consist mostly of clothes, toiletries, and a few odds and ends I thought we'd need.

I'm taking a mental inventory of everything I brought in a vain attempt to forget that we're alone now. Just me and Booker. *Booker and Poppy...sitting in a tree...K-I-S-S-I—*

My thoughts stop when I hear his footsteps approach behind

me. I steel myself and turn to look at him. He's smiling at me—that same boyish smile that's always a little bit soft around the edges, like he has a secret that no one else knows.

He crosses his arms and leans against the kitchen counter. "Poppy."

I smile and blow a piece of hair out of my eyes. "Booker."

"It's really good to see you, even if you do have a lot less hair than before." He narrows his eyes on me speculatively.

I shake my head so my fringe fans over my eyes. "Look. There's more than you think." I grab hold of the tresses in a fist. "It's still a good fistful."

His eyes widen. "And what were you getting up to in Germany that required enough hair to grab hold of?"

I release the locks and pin him with an odd look. Booker and I don't really talk about our romantic relationships. It's one area we've always avoided. Is that really where he's going with this line of questioning?

"Probably nothing different than what you get up to in England. Or wherever your football travels take you, I'm sure."

He quirks a sardonic brow. "What's that supposed to mean?"

"I mean, I'm sure you don't have to sleep alone very often, Book." He's not going to fool me into thinking he's been celibate these past few years that his football career has taken off. The Harris Brothers are a hot ticket item in London. I'm sure he hardly has to lift a finger for a shag.

He gets an awkward look on his face and then diverts his gaze to my boxes. "Tell me which boxes go to your bedroom."

Good change of subject, Book.

I bend over to shuffle a few toward him. He steps up close to me, brushing his arm against mine. "I'll get these. If you can believe it, I'm even stronger now, Pop." He winks and it makes me laugh.

"So I've noticed," I murmur, grabbing a smaller box and following behind him as he weaves through the flat. I'm not even ashamed to admit I'm totally staring at his arse in those loose-fitting jeans. It's like a peculiar time warp seeing him again, but now he's a man instead of a boy.

He talks me through the flat as we walk, showing me the drawer my keys are in, which will get me into the building, the flat, and the gym on the top floor. The space is cosy, but not small. It's quite perfect actually. The white-washed kitchen has a cute oak table and four white chairs that separate the space from the living room. The front room has a black leather sectional, a big screen, and modern double glazed windows that open up onto a large balcony.

I follow Booker down the hallway to the right of the living room. He points to the first door on the left that's the bathroom where I'll hopefully never have to poo, especially because it's so pretty. It's all glossy white tile with a funky modern sink that sits on top of the counter. And the glass walled shower tub…It's sexy as fuck. I just hope and pray neither of us ever defiles it.

He stops off at the next door on the left and says it's his room. All that sits in there amongst several boxes is a big bed, two nightstands, and two lamps. Halfway down the hall on the opposite side are bi-fold doors that contain a washer and dryer unit. Then, at the end of the hallway, he slides open a white pocket door.

"This is where you'll be staying. It's technically a den, so it's a bit small. But it has its own balcony, so I thought you might prefer it." He looks at me nervously and adds, "Of course if I'm wrong, just say the word and we'll switch."

I stride past him to the glass balcony door and swing it open, smiling as the smell of flowers breeze in like a dream. Fresh floral scent in the city of London. How in the world does one achieve that? It's positively magical. It makes me think of *The Sound of Music*, running through a meadow with dancing children frolicking all around.

"…smells like flowers all the time."

My head jerks at the sound of Booker's voice. "What? What were you saying? I didn't hear all that."

His eyes crinkle with a grin as he watches me. "I said the Columbia Road Flower Market takes place near here, so that's why it's so fragrant."

"It's lovely," I sigh. "This room is exquisite, Booker. Thank you." I eye the daybed along the wall. "I told you I have an air mattress. You didn't have to get me a bed."

"Yes I did," he murmurs and drops the boxes on the floor. "I wish it could be bigger, but—"

"It's perfect. Everything is perfect."

He smiles and looks around the room, stuffing his hands in his pockets and appearing a bit nervous all of the sudden. "Well, I've got unpacking to do as I'm sure you do, so I'll…leave you to it."

He slides the door closed as he leaves and I exhale heavily, not realising that I was holding my breath. This entire scenario may be more difficult than I thought. Sharing a bedroom wall with my best friend—whom I thought I was in love with—has the potential to be epically awesome…or epically awful.

It'll be awesome. I've decided.

I'm not the same girl I was six years ago. I've grown and matured. I've had real relationships, not figments of my imagination. I'm not *in love* with Booker Harris anymore. He's simply my best friend whom I'm excited to spend some time with again. This is great. We'll be like brother and sister!

The Perfect Fistful

Booker

A
FTER SEVERAL HOURS OF SOLITUDE, MY ROOM IS FINALLY A room. Clothes are in the wardrobe, toiletries are in the bathroom. I was able to fit all of my items on the vanity shelves behind the mirror, leaving the large cupboard beside it open for Poppy's items.

It'll be weird sharing a bathroom with a girl. Sure I grew up with a sister. But Vi had her own bathroom that we were never allowed to use, so I don't know how many items Poppy will have to store in there. All I know is that I need to do my best to put the toilet seat down so she doesn't fall in. Vi's been bashing me over the head about that for the past week since I told her Poppy is staying with me for a couple months.

I can handle this.

When I come out of my room to toss the empty boxes, a strange noise stops me in my tracks. It sounded like a tiny yelp coming from Poppy's room. I freeze to see if I hear it again and then the yelp morphs into a whimper. Alarmed, I eat up the small space between our bedroom doors. Without bothering to knock, I slide it open and look around quickly to see what's wrong.

Amongst a sea of cardboard boxes, I catch sight of Poppy on her knees, arse in the air with the top half of her body beneath the bed. She lets out a cry of pain.

"Poppy, are you all right?" I drop to my knees beside her and hesitate with my hands, not knowing where to put them on her for comfort since it's pretty much just her arse sticking out.

"No," she moans.

"What's happened?" I look under the bed and see her face red with pain and her hair tangled in the springs.

"My hair is stuck on the lovely bed you bought for me. I've been trying to free it for ages." Her voice wobbles with emotion. "I think I might have to cut it off, and I don't have that much hair left to begin with. I'm going to look like a boy."

I sit up from my position and try to stifle my laugh. My eyes roam the swells of her arse beneath the tight white trousers she's wearing. A nude lace thong peeks out the top. "You could *never* look like a boy."

"Well, are you going to sit there and feed me lies, or are you going to help me?" she exclaims.

Right. Help. She needs help. I flip over onto my back and pull myself under the bed beside her. Our eyes find each other in the dark. "You've really got a mess here, haven't you?" I begin plucking small strands of hair out of the frame as gently as possible.

"Yes. And my arse muscles are screaming because this position is not comfortable. Remind me to stop skipping leg days."

My brows raise. "You been working out, Pop?"

Her mouth opens in shock. "Yes! Diligently! I had a trainer and all that jazz. I'm disappointed you didn't notice!"

"Oh, I noticed," I murmur. Our eyes meet again and hold for a beat before I quickly refocus back on her hair that's now halfway free.

After a few seconds of silence, she states, "Lots about me is different now, Booker. You'd be surprised."

I inhale deeply, remembering the smell of her alone is different.

She used to always smell like flowers. Whatever perfume she's wearing now is decidedly more…sexy. "I believe it." I free a few more pieces of her hair. "I've almost got you all detached."

I pull the last bit and she shoots out from beneath the bed like a slingshot. "Oh, thank goodness," she sighs.

When my head pops out from under the bed, I catch her eyeing the bit of my stomach peeking out from where my shirt has ridden up. "It's quite obvious you've been working out, too, Book. You seem…massive now." She eyes me appreciatively.

I scoff but enjoy the fact that she noticed. "It kind of comes with the whole keeper thing. Most are big. And if you're not big, you have to appear big. It's an intimidation tactic more than it is about actual size, really. Plus, you've seen my brothers. I'm still playing catch-up."

She eyes my arms as I wrap them around my legs and lean my back against her bed. "I'd say you're on your way to passing them. Although, I liked you when you were a string bean like me."

She beams and I get a glimpse of the young girl that I used to play with in the woods. I hadn't realised how much I missed her until seeing her like this again. Happy. Smiling. She's still so bright and cheery, like always. There's been a void in my life these last few years, and I think it was the absence of her. *God I've missed her.*

"I'd say we've both changed." I smile back at her but then falter when I glance down at her breasts.

A quietness builds between us when our eyes lock and we familiarise ourselves with each other's faces again. It's weird to be looking at her so closely. I see her face and can think of all the fun times we had together growing up, yet she's different now, too. Matured. Beautiful.

She's first to break the intense trance when she rubs her hands together and moves to stand up. "Well, I'm about done here and I'm starved. What do you say we get into our comfies, order in some takeout, and get pissed?"

Her green eyes are ablaze with excitement, like this is her idea of the perfect evening. I don't usually drink much during the season, but considering my next match is local and I won't have to leave early to travel, I'll make an exception. I've always made lots of exceptions for Poppy.

I nod. "No practice tomorrow, so I'm game. Do you start your job tomorrow?"

"Nope," she chirps. "Not until Wednesday. I'm free to get rat-arsed and have a lie in."

I chuckle. "All right then. Since we're both free, let's have some fun. I'm just going to haul these boxes to the bin and shower. Then I'm all yours."

Her cheeks blush and I awkwardly tug at my earlobe at how that came out. God, I don't know why I'm being so unsmooth right now. It's just Poppy. Maybe a few drinks is exactly what we need to help us get back to being good old Booker and Poppy.

She gives me a playful shove as I stand up. "Prepare yourself, Harris. I've been living in Germany and those people know how to drink!"

Showered, shaved, and dressed in a pair of lounge pants and a white T-shirt, I make my way out of the bathroom and find Poppy in the kitchen rummaging through a box on the counter. She's got music playing from a small portable speaker and is moving to the beat like she's been living here for months. It's weird, but she's been here less than twelve hours and she makes my place feel more like home already. My eyes lower to her short grey running shorts, and I can't help but doubt her claim on skipping leg days at the gym. She has been putting in some serious time to have that kind of definition.

Hearing my approach, she turns and catches me checking out her calves. She shakes the two bottles in her hands and asks, "What do you say to a little cream soda and tequila?"

"Pass," I groan, my face crumpling. Just hearing her utter the words makes my stomach heave. "I still haven't recovered from the last time we drank that shit."

She giggles and it makes me smile. "Okay. Just tequila?"

I shake my head. "You've ruined me from tequila. Anything else, please."

"Oh my God, I hate tequila, too! It makes me so sad because tequila is the perfect party drink, but I'm always choking down margaritas. It's such a pity."

Chuckling, I reply, "Completely devastating. I'm more of a whiskey drinker now."

"Perfect!" she sings and turns back to her box of what appears to be loads of booze. I step up behind her to peer over her shoulder as she adds, "I have the most amazing whiskey tea drink! You're going to love it."

I inhale her scent one more time, feeling the aroma all the way down to my toes. I turn and hoist myself up on the counter beside her. "That's what you said about tequila and cream soda."

She rolls her eyes. "We were teenagers then, Booker. You can't blame me for my teen ideas. I was running on hormones back then."

My brows lift with interest. In all our years of friendship, we've never spoken much about our romantic experiences. Now that I haven't seen her for a while, I find myself more curious.

"This drink is different, I promise," she coos. "It's a proper recipe from the Teeling Whiskey Distillery in Dublin. A group of us went there on holiday once and we all fell in love."

She says "all" like she has a close-knit group of mates that I know nothing about. I've never had many friends. By choice mostly. Poppy's pretty much the only outsider I ever committed any time to. It's strange to think she's created this whole other life without me while she's been away. Sure we kept in touch via email and the occasional texting, but we never got into too many specific details.

It was more just talking about things we thought the other would find amusing or ridiculous. I did tell her when Vi had her baby, and she saw the papers when Tanner and Camden both had their media scandals this past year. Cam's wasn't quite as major as Tan's, but that's bloody twins for you—they have to do everything the same. Aside from that, our chats have been pretty impersonal.

Poppy dumps some ingredients into a shaker before grabbing a couple of rocks glasses from the cupboard. She cringes as she goes to the ice dispenser on the fridge and then thrusts a fist in the air when it spits out ice. "I wasn't sure there'd be ice in here since you just moved in and all. Did you know the key to a great mixed drink is lots of ice?"

Her face is so serious, I laugh and then laugh some more when she sticks her tongue out as she works. Poppy has always had this great way of turning the most mundane tasks into a show. Like her everyday life is a performing art.

I watch curiously as she pours the ruby mixture into the glasses. She seems to really know what she's doing. "Did you learn to bartend over there in Frankfurt, as well as become a bilinguist?"

She hands me one of the drinks and narrows her eyes. "Ja, habe ich." She winks and adds, "Yes, I did tend bar. It was a great way to meet people while being forced to learn the language. Although, most speak English around the campus, but they were happy to slip into German for me if I asked them sweetly."

"I'm sure there are not many people who would ever say no to you, Poppy." We clink glasses and take a drink. It's got a raspberry flavouring to it, but it's not overly sweet. The burn of the whiskey sets it off perfectly. "This is much better than tequila and cream soda."

Her giggle is adorable.

"How's your hair?" I ask as she hoists herself up beside me on the counter and runs her hand through the locks.

"It's fine, thanks to you." She takes a sip. "Good God, I was in a panic thinking I'd have to shave my head to get myself out of there."

"And then you thought you might look like a boy." I mimic her whiny tone and can't hold back my immature chortle.

She nudges me with her shoulder and then asks, "Do you remember that boy on the playground in primary school who said I sounded like a boy?"

I nearly choke on my drink. "I'd almost forgotten him! What a fucking wanker. What was his name again?"

"Giles Windsor." She gets a weird look on her face and drums her fingers on her dewy glass. "In all fairness, he was only nine. You were more upset than I was."

I puff out my chest in defense. "Well, he was ridiculous. He deserved the Harris Shakedown we gave him. You have a great voice."

"I have a raspy voice," she argues and licks a dribble of whiskey drink off the side of her glass. "I sound like Lindsay Lohan on a bender."

"You do not!" I argue and stare at her mouth as she licks her lips. "Your voice is sexy." My face heats. I've never used the word sexy to describe Poppy. I take another drink. How quickly things have shifted. To get the attention off of me, I add, "It makes you a brilliant singer, too."

Her eyes find mine as she laughs around the rim of her glass. "You would know. God, I can still remember singing at the very top of my lungs on that fallen tree when we played in the park. I can't believe you even liked hanging out with me. I was such an odd little duckling."

"You were normal compared to Cam and Tan."

She smirks and grabs the shaker to top off my drink that I didn't even realise I'd finished. "We had some great adventures growing up, didn't we?" She pins me with a twinkle in her green eyes. Man, they really pop out so much more. Must be because of her short hair.

I roll my glass in my hands and silently muse for a minute. "Except for that time we got caught by the park warden."

Her eyes fly wide. "Oh, I know! What a twat! None of the other wardens ever looked twice at us being back there after eight p.m. Then one tiny prick fopdoodle who flunked out of copper school thought he'd make an example of us. What a dick."

"You can say that again," I reply.

"What a dick!"

We both laugh and cheers and drink again, slipping back into the comfort of our memories.

Around a chunk of ice, Poppy adds, "That was the warden who wanted to break down our fort. Do you remember?"

I nod. "That was the first time my dad actually gave two shits about anything besides football. He completely reamed out the council about the wardens treating the park like the 'wild fucking west.'"

We both giggle at that. "This drink is good, Poppy."

She slides off the counter and throws her hands up in the air. "Redemption is mine!"

A song she likes comes on the radio at the same time, so she rushes over and cranks up the volume. She begins dancing with her drink in her hand and I can't help but laugh at her cheesy moves. To help set the mood, I reach back and flip the overhead light off in the kitchen. The room is cast in blue hues from the backsplash lighting, giving the perfect illusion of a nightclub.

"See, Book? Who needs to go out when we have all the fun we need right here?" She downs her drink and throws her hands above her head as she drops into a low squat. Her curves are accentuated with every move she makes. Curves that she had to have spent a lot of hours in the gym to achieve. She's completely lost her little girl features. Now she's powerful, like she could go all night.

Shaking my head, I slide off the counter and jiggle the martini shaker at her. "Show me how to make these so I can make the next round."

She shimmies over to the counter playfully, rubbing her butt on my hip as she makes quick work of explaining how much to measure out of each component. We're standing shoulder-to-shoulder. Or I should say shoulder-to-elbow. Poppy's maybe five-seven on a good day. Barefoot in the kitchen, she's lucky if she's hitting five-five.

"I think I can handle this," I say, but her smirk is saying otherwise. "You don't think I can?"

She takes a drink and draws closer to me, a challenging curve to her lips. The glossiness of her eyes sparkles in the dim blue lighting as she husks, "You never were much use in the kitchen, Booker."

I place my hands on my hips as she refills my drink. "Bartending isn't exactly high-level chef work."

"True, but it does require some math skills." She giggles as if she knows she's poking the bear.

"I was always great at numbers!" I exclaim, reaching out and giving her a cheeky squeeze on her side. "You were the one who was crap at them!"

"I've been cured," she says, laughing and squirming out of my reach. I want to tickle her more, but I hold back. "Two years of slinging drinks and flirting with customers for tips earned me an education in all things number-erical."

She slurs the last word. I'm not even sure it was a word. "Good Lord, you're going to be teaching English?"

"Numerical!" she bellows. "I know the word. It was simply a silly slip of the tongue." She leans into me and whispers, "Haven't you ever had a slip of the tongue, Booker?"

The way she says it makes my body react surprisingly. A rude thought involving my tongue on Poppy invades my mind. I quickly shake my head and say, "We should order some food."

"That we should," she says before she downs another drink. How many have we drunk now? I've lost track. "You can use my mobile. Go ahead and order for us. You know what I like."

She turns to head to the loo, and I momentarily realise I like the way she said "us." I like having a flatmate. Why would anybody ever want to live alone? Having a flatmate is loads more fun than eating by yourself over the kitchen counter. I think if I lived alone, I'd be like Vi and have a dog. Maybe not a big slobbering mutt like her dog, Bruce, but something small that I could talk to when I'm lonely.

The pizza takes forever to arrive. We've been on straight whiskey and water for the past hour, both becoming too impatient for the sweet tea concoction. I'm impressed that Poppy is keeping up with me drink for drink, but I'm a lightweight during the season.

When the food finally arrives, it's nearing ten o'clock, and we devour it like starved animals. I realise a bit too late that we could have used sustenance a while ago, but the hunger hasn't stopped our humourous walk down memory lane.

"I'm stuffed," I say, shoving the pizza box to the side of the coffee table and stretching out on the centre of the sectional sofa.

"Well, you ate six slices," Poppy jabs.

I frown. "Did I? I lost count." I quirk a brow at her. "I don't think I like your tone."

"No judgement! I lost count with these drinks." She shakes her tumbler and then sets it by the pizza box. Dropping down beside me on the couch, she rotates and presses her back to my shoulder. She kicks her muscular legs out and mirrors my position as she extends toward the other end of the sofa. She sighs, "This was fun. I much prefer this than going out on the town."

"Did you go out a lot in Frankfurt?" I ask because I'm still curious to hear more about her time over there. "Did those German blokes you flirted with for tips show you a nice time?"

She twists her head to frown up at me, puzzling her brows at my random question. "Are we really going to talk about this?"

I shrug because, well, now that I've opened the can, I don't really want to stuff it all back in. "Did you leave anyone behind broken hearted?"

"No," she murmurs and a tense silence stretches out before us. "What about you? You have a girlfriend I should know about?"

I roll my eyes. "I wouldn't have invited you to stay if I had a girlfriend."

"Why's that?"

"Because…look at you," I scoff.

That tense silence returns, but this time I can hear her breathing. I can feel the rise and fall of her shoulders as she leans against me.

Her voice is soft when she asks, "What do you mean, *look at you*?"

I tug on my earlobe, feeling a stirring in my stomach that doesn't have anything to do with the massive amounts of whiskey I consumed tonight. "I think it's quite obvious, Poppy. You're not merely a girl anymore. You're…a woman. And that haircut. I don't know. It just…suits you."

She turns her head up and looks at me curiously. I return her gaze, noting the light dusting of freckles across the bridge of her nose. I don't think I've ever noticed those before. She draws my eyes downward as she licks her lips and a warmth spreads between us.

All of the sudden, she sits up, pulling me out of the trance I have on her lips as she situates herself crisscross to face me. I inhale deeply as her hand slides into my hair right above my ear. "Looks like you could use a cut," she croaks, combing through the thick locks. I expect her to pull away, but she lingers, her scent wafting over me. My eyes fall closed as she slices through every strand and traces her fingertips along the nerve endings on my scalp, massaging in slow, languid movements.

God, that feels good.

My head nods to the side as I slur, "I've missed you, Poppy."

She exhales. "I've missed you, too, Booker."

"No, I mean, I've seriously *missed* you." Groaning from her touch, I add, "I put one of my lamps in your room. I know how you hate the dark."

Silence ensues, so my eyes lazily open and find she's watching me.

"I don't know why I said that just now," I husk.

Her hand falls away from my head, but I catch it with mine

because, well, I'm not ready for her to stop touching me yet. I want to be close to her like we always used to be.

I slide my fingers between hers, loving the softness of her hands against the hardness of mine, the smallness of hers against the largeness of mine. She feels so good against my skin. I never want to lose Poppy again. I've missed having her near me like this.

Aching for more, I pull her to me. Her legs unfold as she tucks into my chest, one hand over my heart, the other still entwined with mine. She nestles into me like she did when we were kids and she'd been crying about one of the many animals that died at her dad's clinic.

Pressing her nose into my chest, her shoulders rise as she inhales deeply. I can feel her warm breath through the fabric of my shirt and it feels *good*. Really good. I want her mouth to open so her breath goes from warm to hot. I want her lips to part, and I want to feel her tongue on my body. On me. Flesh against flesh.

I crook my finger beneath her chin and lift her face to mine. She looks beautiful. Familiar and comfortable, like a memory that I once lost. I lower my head so we're eye-to-eye and softly brush her lips with mine. It's a kiss of friendship. Of history. Of knowing someone so completely that you assume you know what their lips will taste like before you even touch them.

But I didn't know.

I had no fucking idea.

A soft whimper travels from her throat to my lips still pressed against hers. It ignites a lust inside of me that I've never felt before. Desperate for more, I swipe my tongue across the seam of her mouth and she opens herself up to me like a blossoming flower. She moans when I taste her tongue and hearing her voice reminds me that I'm kissing my best fucking friend. But I can't stop. I've kissed her head, her cheek, maybe even her hand when she made us play make believe shit. But never her lips. Never her soft, lush mouth that feels like an oasis I could get lost inside of.

In my mind, I know I should stop. *We've had too much to drink. You're taking advantage. This will terrify her. She will leave you.* But my body can't get close enough to her. I want to feel her. All of her. I want to claim her in a way that will make me feel secure about where she is right in this moment. I know I might regret this, but fuck it. I want her.

Clumsily, I begin pushing Poppy backwards on the couch. Her legs wrap around my hips, making our connection more snug. Her hands press against my chest, clutching my shirt as our breaths mingle together with strenuous, confused pants.

"Poppy." My voice wavers with equal parts bewilderment and lust as I stare into her eyes only a few inches from mine. She looks as shaken as I am.

Her gaze drops to my lips. "Kiss me, Booker." Her deep, throaty request is needy. "Kiss me like you mean it."

So I do. I do because there is nothing I want more right now. I close the distance between us and mean every lick and nibble and swipe I place on her. My lips part to devour her, and she's warm and compliant against me, desire and yearning evident all over her body as I make a complete sweep of her mouth. The heady tension generating between us is so electric, I'm not sure I have the strength to pull away and draw breath.

Somehow, I manage to break apart for a split second because her hands are yanking at something between us. When I realise she's trying to take my shirt off, I help her pull it up over my head. It gets stuck on my ear, but as soon as I'm free, I do the same to hers. And before I can get my trembling hands to grip the zipper on the front of her sports bra, she's already got it undone and her breasts tumble out.

My eyes catch a glint of metal on the tip of her left nipple, and I stare for a second before it registers that she has a piercing on one of her breasts. A frenzy erupts inside of me. My hand isn't gentle as it grabs hold of her breast, squeezing hard with the urgent need

I have to claim it as mine. Every change about Poppy—every surprise, every subtle difference, every hair cut on her head—feels like a betrayal. Poppy is *my* friend. She is mine. I should know everything about her. The surprise of this piercing is hurtful.

In a haze of hunger and the need for some more intimate skin-on-skin contact, I pinch her pierced nipple so unapologetically, a hoarse cry rips from her throat. The pitch of her voice is so hot, I want to taste it. I slam my lips back to hers, clinking our teeth as I plunge my tongue deep inside her mouth, massaging hers with mine. She tastes so good. Like raspberries and whiskey. Combined with the scent of her perfume, it makes me want to lick every inch of her body.

Her hips thrust up into me as I dive down to pull her nipple into my mouth. She keens as the metal clinks on my teeth. Her hands rake through my hair as she pulls me away and then yanks me to her chest repeatedly, like she can't decide if she can take any more.

I pause my assault on her breast to slip a hand inside her shorts. My head drops into the crook of her neck when I find her hot with arousal. "Oh my God, Poppy. You're soaked."

"Booker," she whimpers, gyrating her hips up into my palm with desperate thrusts. I slide a finger deep inside her, but I know that's not what she needs. I've never heard Poppy's sex cry before, but I've known her long enough to know what she needs from me.

It's instinct.

I sit back on my knees, nearly tipping backwards as she rises with me, frantically fumbling with the drawstring on my trousers. When she frees me from my boxers, her hand wraps firmly around my cock. All of the sudden, she pauses and looks up at me. Her eyes have a hint of apprehension in them and everything freezes. Her grip, our bodies, our breaths, our hearts, even our eyes lock on one another...and it feels like a dare. Like she's daring me to stop her. Daring me to grant her permission. Daring the world to crash all around us.

"Poppy." I utter her name like a secret password to grant us permission.

Without a reply, she bends down and sweeps her tongue over the moisture leaking from my tip. My hips jerk at the shocking contact of her hot tongue touching my most erogenous spot. When she pulls me into her mouth, a grunt rips from my throat. She takes me so deep that my thighs begin to quake with each bob of her head. I reach and grab a fistful of her hair for balance. *The perfect fistful.*

My mind leaves my body as I fuck her mouth, thrusting myself down her throat. God she feels so fucking good. If it weren't for the whiskey in my system, I'd be coming in her mouth by now. But I need more. More than just her mouth. When I pull my dick away, she looks up at me with annoyance but then quickly understands as I shift to pull off her shorts and knickers. Everything is rushed and desperate and manic. Sloppy.

When she drops onto her back—staring up at me with lust-filled eyes, wild, messy hair, and one metal barbell twinkling in the dim light—everything slows. Her chest rises and falls with her breaths, her eyes blink a slow blink of readiness. Her familiar face displays our past, but her mysterious body taunts me with secrets.

She is Poppy. But she is not.

"Booker." She whispers my name and I meet her gaze with mine. It's her granting permission this time. She reaches low and grabs hold of my length. My eyes close when she squeezes me and swipes her thumb over my sensitive tip that's aching for a place inside of her. She positions me right where I want to be and croaks, "Make love to me."

I instantly tense. Her words like a bucket of ice cold water in my face. *What the fuck am I doing? This is Poppy. This is my best friend. I can't be doing this.*

Suddenly, I pull back. The couch is sticky and uncomfortable, the air heavy and damp. Our slickened skin against each other feels odd as our laboured breaths work to slow down our heartrates. She feels the shift in the air, too. It's like waking up from a dream and trying to figure out where sleep ends and awakening begins.

Poppy is beneath me.

Reality has fully returned, and all that's left is a whiskey buzz wearing off much too early. *I almost fucked my best friend.*

Stress-Induced Migraine

Poppy

Mind-blowing almost hook up, followed immediately by earth-altering awkwardness.

I can't even look Booker in the eyes when reality dawns on me over what's just happened. How much did I show him? How little control did I have over myself? *God, I hope I didn't scream out "I love you" or something moronic like that!*

No words are spoken as I wiggle out from under him and grab my clothes up off the floor. I scurry into the loo as fast as my shaky legs can take me. Dropping down on the toilet, I run my hands through my hair as I desperately try to shut off my libido and wake my brain the fuck up.

I finish peeing and wash my hands and face before putting my clothes back on. Glancing at my reflection in the mirror, I shake my head in disgust as I dry-swallow my birth control pill like it'll somehow calm my anxiety-filled head.

I came back to London under the guise that I had changed. That I no longer needed, wanted, or cared about Booker Harris like I once thought I did. And what's the first thing I do? Nearly sleep with him hours after I've moved in to his flat.

I'm officially ridiculous.

A knot forms in my throat as disappointment and shame cloud over me. I brush my teeth, trying to stop the tears from falling, but it's no use. I've really fucked things up, and this splitting headache creeping over me isn't helping matters. I don't even feel drunk anymore, but surely that's the only excuse I can claim after such an outrageous display of affection.

Swallowing hard and praying I can sneak out of the loo without being noticed, I open the door and dash out with my head down. When I pass his room, I think I've made it, only to collide with a shirtless Booker propped against the wall beside my door. Nerves explode in my chest as I eye his abs—hard, corded abs that I was stroking only moments ago.

I look up to see Booker's sympathetic gaze in the dark. Christ, he's mortified. "Poppy, I didn't mean to…I hope you don't think I—"

"It was nothing, Booker. No need to apologise. There's really no need to say a word."

The very last thing I need to hear him say right now is that he doesn't have feelings for me. He couldn't put a bloody shirt on for this?

He frowns and tugs on his earlobe. He's had that nervous tic since we were kids. "That wasn't what—"

"Let's just forget it. It's late. We've had too much to drink." I make a move for my room, feeling like the cheapest kind of whore, but his hand shoots out, stopping my retreat.

"You're not leaving, right?" His eyes are wide and fearful. His hand clenches the doorframe firmly, like he's trying to stop himself from flipping out.

I shake my head. "Not unless you want me to leave."

He closes his eyes with a heavy sigh. "That's the last thing I want. I just hope you don't think I was trying to take advantage of you." He rushes the words out, tension radiating from his thick forearm. "I'd rather kill myself than have you think that's why I asked you to move in with me."

I shake my head awkwardly, eyes downcast. "No need to get suicidal. I'm equally as guilty, Booker. You have no idea." And he never will. I'll never tell him that this isn't the first time I've thought of him naked with me.

"What do you mean?" His voice sounds curious more than accusatory.

My mouth opens and closes a few times before I stammer, "I was the one mixing the drinks." I laugh nervously and hate the sound of my voice right now. "Please, Booker. I'm drunk and I need to pass out."

He stiffens with a sharp intake of breath and then slowly drops his arm. I scurry past him like a shameful child who got caught shagging the neighbour boy, which I very nearly did.

I slide the door closed.

Sleep. I just need sleep. I'll deal with this monumental fuck-up in the morning.

In the early morning hours, I wake with a horrid migraine that could kill all other migraines. I get them from time to time, but they're usually stress-induced, centred around exams and that sort of thing. Are sexually frustrated migraines a thing? I'd think nearly sleeping with your best friend from childhood constitutes migraine-worthy stress.

The pain is so intense, it's accompanied by heavy nausea. This is usually how my migraines go: I wake up, puke, and then disappear for as many days as it takes the fucker to subside. I have medication for them, but all it does is dull the murderous pain from homicide to manslaughter.

I slide out of bed and step into a pair of sweats. Sure enough, the gagging sets in. Sprinting out of my room and straight to the loo,

I spew the contents of my belly—mostly whiskey—into the toilet. The light shining through the foggy window is near crippling. This is either the worst kind of hangover or the worst kind of migraine. Probably both. *Fuck me if I don't deserve this.*

When the nausea wanes, I slowly make my way out of the bathroom. As I open the door, I glance over and see Booker drinking a glass of water in the kitchen. He's wearing a pair of football shorts and a sleeveless T-shirt, the back of which is soaked in sweat. He obviously just came back from a workout.

He turns when he hears me, and I give him a slight head nod. "Crippling hangover or migraine. Either way, I'm going back to bed."

He looks uneasy for a moment, like he wants to say something but then thinks better of it and nods politely. Watching his head shake hurts my brain.

I return to the comfort of my room, yank the curtain closed over the balcony door, and blanket myself in darkness. I hate the dark, but in these scenarios, I need it. Migraines are nature's cruel joke on my childish phobia.

Closing my eyes, I pray for sleep to find me. I pray even more that I'll wake up and find that last night with Booker was a stupid nightmare.

When I wake up, it's dark outside. I sit up and exhale a huge sigh of relief that my head no longer feels like there's a vice grip on it. I lean over to the lamp that Booker left on my floor and flick it on, as appreciating that my room is now bathed in a soft yellow glow. I'm alive. I made it.

Itching for a shower, I gather up some clothes and slide open my door, nearly tripping over a bottle of water on the floor, accompanied by two pieces of toast on a plate. Tummy grumbling, I grab a slice and take a bite. It's definitely more than a few hours old, so I wash it down with a sip of water before making my way down the hall.

Booker must be out because the flat is dark, aside from the blue backsplash light in the kitchen. That's good. Space is precisely what we need. And since I'm just now feeling human again, I'm grateful for the solitude.

The shower is glorious. It has eight sprayers that hit me in all my favourite places, rejuvenating in more ways than one. I dry off and yank a brush through my short tresses, staring at myself in the foggy mirror for a mental pep talk.

Okay, Poppy. You can handle this. True it wasn't the best twenty-four hours of your life. But that doesn't have to mean anything has changed. Booker left toast and water at your door. That's a very friendly thing to do, and that's all you want from him anyway. You're not the same girl who pined for him in your teen years. You've changed. You have a nipple ring to prove it! You've experienced men. Only a few, but still. That basically means you're the shit, and a little foreplay with your best friend changes nothing.

Even if it was…really…fucking…good.

6

Half-Truths

Booker

"GOOD ENOUGH IS NEVER GOOD ENOUGH!" COACH SHOUTS AS my teammates and I stand at the goal line, preparing to run another killer. "We only have three matches left in the season, and I see a lot of you prancing around like this is for fun and relaxation! Tomorrow is a home game, and I refuse to let our disappointment over not getting promoted this season earn us a loss. Now fucking run!"

He blows the whistle and we sprint toward the closest line, then turn back and hit the midfield line. Then farther still. Then the rest until we're all the way to the end of the field and back.

"Harris!" Coach shouts. Both Tanner and I stop midstride to look at him. "Not, you…You! Well, hell, both of you is fine. Get over here."

We jog up to Coach and he hits me with a stern look. "Now, Booker, you have the best hands in the Championship League, but I'd like to see you work on becoming more explosive. Keep pushing the areas that aren't your best and soon we'll have nothing left to push, all right?"

I nod and head over to the net where my gloves are as he yells, "Do sixty-second sets of ab killers. Tanner, you shoot for him. I'll tell you when to stop."

I glove-up and drop down on the goal line with my legs straight out in front of me while Tanner positions himself ten yards out. I gesture for my right side first and he kicks the ball three feet over. I stop it and toss it back. Then he switches to the left.

After the first set, Tanner waggles his eyebrows and asks, "How's the roomie?"

Frowning and chucking the football back at him, I reply curtly, "Fine." I pause to squeeze a drink of water into my mouth before resuming my position on the goal line.

"That's it? Just…fine? It's been almost a week of living with her, and that's all you have to say?" He kicks the ball at me again.

I catch it and shrug. "She started her new job. I'm at practice. We haven't been seeing much of each other." I throw the ball back to him and try to ignore the fact that Poppy and I have been avoiding each other. I've been working out more than usual. She's been going into work extremely early. Hell, she could be sleeping at her parents' house in Chigwell for all I know. I've been checking for evidence that she's still staying at my flat, and the fresh groceries and occasional dirty dishes in the dishwasher lead me to believe she hasn't been abducted.

"You're bloody flatmates!" Tanner stops the ball I fling at him and stands with it below his boot. "Don't your paths cross on the way to the toilet? My fiancé is a high-risk baby surgeon and we still manage to find time for morning shags."

"Will you just shoot the bloody ball?" Tanner's playful smirk drops and he jukes me out, drilling one the opposite way I was expecting. I flinch as a muscle in my side pulls. "Fuck!" I growl and punch the ground in frustration.

A nervous expression breaks across his face. "Sorry, broseph. Are you all right?"

I stand up and grab my lower back on one side. "Yes. I just tweaked that fucking muscle in my back again. That was a cheap fake-out, you prat. It's a fucking strength training drill."

"Well, you know I get agitated when you don't answer my questions." Tanner's bearded face looks apologetic, but it's too late. He's a fucking wanker.

"What's going on, guys?" a female voice interrupts.

I turn to see Camden's girlfriend, Indie, stride up to us in her Bethnal polo and trousers, a med kit in hand. "Tanner's a moron," I answer.

"That's nothing new." Indie grins and pushes her bright green glasses up her nose. She gestures for me to sit down where I'm at and drops down on her knees next to me. "You tweak that same muscle again?"

I nod and she begins rooting around in the kit for the Deep Heat. "You need to be stretching this out every night, Booker. I've told you this. This muscle needs strength training for a solid six months. Playing with injuries isn't necessary if we do things to prevent them instead."

"I know. I keep forgetting," I groan.

Tanner eventually gets yelled at by Coach to rejoin the team. I exhale heavily, relieved to see the back of him.

"Tanner getting on your nerves again?" she asks, looking up at me as she squirts the cream into her hand and twirls her finger in front of me so I turn around.

Indie and Camden have been together for nearly a year, so she's practically part of the family. I think he would have proposed already if Tanner hadn't stolen his thunder by proposing to Belle first.

"He's trying to wind me up about rooming with Poppy."

She chuckles. "Oh yes, the childhood friend I've been hearing so much about. I don't know why you're surprised by Tanner. He has a go at people for much lesser things. You shacking up with a girl is high-level gossip in the Harris family."

I flinch as Indie rubs the cream on my side, working out the knot that's already formed. Indie is good at this—sports medicine. She's been with Bethnal for less than a year and has already been promoted from shadowing our team doctor to assisting and travelling with us on a regular basis. She's quick, she's efficient, and she has a great way of knowing exactly what we need before we even need it. Injury numbers have gone down since she joined the team because she knows all these strange new stretching techniques for injury prevention. We all laughed when she first demonstrated how to do them. But after one session, we all felt an ache in muscles we didn't even know we had.

"Poppy and I are not shacking up," I sigh. "Actually, we're hardly speaking."

"Oh?" Indie asks. "Did you do something to piss her off?"

I shrug my shoulders and remain mute because I'm not proud of what I did. I can't believe how far it went, and it's all my fault. I was the one who kissed her first. I was the one who climbed on top of her. And I can't stop replaying it all in my mind in vivid detail. I can't stop seeing that fucking nipple ring of hers.

"You going to bring her to Sunday dinner?" Indie asks, applying a warm bandage over the affected area.

I clear my throat, annoyed by my graphic memory. "I'm not sure she'd want to come. We're kind of in a strange place." It's amazing how much easier it is to reveal even half-truths to Indie. I think she must have her degree in psychology, too.

She tsks and replies, "Well, get out of it and invite her. Harris Sunday dinners are great at bringing people back together. It's where you both grew up. This seems like a no-brainer."

That's actually not a bad idea. I've been avoiding her because I don't know what to expect from her. I'm afraid that if I push her too soon, she might bolt. But maybe going back home will help us remember what we were like as kids and not focus so much on how different we are as adults.

Indie caps the cream and stands. "Stretch and ice that tonight. Other than that, get your arse back to work. We have a game to win, and we won't be able to do it without you."

Keeper of My Own Heart

Booker

Iт's game day. As usual, I'm on edge as I get ready in my room. I don't get jovial and excited on game days like Tanner. I don't wax lyrical about the majesty of Tower Park. I retreat into myself and focus one hundred percent on the game.

Goalkeepers are more often goats than heroes. It's a role on the pitch that is always more criticised than praised. Maybe it's because I never play a dramatic game if I can help it. I'm not setting up those Sky Sports-worthy saves and creating headlines because I grew up learning that dramatic diving saves happen when you're not paying attention. Instead, I prefer to be prepared for anything and everything. I calculate every slice a football makes across the pitch and ready my subconscious for the speed and trajectory their kick would have if they shot at me right then.

I apply this same strategy to my life. Low drama. Love is an unpredictable emotion. It causes extremes and, as a footy player who prepares for worst case scenarios, I can't overextend my inner circle or I risk getting burned. That's why I don't have relationships with women. I usually date them a few times before I sleep with them. Then I lose interest and stop calling. It's a cycle that I repeat and causes very little commotion. I can usually tell when I've come across someone who's clinging on a bit too tightly and detach before things go too far.

Luckily, I'm the keeper of my own heart.

I stuff my boots and gloves into my team bag and zip up my jacket. Making my way out of my room, Poppy's voice surprises me as I enter the kitchen.

"You have a match today, right?" I look up to see her perched on top of the table with a bowl of cereal in her hand. She ruffles her hair off to the side, avoiding eye contact with me despite the fact that she just asked me a question.

Effectively snapped out of my tunnel vision, I nod woodenly. "Yeah, I do. Are you not working today?"

She shakes her head. "I'm off. And since I've never seen you play, I thought I'd come. If that's okay."

Frowning, I pull my bag up on my shoulder, shocked by her request. Having Poppy at a match will be a completely new experience for me.

"I'll erm…organise a ticket for you to pick up at the window," I stammer.

Her face flushes a crimson colour. "You don't have to do that." Her eyes finally find mine. They seem sad and insecure. They've lost the joy she had when she first arrived. I hate that I did that to them. I hate that this is the most we've spoken since night one. I wanted this flatmate situation to make it easy for us to be mates again, not hard. I miss her light tone. I miss the way she sometimes sings the last word of her sentences. This Poppy feels awkward. I have to fix it.

Steeling myself, I reply, "I'd really like to, Poppy. You wouldn't be sitting alone then. My sister will be there, and I'm sure she would love to see you. You could finally meet my niece." I pause, feeling a bit uncomfortable and then rush out, "Our seats are separate from the WAGs in the upper tier boxes. Vi has always refused to sit anywhere but first row at the halfway line, so it's a much better experience watching the game."

Poppy frowns as she ponders my verbal diarrhea. It was way more information than she needed to know, but I realised that I want her in those seats. I want her to see me play. It's…important to me.

"I'm surprised Vi hasn't come by actually," she says, interrupting my internal reverie. "I'd have figured she'd be in here rearranging your cupboards by now."

I laugh. "She and Hayden spent the last week out in Essex with his family. They are as obsessed with the baby as we are."

Her smile is genuine. "That's really nice. Well, if it's not too much trouble, I'd love a ticket. Cheers, Book."

"Don't mention it." I move toward the door and then pause, looking back over my shoulder. "And hey, if you want a Bethnal kit, there are loads hanging in my wardrobe. Help yourself." She frowns and gazes nervously at my bedroom door. "Don't look like that. They're clean…Most of 'em." We both laugh and it feels really fucking nice.

Still smiling, I turn to leave and she adds, "Hey, good luck…I erm…want to say break a leg, but that has a much different connotation in sports than it does in theatre. So I'll simply say have fast hands." She wiggles her fingers up in front of her with a laugh.

My smile grows. "I'm told my hands are the best in the league."

Her smile falters. "I believe it."

With that parting exchange that travelled right to my fucking dick, I stride out of our flat, trying desperately to erase the rude images I have of Poppy and that nipple ring I can't ask her about.

Poppy

Tower Park is packed with people milling about in green and white, many with heaping cups of beer spilling onto the pavement of the communal areas as they wait to file in to their seats. I'm grateful Booker offered up a shirt because I'd be sticking out in anything else.

I'm a bit embarrassed to admit the length of time I spent sniffing all the options in his wardrobe, and it wasn't because I thought they were dirty. Booker has always had an intoxicating smell about him. It's like the scent of the woods after a light rain—clean and elemental. His wardrobe is bathed in that same fragrance, hanging there like an unmitigated longing.

Not longing. Just memories. Memories of a dear friend. Get it together, Poppy. You're wearing his shirt, not walking around in his bloody boxers!

I decided to come to his match today as a peace offering. As a way to mend fences after our awkward first encounter. What happened between us was a massive mistake. We were simply caught up in the moment after not seeing each other for so many years. Nothing has changed.

You're still you. He's still him. This isn't the beginning of a love story. You tried that once and it ended horribly. Booker Harris is not the guy for you.

Poppy
18 Years Old

"I passed my A-Levels with flying colours, and now the world is my oyster!" I sing to myself as I get dressed for the party at Giles Windsor's house tonight. Normally, I wouldn't be caught dead at a party with kids from my school. It's a stuffy private institution for privileged kids, and none of them have any imagination.

However, Booker Harris will be there.

And that's why tonight is so important.

Booker is my best friend. From the day I met him on that fallen tree in the woods behind our houses, I knew he was someone special. He never looked at me sideways when I sang at the top of my lungs on my makeshift tree stage. He simply hunkered down beside me and built a fort, pausing to answer all my random questions about the world.

He even indulged my Grimm's Fairy Tales obsession. On my eleventh birthday, I had an aunt gift me the complete collection of folk stories. I was always too afraid to read them by myself, though, so Booker sat out on our tree with me while I read. Sometimes he'd even ask me to read aloud.

The stories terrified me, but I loved the incredible contrast of magical tales with gruesome twists. My entire life, I've always felt like I, too, am an odd juxtaposition. I have a horrible raspy voice, but I love to sing. I'm klutzy, yet I feel like I was born to dance. My mother calls me flighty, but when I look at other people, I feel like I'm incredibly down-to-earth. None of that makes sense. None of that fits the moulds of society. It all has the makings for a horrible identity crisis!

But Booker always told me to never stop chasing butterflies. He was the one who gave me the strength to tell my parents I was going to take a year off of school to find myself.

When I'm with Booker, I feel completely free. That's why I have to talk to him tonight. I have to tell him the truth…

…That I am in love with him.

I can't pinpoint the exact moment I fell for Booker Harris. I compare my love to the giant Himalayan lily I read about in school. For most of its life, it's a mess of glossy leaves. But after seven years, it shoots up to almost ten feet tall and produces beautiful trumpet-shaped flowers that are simply magical. And they had been there all along, waiting for the perfect time to bloom.

That is how my feelings for Booker came about. One day, I woke up and allowed myself to bloom. I thought the flowers might fade, but *they haven't. They are still madly, completely, and irrationally in full bloom.*

So my plan is to tell him tonight before the party. I haven't seen much of him lately because he's been so busy with football. But with big life decisions coming up for me, I can't wait any longer. I'm going to march into his bedroom and tell him that we belong together.

Dressed in a long black dress with my hair in a bun on top of my head, I make my way through the park, feeling foolish for wearing these heels out here. But I need to look my best so Booker will see me as more than his good buddy, Poppy, who normally doesn't think much about what she wears. I want him to see me as a beautiful woman.

As I approach the halfway point between our houses, our tipped over tree comes into view. My heart flutters when I see someone sitting over there. Could it be Booker? How perfect if it is. What better place to profess my love for him than by our tree that first introduced us!

I squint as I draw closer and then realise that Booker is not alone. He's sitting on a blanket with a girl. The moonlight casts just enough light for me to make out their faces.

I stop behind a nearby tree, and my heart plummets when I see them lie down. His mouth is on hers, and her hands are running the length of his back like a spider. I gasp when I see his hand slide up her skirt.

"Booker, wait." The girl's voice is high-pitched and smooth. I instantly recognise her as Sidney Carmichael—one of the more popular girls in school who lives down the street from us. Everyone loves her because her family has a pool in the garden of their summer house.

Booker pulls his hand out from under her skirt, and she sits up, digging around in her purse. She pauses, looking into his eyes. "Are you sure Poppy means nothing to you? This fort you built out here together seems very special."

My breath hitches when I hear my name, and I cover my mouth to silence myself for his response.

"She's just a mate is all. I could never look at her the way I look at you."

Her white teeth sparkle in the moonlight, and she pulls a tiny foil packet from her purse and holds it up to him. I watch in horror as he reaches out to grab the condom, but she holds it back and says, "I love you."

I turn away, cupping my mouth as tears well in my eyes. I think I might be sick.

When a sob attempts to rip its way up from my throat, I begin running in the dark, tripping on a tree root and buggering up my ankle. I limp the entire way through the dark woods, tears falling down my face as my love flower morphs into complete and utter betrayal.

Of all the places Booker could have taken her, he brought her to our tree. The place where we've spent countless hours together. The place where we complained about our overbearing families and made our life decisions. The place where we laughed and grew closer.

The place I thought was sacred.

Witnessing what I just saw makes one thing perfectly clear. Whatever blooms I had for Booker Harris aren't flowers of love. Not at all. They are shrivelled up weeds that need to be pulled.

I make my way down the aisle and spot Vi's blonde hair right away. She turns and when we make eye contact, she looks like she's just seen Santa Claus himself.

"Poppy!" she squeals and hands her baby off to the guy next to her. She rushes up the concrete steps and scoops me up in a tight squeeze. "I haven't seen you since you were a child! Just look at you!"

Her blue eyes are raking over my entire body. I get this a lot when I come home. It's the hair. It was a shock to my parents, too. But as soon as I cut it, I knew I'd never go back.

"Look at you," I reply with a smile. "Vi Harris, officially grown up and a proper mummy. Congratulations on the baby. Booker said you guys call her Rocky?"

She beams. "Yes. Her name is actually Adrienne. She was a bit of a fighter when she was born, so we were inspired by Sylvester Stallone when we named her. Come and meet her!"

She grabs hold of my arm and leads me down the rest of the stairs to our seats in the front row. "This is Hayden, my fiancé. We're getting married this summer, after football season is over, of course."

"Oh, do you play, too?" I ask, looking up at the stunningly hand-some man holding an equally stunning baby.

He laughs, his eyes narrowing on Vi. "No, but Vi is an unpaid sideline coach, so football comes before our wedding apparently."

Her jaw drops in mock offense. "It's not like that. We're planning to go away for the wedding and I want all my brothers there, so we're waiting until July when their schedules are a lot more manageable."

"That sounds fun!" I beam, enjoying the sight of Vi and her happy little blonde family. My eyes zero in on Rocky. "Hello, you." I reach out and clutch Rocky's perfectly chubby baby hand. She has the bluest eyes I've ever seen on a child, and her blonde hair is so thick and feathery, I can't help but run my fingers through it. I laugh at the little sweatband they have around her forehead. "Vi, she is ab-solutely beautiful."

Vi looks from the baby to Hayden for a moment, absorbing the compliment. "She really is. You won't hear any arguments from me."

Hayden chuckles. "I've never been more grateful for all of Vi's brothers than I am now. When she's older and boys start knocking down our door, I won't hesitate to call in a Harris Shakedown."

This makes me giggle because it's such an easily conceived scene.

Vi gestures to the brunette standing on the other side of Hayden. "Sorry…This is Belle! Tanner's future victim, I mean wife."

Belle's laugh echoes as she reaches around Hayden to shake my hand. She's a stunning tall, dark, and curvy brunette whom I can't help but stare at.

She cuts a look at Vi. "If anyone's the victim, it's him. Believe me, I'm no picnic. You should see me after a twelve-hour surgery. I'm a nightmare."

"Please!" Vi argues. "Tanner is marrying up and there's nothing you can say or do to change that fact."

The two laugh with each other momentarily until the Bethnal Green Pride song starts and the players begin to march out. Hayden passes Rocky off to Vi and says he's going to go grab some Pukka Pies for us before the match begins.

After he leaves, I have to doubt Hayden's judgement skills a bit because Rocky is getting all kinds of jostled by Vi's exuberant screams to sing along with the song. It's quite a comical sight. Rocky's big blue eyes stare up at her mother in wonder as Vi focuses all of her energy toward the pitch and projects her voice as loud as she can.

"Do you want me to…" I hold my hands out to the baby and Vi nods eagerly.

"Thanks!" she says as she passes Rocky off to me and then stands up on her seat to sing even louder.

I clutch Rocky to my side, enjoying the weight of her. I've always loved babies and have never shied away from holding someone's if they let me. Rocky nestles into me, all cuddly and soft and oozing warmth and cosiness. I smile brightly at her and wave her hand to the anthem. Her smile is heart-melting, and I laugh when I look up to see Vi still cheering at maximum volume after the song has ended.

I press my lips to Rocky's ear and whisper, "Your mummy is a little nutty for footy, isn't she?"

Rocky coos and giggles at me as if she's saying I'm late to the party and this isn't new information. I laugh and nuzzle her with a hug, finally turning to look out at the pitch. I'm surprised to see Booker lined up with his team right below us, only twenty feet away. But while everyone else is facing the pitch, he's facing us.

Our eyes lock and it's a peculiar exchange. He's not smiling or frowning. He's simply…watching. The intensity in his gaze makes my chest flutter. And he won't look away, which makes it impossible for me to look away. It's like his glower is holding me captive. As I stand here, feeling the weight of his eyes on me, a pressure-filled sensation moves up my chest and into my throat. It continues all the way to my eyes, blurring my vision.

Finally, Hayden breaks our eye contact as he attempts to shuffle past me and Rocky with a tray full of food. While he returns to his seat between Vi and Belle, I shake my head to try and clear my foggy brain.

I manage to hold Rocky for most of the first half of the game, but she begins fussing around halftime. Hayden takes her from me and tips her into a sideways position in his arms. He starts rocking her back and forth in a swinging motion. I watch in awe because it seriously takes all of three minutes for her to pass out in his arms, asleep like a baby. He holds Rocky the rest of the game while Vi continues screaming at the refs. Hayden is too busy laughing at her to mind. Belle is a bit more of a silent sport watcher. She looks nervous and completely focused on Tanner.

In the end, the match was quite exciting for the Bethnal Green offense as they racked up five goals to the opponents' zero. Bethnal truly bossed the game in the first half, only allowing the opponents one shot. It was a sudden, unexpected back kick to Booker that had my heart in my throat, but it was all for naught. He caught it with ease and punted it so far back down the field, my jaw dropped. So much power in his legs. So much precision in his hands. He really has blossomed into an incredible athlete.

The attacking duo of Tanner and his fellow striker, Roan DeWalt, was impressive to witness. The two volleyed off each other and went goal for goal, earning a pair each. The fifth goal was from a gorgeous back-pass assist from Tanner to a midfielder who shot high, right past the keeper's gloves.

The second half was when Booker truly had his shining moment in the game. After a poor tackle from a Bethnal defender, the opponent earned a penalty kick. My nerves were at an all-time high as I watched the player standing so close to Booker, preparing for his shot. The chances of Booker stopping the kick were small. The striker clearly had the advantage. But Booker held his ground—gloves out, eyes narrowed, legs bent. That boyish face of his was gone and replaced by the image of a supreme career athlete.

He has never looked more intimidating.

The kicker had a delayed run up on the penalty shot. He angled like he was going to kick to the right, but it ended up whizzing low and down the middle. Booker took the fake and dove left, overshooting by a lot. I cringed because it looked like the ball was going to skate right past his legs. But at the last second, Booker stretched his boot out and blocked the ball with his foot, sending the fast kick flying out of bounds.

The crowd was absolutely deafening. It was an incredible save. And watching Tanner rush the goal and pick Booker up to celebrate such a miraculous stop was even more incredible. Booker's reaction was far less animated than Tanner's. His control still evident, his body still tense from the near miss. But he was happy. I could see his beaming smile easily from my seat, and it was a beautiful Harris moment to witness on the pitch.

Booker

After the game, I'm on a high like I've never been. Maybe it was the trick save. Maybe it was the fact that it was a home match and we won. Or maybe it was the fact that Poppy was in the stands.

Watching her up there with my family felt so right, like the stars had aligned and she was exactly where she belonged. My best friend, cheering from the front row.

When I started playing football in my teens, I never let Poppy come to any of my matches. I was always on the sidelines, never playing. The first choice keeper was older, more experienced, and at least twice my size. It was depressing because my brothers walked on the pitch and owned it from day one. That's the shit thing about the keeper position. You're competing for one, single, solitary position. If you're not the best, you're as good as nothing to the team.

So football and Poppy were always kept separate. It was easier that way at the time. But having her here today felt like an immense relief. Like she was extending a peace offering. Like she was saying, *"Look, I know we buggered up on night one, but that doesn't change anything. We're still mates and I'm not going anywhere."*

Whatever it was, I can't get up into the stands to see her fast enough. The endorphins coursing through my veins are at an ultimate high, making me feel like I could run ten miles.

I manage to sneak up beside her as she's chatting with Vi, and she jumps nearly a foot in the air when she lays eyes on me.

"Booker!" Vi yells, pulling my focus off of Poppy. She wraps me in a hug. "Fucking aces game, my love. That last save. It was amazing! I can't wait to watch it on the highlights I recorded at home. Seriously, career best save by far."

I smile sheepishly as everyone else gives me a pat on the back, but the one I'm most curious for a reaction from remains silent. When their attention turns to something Rocky does, I step toward Poppy and nudge her with my elbow.

"Hello." My voice is quiet as I lean over her, inhaling her scent—a vast improvement from the sweat and dirt wafting off of me.

"Hello," she replies, looking up at me as she frowns with a puzzled expression.

I smirk as I continue to tower over her. "How'd you like the game?"

Her eyes fixate on my mouth as I lick my lips. As if in some sort of daze, she twitches slightly and swallows. "Good seats." Her cheeks flame red.

This amuses me and I have to bite my lip to stop from laughing. Of all the things she could have said after never having seen me play, she comments on the seats. It makes me want to tackle her to the ground and tickle her until she admits how bloody good I am.

I quirk my brow. "That's all you have to comment on?"

"Oh yeah, good game or whatever." She flicks her wrist in the air like today is any old Saturday and she didn't just witness my career best save.

This makes me snicker. She can be stubborn as a mule sometimes. Determined, I straighten my posture, looming over her even more now and trying to silently intimidate her into admission. I want to hear her fucking say it. I want to hear her say I'm great. I'm not usually a cocky sod. My ego isn't one that needs constant attention. But fuck me, after a game like tonight, I can't help but want praise from my best friend.

I pierce her with a challenging look. "Did you really just say whatever?"

Her tongue swipes across her glossy lips as I move in even closer. She starts twitching and murmurs so low I can barely hear her, "Are you seriously trying to keeper me right now?"

"Am I what?" I ask, not sure I heard her correctly.

Before she gets a chance to reply, Tanner's boots clack up behind Belle. He cops a feel and she squeals, turning and whacking him on the chest. The two kiss for a bit longer than is appropriate, but no one seems to mind.

Then, all of the sudden, Poppy gets a tap on her shoulder.

"Jaysus Christ, Sugar Pop. I thought that was you!" An Irish voice bellows from behind us.

Poppy and I both turn to look at the man who is addressing my friend so casually. He wraps his inked arms around her trim waist and pulls her into a hug, lifting her off the ground before kissing the top of her head.

"Oh my God, Nigel! What are you doing here?" Poppy exclaims, her face the picture of shock.

"I'm just over with a few of the lads to catch a match," he answers, his Irish lilt thick and heavy. "One last hurray before we join the working stiffs and earning a proper wage." He chuckles and strokes his long beard.

I already don't like him. He's a hipster personified with his ten-inch beard and curls on the ends of his mustache. It's too much. He's trying too hard. It looks like he tried to rough up his appearance with copious amounts of ink and piercings. None of it looks authentic.

"I can hardly believe it," he scoffs, shaking his head. His eyes rake down Poppy's body in a familiar way that raises my hackles. "What are the odds of running into each other at a footy game of all places? What brings you here?"

I brush up against Poppy, indicating in no uncertain terms that I want to be introduced. If this guy is after her, he needs to know I've got her back.

Poppy clears her throat and looks up at me nervously. "This is my friend, Booker Harris."

"The goalie!" Nigel's eyes fly wide. "Wow, I didn't know you knew him. Hey, pal, brilliant save out there with that penalty kick. Feck me, that's highlight-worthy shite right there."

He reaches out to shake my hand. Maybe he's not all bad, but my brows are still furrowed as I reply, "Thanks. How do you two—"

"Sugar Pop and I met at Uni." Nigel tosses his arm jovially around her shoulders, pulling her into him and away from me. "We were having the craic at this party we were both at, and I couldn't take me eyes off her."

My jaw tightens as I watch how he holds her. It's a familiar embrace, like he's touched her before. I look him up and down, and my eyes lock on his lip piercing. Then it dawns on me. I look at Poppy, who's still a ball of nerves. I glance down at her breast and then back to her eyes. It's confirmed.

This wanker pierced Poppy.

"Do yous have time to grab a pint, Pop?" Nigel asks with a smirk. "I'd love to catch up."

She smiles and squirms under his arm. "You know, Nigel, I'm really busy. I have a job here in London and my schedule is full I'm afraid."

"Oh, that's a shame," Nigel whines. "Well, I'm here until Tuesday. You have my number, so give me a ring if your schedule lightens up."

"Sure, sure," she replies. "Either way, it was great running into you." She gives him a quick hug and all but pushes him away as he strides over to rejoin his friends.

That was fucking interesting.

Poppy seems to be avoiding eye contact with me as she says her goodbyes to my family and excuses herself.

As I watch her leave, I can't help but wonder more about what Poppy got up to in Germany.

A Hundred Poppies

Booker

Bringing Poppy back to the Harris house feels like a blast from the past. Seeing her walk through the foyer again makes it feel like nothing has changed. Sure she has more curves than she used to. And her hair is shorter. And she has a fucking nipple ring that I'm about ninety-nine percent sure that prat Nigel had something to do with. But when she walks into my dad's kitchen and he sweeps her up in a big hug, it's like the world makes sense again.

"And how are your parents?" Dad asks Poppy as he pulls a stool out for her at the counter.

"They are great. Dad's still running the veterinary clinic with Mum right alongside him. My sister is married now, and they live in Oxford. Other than that, things have been quite boring."

Dad chuckles. "You know, we live close enough you'd think I'd see them from time to time, but I'm afraid football is all I make time for. I should try harder."

"Oh, that can't be all true," Poppy croons. "I hear you're a top-notch Grandad."

Dad's eyes twinkle at the mention of Rocky. "She's quite the stunner, isn't she? I wouldn't mind half a dozen more grandkids."

Poppy laughs and Dad continues catching up with her as everybody else begins to show up.

Sunday dinners at the Harris' became a ritual right around the time that Gareth signed a contract with Man U. Dad was decidedly upset that he signed without telling us first, but I think it had more to do with the fact that it was Dad's former team and the history surrounding that time in his life.

Dad was a star striker for Man U at the time our mum died from cancer. I was only one year old when it all went down, but I'm told he lost it, broke his contract with the team, and sold the Manchester flat we lived in half the year.

He moved all five of us kids up to the Chigwell home without so much as a part-time nanny. The home is gated and secluded. If it wasn't for the wooded park behind our house, we would have felt completely isolated. But I think that's exactly what he wanted. To disappear from the world. Gareth was eight when it all happened, so he remembers the worst bits…but he rarely speaks of it.

Gareth has always been headstrong like that. Where the rest of us lean on each other and rule by committee, he's always been a bit of a loner. Vi could sense the disconnect with him after he bought a place in Manchester, so she instated the Sunday night dinners, no exceptions. For the most part, we all make it unless we're away travelling or moving into a new flat, of course. It's really brought our family back together.

"Booker," Belle says my name, snapping me out of my internal reverie. She strides right toward where I'm seated at the counter watching Vi cook while I hold a sleeping Rocky in my arms. "Indie and I are going to steal Poppy for a moment. We're talking wedding stuff outside and we need an unbiased moderator."

Poppy looks up from where she's seated with Dad at the table.

"More like Belle needs her head examined," Indie retorts, wiggling her red frames on her eyes. "The wedding is six weeks away and she's talking about changing the venue to Tower Park! I told her to go for it if she likes to get rained on."

Belle rolls her brown eyes. "It's a small wedding. If I have to change venues, it won't be that big of a deal to call everyone and let them know. It's where Tanner and I got engaged…erm…officially. I've already talked to Vaughn."

Dad shoots Indie a guilty look. "Well, don't let me keep you, Poppy. I've got to go check the barbecue anyhow." He makes his way out of the line of fire.

Indie exhales heavily, ruffling the top-knot of red hair on her head. "There are details we already have in place, Belle! A list. I love my lists. We had everything figured out."

Belle pins me with an exasperated look. "See why we need a third party?"

Indie and Belle look at me like I'm Poppy's keeper. My eyes find hers. "I was going to see if you wanted to walk out to the park actually. Go visit our old stomping ground and see if our fort is still standing?" My face feels hot as her expression turns uncomfortable.

"Erm…no." She shakes her head rapidly. "I'd actually love to help the girls."

I frown, feeling rejected as Belle beams and all but drags Poppy out the back door to the garden. My eyes remain fixated on where they exited, wondering what the hell just happened. Poppy seemed weird when I mentioned the park, like she wouldn't be caught dead out there. I don't understand. It's where we met. It's our special place. We spent hours out there building that fort and playing together. Why wouldn't she want to go out there?

Annoyed, I move to go outside so I can try to talk to Poppy, but Vi stops me in my tracks. "Stay where you are." Her tone is bossy as usual. She stands at the counter, stirring a pot of sauce on the stovetop and eyeing me over her shoulder. "Don't think I don't see what's going on here, Booker."

"What?" I ask, clutching Rocky to me to serve as a buffer

between me and my sister. Vi and I have always had a close connection. Probably because I was the youngest and she was trying to protect me from my brothers. But bloody hell, she can be overly insightful sometimes.

"You seem to be getting awfully territorial over your *friend.*" She emphasises the last word as she slides a pan of dinner rolls into the oven. "First yesterday at Tower Park. Now here at Dad's." She shakes her head with a sigh.

"I'm protective over lots of people," I argue. It's the keeper in me. I'm not going to apologise for that. "I remember having to give Hayden the Harris Shakedown not too long ago when he lost his bloody mind on you."

She rolls her eyes. "What Hayden and I endured wasn't easy for either of us. We've come a long way from those days, though. You and Poppy are different."

"How so? Poppy's been my best friend for ages. Why wouldn't I want to protect her the same way I protect you?"

"Because you don't look at me the way you look at her."

"And how do I look at her?" I ask, lowering my voice when Rocky stirs in my arms.

She presses her palms flat on the counter, pinning me with a glare. "Like a man who wants more than what he has."

Her words stun me into silence. Complete and utter silence. I don't want more than what I have with Poppy. I want exactly what we had before. If anything, that's all I'm trying to gain. The "more" we had the other night was a mistake. Getting that kind of more with Poppy would eventually end with a lot less, and I can't lose her again. Losing her once was bad enough. When she left for Germany, I thought she wasn't coming back. There was a look in her eyes that I still can't shake.

Booker

19 Years Old

Standing in front of the McAdams' home feels a bit surreal for some reason. I used to walk right in without a care in the world. But the past few months, things have been quiet between Poppy and I. We've both been busy. She's been doing a bit of travelling with her sister, and my football schedule is completely stressing me out. I'm the reserve keeper and have been killing myself trying to become the starter. The anxiety of it all has caused me to forget the fact that Poppy has always been the perfect reprieve.

I miss my best friend.

I knock firmly on the door. My mood brightens when Poppy is the one to answer. "Hiya, Poppy, how's it going?" I ask, feeling odd and a bit more formal than usual.

"I'm okay, Booker. How are you?" She looks away, tugging a long strand of hair. Her face isn't the normal bright and cheery it usually is.

"I'm all right. I erm…miss you." I reach out and touch her shoulder playfully, trying to seem light-hearted but feeling anything but. "We haven't talked in a while, so I thought maybe we can go do something. I was getting ready to go for a run, but I thought I'd see if you want to go for a walk instead."

Her brows knit together. "I'm a bit busy at the moment."

"Doing what?" I ask with a laugh. She doesn't look busy, and I can't recall many times when Poppy has blown me off.

Her lips form a thin line. "I'm…packing."

"Oh?" I ask, wondering if she's talking about packing for Uni in London. "I thought you were planning to live at home for the first couple of years."

"Yeah…I erm…was going to tell you." Her eyes flash downward. "I'm going to Goethe University in Frankfurt."

My heart stops. Wait, she's what? "Like…in Germany?" I ask stupidly, but the concept of her leaving seems unbelievable to me.

She exhales and pinches the bridge of her nose. "Yes, Booker. In Germany. You know how much I've always wanted to live there. And they have a great program for teaching German as a second language, which is what I want to do, so it's pretty perfect for me."

I grip the back of my neck and squeeze, completely stunned by this new information that she's spouting out like the daily bloody news. "You're moving there permanently?"

She shrugs. "Probably not permanently. I don't know. I haven't decided. They have a Master's program there, too."

"When do you leave?" I snap. Poppy has always been a bit nutty for Germany ever since she got hooked on the Brothers Grimm, but moving there is coming out of fucking nowhere. This is the kind of decision we usually discuss.

She swallows slowly. "One week."

I huff out a laugh, heat pulsing through my veins. "One week! When were you planning on telling me, Poppy?"

"I was going to tell you," she stammers and looks away from me.

"From where? The plane?" I exclaim, feeling my heart sink over the finality of all of this. Poppy is leaving and she's acting like I'm a fucking afterthought. Like when Gareth buggered off to Manchester without a look back. Like how Dad barely cares what I have to say if I'm not talking about football. Like how Camden and Tanner only care about themselves. Like I'm nothing.

Unable to look at her any longer, I turn away and jam my hands through my hair, trying to dampen the rage billowing up inside of me. I don't know what the fuck is going on. Last I knew, Poppy was going to Uni in London. She was going to live at home. I was going to live at home. Things were going to stay the same. London is where she belongs. Now she's leaving?

I swerve my accusing eyes at her. "I thought I was supposed to be your best friend, and moving to another country seems like the kind of thing you tell a friend." My tone is acerbic. I'm fucking furious.

Her eyes narrow on me as she steps out onto the front porch and backs me up a foot. She stabs her pointer finger into my chest. "I'm sorry I didn't get around to telling you, but we haven't really been hanging out much lately."

"So what? That doesn't mean we're not still mates!" I exclaim.

"Actually, that's precisely what it means. Friends tell each other things. Friends talk. Friends don't betray one another."

Betray one another? Her anger gives way to hurt as her raspy voice cracks on the last word. Her green eyes look sad and defeated. I want to reach out and hug her. Hold her until she tells me what's going on in that wild, imaginative head of hers. But I feel like I'm looking at a stranger.

She's fucking leaving.

My voice is soft as I look around at anything but her and ask, "What does that mean, Poppy? Are you saying I have betrayed you?"

I look up to find her staring at me so hard, I feel small. I shrink in my own shoes and search my brain for whatever she might be accusing me of. I'm the one who feels betrayed, though. She is the one who changed the plans. She's the one moving away and treating me like our friendship has meant nothing to her.

Her face softens as she takes in my confused expression. "I'm sorry, all right. It all came up rather quickly, and an international pre-course for all the non-Germans starts earlier than I realised. And, you've been so busy with football, I didn't want to distract you."

That sounds like an excuse. A shitty lie. And it doesn't sound anything like my best friend. This is why you keep your inner circle of people you truly care about small. This kind of pain. I've reached my limit.

I turn to walk away as her voice calls out, "Booker, where are you going?"

I stop and scuff my foot on the pavement. "Home." I could laugh as everything I thought I knew about my friendship with Poppy vanishes completely. "I have a match tomorrow in Birmingham that I have to ride the bench for. If hell freezes over and they put me in, I'll try to send you a postcard."

She huffs out a frustrated growl. "So you're going to leave without hugging me goodbye?" Her angry eyes blink rapidly. I think I might see tears forming in their depths, but there's no use in worrying about her anymore.

I give her one last look. "This isn't a goodbye I want, so I'm not giving it."

Vi calls everyone into the house when dinner's ready. All seated around the table, Tanner and Camden fight over who gets to hold Rocky next because she can't ever just be sat in a pram or a car seat. She must be held at all times. Meanwhile, I'm still holding the prize. I hunch over her in my arms, kissing her head over and over. *God, how do they make baby's heads so bloody soft?*

In the end, Gareth sneaks in and swipes Rocky next. I smile at Vi as I pass her over. "She really is the cutest baby that ever existed."

Vi nods but then points to me and Poppy, who's seated across from me. "You and Poppy were pretty cute kids, too, if I recall. You were always the talk of the neighbourhood because you'd stop traffic with your cuteness."

"We did not," I scoff and look at Poppy, whose cheeks are red with embarrassment. It doesn't deter Vi a bit, though.

"When you were about eight, I remember finding you two playing out back. I walked up just as Poppy said to you in her adorable little voice, 'I wish there were a hundred Bookers in the world.' And Booker, you looked right at her with the straightest face and said, 'I wish there were a hundred Poppies in the world.' And the two of you laughed like you just shared the most hilarious joke. I could have died from cuteness overload. You two were always in your own little world."

Belle and Indie croon, and Tanner and Camden chortle like the prats they are. Tanner sighs and looks at Camden with his hands clutched against his heart. In a high-pitched voice, he says, "Camden, I wish there were a hundred Camdens in the world."

Cam smiles hugely and replies in a similar tone, "And Tanner, I wish there were a hundred Camdens in the world, too."

"You wanker," Tanner bellows and yanks Camden down into a headlock.

Dad yells at them to grow up, but nobody listens until Vi places her hands on the table and shouts, "Oi, not around the baby."

They stop instantly, and we all laugh and roll our eyes at the ridiculousness of the twins.

When things settle down and we all begin to eat, my eyes find the one person in the room I actually would take a hundred of…And that thought scares the shit out of me.

Spine-Shivering Forehead Kiss

Poppy

I NEVER THOUGHT I'D SAY THAT TEACHING GERMAN TO ENGLISH children is easier than teaching English to grown adults, but bloody hell, no wonder this job pays so well. The next few weeks of teaching are a nightmare. If I'm not hand-holding the small Vietnamese grandmother as she weeps about having to do homework, then I'm shouting at the Italian *Godfather* wannabe to put out his cigarette. Cultural stereotyping is something I am very conscious of, but these people walk right into it! Though I will say the group of Scandinavian men—Denmark I think—are a laugh. They have no clue what I'm saying, but they smile through every lesson. I think they were even trying to ask me out for a drink one day after class. My Danish is a little rough, but I was able to politely say, "Nej tak, no thank you."

Quite honestly, though, I wouldn't mind a little company. Booker has had some away games, so I've seen very little of him. The bit I have seen him, he's been busy stretching. One day I came home and he was in the living room bent over with his arse high up in the air in the downward dog pose. When he took off his shirt and started massaging Deep Heat onto his lower back, I had to get the hell out of there. Avoidance seems essential for my mental health, especially when he looks like that.

After being at the Harris house a few weeks ago, my old feelings for Booker started to creep back up. And the way he looked at me at his game and across the table with his family all around didn't help matters.

But tonight is a new night. It's Friday. I'm done with my final course for the week, so I'm plotting the beverage I'll make myself as I let myself into the flat. When I walk inside, I'm shocked to find Booker sitting in the living room.

"Oh hi, Booker," I say, dropping my keys on the kitchen table. "I'm surprised to see you home."

He stands up from the sofa, thrusting his hands in the pockets of his worn jeans. His dark hair has been freshly cut—close on the sides but with a longer quiff in the front. It's lightly gelled back away from his face, which displays the full moody colour of his eyes. "Our last match was Wednesday night in Sheffield. We got back late last night."

I walk over and stand near the sofa, trying to ignore that he was sitting exactly where we got naked. "Erm…right, I saw the score. Congratulations."

He nods, running a lazy hand through his tresses. "Thanks. I'm glad the season's over, though. I'm ready for this break."

"Oh yeah?" I drop down and perch on the arm of the sofa, far enough away that I can't smell him but close enough to be friendly. "So, what do you do in the off-season? Pig-out and become a lazy sod?"

He laughs. "Hardly. I might eat a little more indulgently, but I still workout nearly every day."

"That's cool. The gym here is brilliant," I say stupidly. Of course he knows the gym here is brilliant. It's his flat and he's probably been in it tons of times.

"When do you use it?"

"Mornings usually. Around ten o'clock."

"We should work out together tomorrow." The corner of his mouth pulls up into an adorable boyish grin that reveals one of his dimples. "I want to see this exercise lover, Poppy McAdams, at the gym. Is it awful that I'm imagining you falling arse over tit on the treadmill like a cartoon character?"

"Yes, it's awful," I baulk and immediately try to school my features so he doesn't see recognition dawn on my face. I have fallen off a treadmill not once, not twice, but three times. "I'm much more agile on my feet these days. It's been at least a week since the last time I fell."

He laughs and it sounds good. I've missed his laugh.

"Want to watch a film?" He lifts his brows hopefully.

I narrow my eyes at him. "Only if I get to pick it."

"No," he argues, shaking his head and moving to guard the TV. "No bloody way. I'm not watching a *Twilight* vampire marathon. Or *Step Up*, or *Center Stage*, or some other ridiculous dance movie where the kid from the wrong side of the tracks gets a big break at a prestigious dance academy and then saves a puppy."

My jaw drops. "No one ever saves a puppy." He pins me with a hard look. I cross my arms and add, "Fine. If you pick the movie, I get to pick the workout music tomorrow."

He chuckles and replies, "Deal."

I do a mini victory dance on the spot because what I listen to for workout music will probably kill him. I move my dance down the hallway toward my bedroom to change into some comfortable clothes and call back over my shoulder, "Let's order takeout!"

Nearing the end of *Moneyball* with our bellies full of Chinese food and legs stretched out on our respective sides of the sofa, Booker is shaking his head at the screen. "I have a newfound respect for what my father does." He pauses to lean forward and tosses some popcorn in his mouth. "But I haven't a bloody clue how to play baseball."

"I know! I can barely keep up with football. With baseball, I have no idea what they are going on about."

He chuckles and then looks sideways at me. "Are you ever going to tell me how you're liking your job?"

I shrug. "It's all right. The majority of my students are complete lunatics, but it's temporary."

"Then you'll be teaching German," he states.

"Ja, das ist richtig," I reply with a wink.

"You're completely fluent?" He looks impressed.

I nod.

"Well, that's one good thing that came out of you moving away."

This makes me frown. "There are lots of good things that came out of my education."

He nods his head. "Right, of course education is good. But did you have to go all the way to Germany to achieve it?"

"It's not the moon, Booker," I snap. "It's a two-hour flight."

"But why Germany?" I don't like his flippant tone.

"I needed a change."

"A change from what?" he barks.

"From the *normal*! I was stuck in a rut, and everybody else was having adventures but me. And I've always been like the queen of adventures, so I wanted to reinvent myself a bit." I sit up and sass the last bit for dramatic effect.

"And Germany is where you got your…" He stops midsentence and waggles his finger toward my chest.

Heat moves across my cheekbones and I reflexively curve my shoulders in. "Yes."

"Was it that Nigel bloke who did it?"

I cringe as flashbacks hit me all at once. Nigel was the best kind of distraction at a time when I needed a distraction. Booker and I had such a rough goodbye before I left for Uni that I was in an odd place. I was hurt by him taking Sidney to our tree in the woods. That betrayal was still fresh.

So when I met Nigel at an international student mixer my first year in Germany, I dove in head first. I was struggling with the language, and he was simply…easy. And a bit naughty, which is precisely what I was looking for at the time. He's Irish and rough around the edges. He has piercings in places I never knew you could pierce.

Eventually, he convinced me that piercing my nipples would increase sensitivity and make our sex even more enjoyable. I was excited to do something a little wild, but after the first barbell pushed through my nipple, I cried like a fucking baby. It was horribly awkward. I had planned to pierce both, but I couldn't stomach the pain again. Instead, I rushed out of there with my tail between my legs, cupping my tender nipple.

Quite honestly, I probably would have taken the piercing out right away if I could have stomached it. But every time I looked at it, I remembered the pain and my belly heaved.

When Booker and I *slipped* the other night, I thought I was going to explode in my knickers when he put his mouth on it and sucked. After the traumatic piercing experience, I never let any guy near it. Not even Nigel. Actually, guys rarely saw me without my bra on because I was so protective of the area.

But with Booker, I lost my mind. I didn't even have time to think before he gripped it in his rough hand and claimed it as his own. The entire scene was the most erotic thing I've ever felt.

And Nigel was right. Holy fuck was my nipple sensitive.

Booker's posture straightens as he scoots to the edge of the sofa. His shoulders seem broad and tense, his eyes extra shiny as he watches me with a determined stare. He repeats himself. "Did Nigel pierce your nipple?"

I shake my head. "No."

"But he was there," he pries.

"Yes."

"Did he pressure you to do it?"

"No."

"Bollocks," he snaps, his tone assertive, making me feel three feet tall.

I examine the way he's looking at me and note the slight lift of his shoulders. The tension in his arms. *Is he trying to fucking keeper me again?*

I straighten my posture, brushing back some wisps of blonde hair from my eyes so I can meet his stare. "He suggested it, but in the end, I did it for myself. He never got to…play with it or whatever."

"What?" He's staring even harder at me now.

"It was bloody painful!" I exclaim. "I was so traumatised I couldn't do the other one and I blamed him. I never let anybody…" My voice trails off as I realise what I've admitted out loud.

The room is quiet as Booker processes what I've just said.

Thankfully, he shows mercy by changing the subject. "Did you date a lot of guys in Germany?"

My shoulders slump. "Didn't we already try talking about this?"

"No," he scoffs.

"Something close at least."

"So what?" he baulks.

"Well, Booker, considering we've never talked about relationships, I don't see why you're so curious now."

"Things change." He shrugs like we're having a normal conversation.

I exhale heavily. "What do you want to know?"

"How many?" The question is instant. No pause, no hesitation. He's been sitting on it for a while.

I'm going to make him sweat. "How many what?"

He rolls his eyes. "How many blokes did you sleep with?"

I scoff, "I wasn't a virgin when I went to Uni, Booker."

"You weren't?"

"No!" I screech.

"Who was it?" he asks, sitting up and looking almost perturbed by the revelation that my innocence was taken without his knowledge.

I cross my arms over my chest and shoot him as much attitude as I can muster. "I don't see why it matters, but it was Giles Windsor."

"What?" Booker says with a laugh. "You're lying."

"I'm not lying!" My fists clench.

"You let that prat Giles Windsor take your fucking v-card?" Now he looks really unamused.

"Yes." Why is this so hard for him to believe?

"When?" he asks flippantly, obviously thinking he'll be able to trip me up and catch me in a lie.

I huff hard and lean forward, pinning him with my own keeper stare. "The same night he threw that party after we all finished our A-Levels."

This knocks Booker back on the couch, the wind evidently taken out of his puffy keeper sails. He frowns, trying to cycle back through his memory bank to see what clicks into place. I recall plenty of things that click into place that night.

"What about you?" I ask, a sharpness to my voice.

"What about me?" He looks distracted.

"How many girls have you shagged?" My head jerks with challenge. Now it's his turn to be in the hot seat.

He looks prickly, so I add, "Whatever you say, I'm going to multiply it by two. That's what a quiz in *Cosmo* says to do."

His jaw clenches. "I'm not sure without really thinking, but I'd guess like…twenty."

I pull back. That's actually not as bad as I expected. *Unless it's really forty.* He looks uncomfortable, but I continue, "Most of them after secondary?"

He frowns. "I don't see why that matters."

"Did you sleep with Sidney Carmichael?" It's my question that is instant this time. On the tip of my tongue, waiting to be unleashed.

A flicker of confusion in his gaze doesn't go unnoticed. I want to scream at him that I know what he did. I want to push him back on the couch and ask him why he did it. Why he brought her to a place that was supposed to be sacred. That was supposed to be ours. Of all the trees in the world, he had to tell her that he loved her and fuck her *there*.

But I don't. Because I don't care. Because I'm not a naïve little girl anymore who thinks her best friend is the man of her dreams. Booker is a good mate and that's enough. It's not his fault my adolescent fantasies tried to twist him into something more.

After a moment of tense silence, I exhale. "Don't answer that. I'm knackered and I really don't need to know. I'm going to bed."

I pick myself up off the couch and walk past a frozen Booker. He's evidently still processing, but there's no need to continue a conversation that doesn't matter anymore. This has all gone far enough.

My feet feel like a hundred pounds as I trudge down the darkened hallway. The dim lamp in my room is on, providing a clear path to my reprieve. I hear Booker's footsteps behind me. Suddenly, a warm hand wraps around my forearm, bringing me to a spinning halt as he presses me up against the wall.

I don't have time to react before he rushes out, "I'm sorry, Poppy." He presses his other hand on the wall beside my face, caging me in. Regret colours his features, but I'm not sure what he's actually apologising for. "I shouldn't have pressed you so hard about Germany."

I restrain myself from rolling my eyes and try to ignore his hardened torso brushing up against my chest. I'm also trying to ignore the way his grip on my arm has softened, and how he's rubbing soft circles in the crook of my elbow. His callused thumb in that tender spot apparently touches a direct nerve that shoots right between my legs.

My knees wobble. He's doing that tall and intimidating thing, consuming my senses so all I can do is breathe in his fresh primitive scent. I clear my throat and say, "I just want to get back to normal with you, Booker. We seem so different now."

Irritation tremors in his square jaw as his eyes flash back and forth between mine. "We're still Booker and Poppy. We have to be."

He slides his hand through my short hair to cup my cheek. I inhale a shaky breath as he closes the distance and presses his lips to my forehead. That simple caress on a seemingly innocent part of my body sends shivers up my spine. *What is it about a man kissing you on the forehead that's so damn sexy?*

Murmuring against my skin, he adds, "We're just a bit more grown up now." I'm limp in his arms as he rubs his nose down my temple and my cheek, his breath mingling with mine as he nears the corner of my mouth. A soft gasp escapes me when he presses his body flush with mine. He feels so good. So warm. So…right.

"What are you doing to me, Poppy?" he whispers, his voice trembling.

His words are a kick to my heart. As I lift my chin for him to kiss me, he pulls back and presses himself against the opposite wall. His hands are still frozen in the position he was holding me. Eyes wide and haunted. With a shudder, he turns and strides into his room, closing the door behind him.

Closing the door on me.

Changed For Good

Booker

I HAD WRITTEN OFF NIGHT ONE WITH POPPY AS A MISTAKE. AN accident. A one-time encounter that happened because I missed my best friend, and we were a bit pissed so we got carried away. It took some time, but we managed to get past it. To get back to some semblance of normal.

But then last night happened. And after a shitty night's sleep, the morning light of day brings no clarity to my mind. What started as an easy, carefree movie night ended in a cluster-fuck of epic proportions.

I can't seem to find even ground with Poppy, and it's terrifying me because I lost her once and I don't want to lose her again. The trouble is, I can't stop pressing her about things. I can't dampen the urge I have inside of me to know her completely again. Like old times when I could see her in the hallway at school and know exactly what she was thinking. What mood she was in. How her day was going.

Being flatmates with her isn't like being flatmates with my childhood friend. It's like being flatmates with her sexy and mysterious twin sister. And *fuck* if she didn't feel good in my arms last night. I wanted to kiss her. I wanted to feel her. I wanted to rip her fucking shirt off and taste the metallic of that nipple ring and relish in the fact that she's never let any other man do so.

But Poppy is Poppy. She's my only real friend. I pretty much grew up on a secluded Harris island with very few outsiders ever breaching our shores. It wasn't bad. I love my family. My sister, Vi, is everything to me. My brothers, while annoying, are still whom I enjoy spending most of my time with. But in a sea of big brothers, I always had a feeling of inadequacy. I was never big enough, strong enough, fast enough, good enough.

Poppy was my escape. She looked at me like I was the tallest man on Earth. I can't lose her. I refuse. I have to start thinking with my head and stop following my fucking dick.

And I won't go back to avoiding her like before. We can be friends again. I just have to go at this in a different way. It's simple. I have to get to know the new Poppy.

Poppy

I wake the next morning and find Booker standing at the kitchen counter in front of a blender. He's barefoot and shirtless in a pair of Adidas training trousers. My gaze unabashedly rakes over his bare back. The way his bones and toned muscles slide and snap beneath the ripples of smooth olive skin…

…It's mouthwatering.

But that's irrelevant. After last night, I'm furious. I'm tired of never knowing which Booker I'm going to get. Will it be Investigative Booker, who drills me with twenty questions and then baulks when he doesn't like the answers? Or will it be Sweet Caring Booker, who looks across tables at me and bats his eyes like I'm the best thing since fish and chips? Or maybe it'll be big, dominating Keeper Booker, who magically grows eight feet tall and emits a sexy musk that I want to lick off every inch of his toned body. Or, worst of all, what if it's Loving Booker, who caresses my hair and kisses my forehead and makes my heart grow inside my chest?

I hit a creaky floorboard and he looks over his shoulder, eyes bright, smile beaming. "Good morning! I'm making us protein shakes. As you know, I'm not much in the kitchen, but I can always do a shake. I figured these would be good before our workout." He turns on the blender, the loud noise causing me to flinch.

My brows crinkle as I shuffle over to the table, trying to smooth my morning hair into a less bunny-boiling style. I slide into a chair at the table and watch him like a complicated painting at a museum that I need to interpret for hidden meaning. Maybe I'm getting Best Friend Booker back today?

"Sleep well?" I ask after the blender stops.

"Yeah, pretty much. I heard the neighbour downstairs come in really late at one point, though. I had trouble getting back to sleep after that. You?"

Huh. Interesting. I inhale deeply. "I slept fine, thanks."

He turns around with two tall glasses of white frothy mix and sets one in front of me. "So, what is today? Leg day? Arm day? Cardio day?" His voice is chipper.

I tilt my head and shoot back, "How about we get nutty and mix it up?"

He unplugs the blender and then brings over two pieces of toast that just popped up. "Sounds good. I'm off my workout routine, so I'm up for anything."

I try not to laugh as he sits down with me and even goes so far as to butter my toast. We begin eating our breakfast in comfortable silence, but I can't stop watching him through narrowed lashes.

"What?" he finally asks, laughing with a bite of toast in his mouth as the morning light bathes him in golden hues.

"You seem…very chipper." I sound suspicious.

"I am," he says and takes a drink of his shake. He swallows and adds, "I'm excited to see what music you have planned for our workout."

Okay, Booker Harris. I'm biting, but I'm not buying. My side-eye kung fu is strong.

The gym in this building is quite ridiculous. It occupies the top floor of a six-floor-walk-up. When you enter, there's an entire wall of industrial glass, restored to perfection with a partial view of Spitalfields Market—an eclectic outdoor shopping mall with vendors from all over the world.

The biggest wow factor of this gym is the view of the twenty-foot mural on the building across the street. It's a comic style illustration of a blonde woman lying horizontally with her eyes closed. Her head is thrown back and her mouth is in the shape of an *O*. Above it in large, bubble lettering it reads: GUILTY PLEASURES.

Talk about workout inspiration.

A long bank of treadmills line the windows, so during your entire jog you can enjoy the image of a woman with a rather nice bust having a massive orgasm. *A far more fun way to burn a few calories.*

"Where shall we start?" Booker asks, turning to me in his long black football shorts. His sinewy legs are tan and have the perfect amount of hair on them to ooze masculinity while bypassing that whole Darwin chimp evolution image. His top half is on perfect display in a white Bethnal Green T-shirt with the sleeves cut so deeply you can see his side abs.

Who knew side abs were a thing?

"Music first," I answer, peeling off my hoody to reveal my sexy workout bra underneath.

Booker's eyes widen.

I smile.

This is what he deserves. He thinks he can act all hunky-dory without a care in the world over a protein shake? Well, he can't. I'm tired of him behaving as if nothing's changed. First, we all but have sex, like an epic, climb-the-walls hook up where the only box left unchecked was a *P* in the *V*. Then he avoids me. Then last night, he's all over me, forehead kissing and pressing all of his—

Nope, I'm done. I'm not a meek little girl anymore who Booker can control. I'm putting on my proverbial fuck me heels in the form of sexy active wear, and I'm showing him the new Poppy.

Booker's gaze lowers to my sports bra that has a fabric crossing in the front, leaving a circular cutout that reveals an ample amount of cleavage. Far more than is appropriate for actual gym workouts, but it's never busy up here this time of day and I like my breasts. I wouldn't have wanted to pierce my nipples if I didn't.

It's irrelevant that Booker was the first guy I let see my rack since then.

His eyes skate over my bare torso and down to my black leggings with sheer cutouts all the way up the sides. My body definitely isn't as cut as his, but I know I look different than before I left.

I was never really into fitness when I was younger. I was far more interested in theatre, art, and other things that used the left side of my brain. But when I went to Uni, I wanted a transformation in more ways than simply chopping off my hair and piercing my nipple. So I started working out. That's when I met a student trainer. A pretty hot student trainer, even if he wasn't the most interesting bloke. He created a diet and exercise routine for me, and I started to see results in no time. Muscles in places I didn't know muscles existed. Curves deepening around my hips and arse. More energy in my daily life. It was rejuvenating and great for my sex life. Working out gave me an overall confidence that I was lacking before, and I became completely addicted to the feeling. Now I feel right at home when I walk into a gym.

Booker looks over my shoulder as I pull up the playlist entitled *Wicked* on my mobile. I have to stifle a laugh when I realise he has no idea what he's agreed to. I turn off the screen so he can't see what's coming and hand him the device. "Let's start with a light jog to warm up."

He follows me to the treadmills, popping his earbuds in on the way. Starting up my own machine right beside him, we both begin with a slow walk. As the speed increases, I can tell the instant the music starts playing in his ears because he gets a contorted look in his eyes.

He grabs my phone and I flail my hand out to stop him. "Don't look!" Frowning, he pops out a bud, so I repeat myself. "Don't look at what the song is. Just listen."

"Is it all instrumental?" he asks, looking confused.

"No, just *listen*." I bite my lip.

He reinserts the ear piece and asks, "Did they just say Oz?"

My shoulders shake with silent laughter. Another moment passes and his eyes turn to saucers as he deadpans, "Oh wait, Glinda just arrived. It's getting good now."

I laugh so hard I almost trip on my treadmill. His voice is loud in the quiet gym and he has no idea. I can't contain my giggles when the few other people here begin to gawk at us. Watching his face as he squints hard to listen to every single lyric is hilarious. This is so much better than I expected.

I've been obsessed with *Wicked* since my mum took me and my sister to see it in London before I left for Uni. Watching Booker's eyes twinkle with amusement instead of disdain only makes me love him more.

Like him, I mean. Like him more. As a friend.

"Nice vibrato," he says, nodding his head like Kristen Chenowith is rocking some Led Zeppelin. I buckle over laughing at his serious expression. He looks over at me like I'm a lunatic. I'm just glad I manage to stay vertical on the machine.

After a few more minutes of jogging, I wave him over to the leg machines. A light sheen of sweat coats his face and arms, and his smooth skin glistens under the fluorescents. He's still immersed in the music, but his eyes fall to my cleavage that is also coated with sweat.

I touch my towel to my chest and he quickly looks away, neck turning red. *Did I catch him checking me out?*

I can feel his gaze on my backside as he tails me to the bank of leg machines. Positioning myself correctly, I begin cycling through a few sets, enjoying the way he's tracking my movements. I pop all the areas of my body to maximise the resistance and he nervously looks away. The entire scene makes me purr with satisfaction.

When it's his turn, I'm extra careful not to check out how hot he looks with his taut jaw and veined muscles working overtime as he pushes his body to its breaking point. I don't bother noticing the drizzle of sweat skating down his temple and falling into his clavicle. It's really quite irrelevant at this point.

After a strenuous set of lat pulldowns, I allow the weight I was pulling to lift me from the bench just as Booker hands me my mobile. "I actually didn't mind working out to that music," he states as I roll the headphones around my finger. "It made me feel like I was at the play." He cuts grave eyes at me. "If you tell my brothers that, I'll make you pay."

A snicker bubbles up in my throat. Is it wrong that I want him to make me pay?

I school my expression. "Free weights?"

He silently follows me as I drop my mobile by a workout bench and head over to the barbells on a rack positioned in front of the mirrors.

Booker clears his throat from beside me. "I was going to see if you want to come with me to a little outing Cam is throwing for Indie on Wednesday night."

"Oh?"

"Yeah, it's her birthday and apparently her family isn't big on celebrating. Cam wants to make it special I guess. It's at a pub in Bethnal. It'll be small. Just the Harris clan and a few teammates and friends. Casual but probably fun."

I consider this for a moment. Is he asking me as a date, or as a flatmate thing? Surely it's only a flatmate thing. I shrug my shoulders to put off a carefree vibe. "I'll probably miss the beginning because of work." His face falls, so I quickly add, "But I can come after if you think it'll go past nine."

"Oh yes, definitely. I'll come back and pick you up." He shoots me a cute boyish smirk. Those dimples on full display.

"You don't have to pick me up," I say, forcing his dimples to disappear. "I can take a cab."

"Yes I do, and no you won't." His words are firm and his jaw is taut. I stare in wonder because he's managed to lose the youthful look he always has by simply using those few words. In this moment, he's all man.

A thick Scottish voice from behind interrupts our peculiar eye contact. "Hello there, Poppet. Nice tae see ye again." I turn to find Andrew William—a fellow gym buddy who works out the same time as I do. We've been running into each other up here almost daily since I moved in, and I have to admit, I marvel at his accent.

"Hello, Andrew," I say with a smile and feel intense scrutiny from Booker watching beside me. "How are you?"

"Aye, I'm no bad. Getting a late start I'm afraid. I had an awfy late one last night, so I'm gonna be hingin at some point today." He laughs a little too hard at himself as he tosses a white towel over his muscle-tee'd shoulder. He turns to Booker.

"Sorry, this is Booker," I stammer. "My flatmate. Booker, this is Andrew. He lives…on the first floor?"

"Aye," he confirms with a wink right at me as he reaches out and shakes Booker's hand. He winks a lot. It's Andrew's thing.

"And how do you two know each other?" Booker asks as I try to shake off the sense of déjà vu.

"We don't," I rush. "I mean, we met up here. Similar workout schedules is all." I sing the last word and rock on the balls of my feet, feeling horribly nervous for some reason.

"We ken each other a wee bit." Andrew winks again. "I ken enough tae know that ye cannae bench more than one forty. Last time ye tried, ye nearly choked yerself oot. Ye would have if I hadny been here tae spot ye."

I laugh self-consciously. "That was a fun day."

Booker doesn't look as amused.

An awkward silence descends upon us, and I can't help but take a moment to compare Booker to Andrew. Standing side-by-side, it's clear they are both athletes in peak physical condition. But my eyes gravitate toward Booker's build of tall, stretched out, well-proportioned muscle. Booker looks lithe and fast. Andrew stands a couple inches shorter than him, and you can't quite tell where his neck ends and his shoulders begin. His muscles are huge and rippling, but overpower his physique to the point where his head appears a bit tiny in comparison. He looks like he could plough through an entire football team, though.

"Well, I'll let ye get tae it." Andrew's eyes stay on me longer than necessary as he turns and makes his way over to the treadmills.

I smile awkwardly at Booker before moving to the nearby bench, ready to work my triceps. I prop my right hand and right knee on the bench to form a ninety-degree angle with my arm and begin lifting.

After several sets, I pause, shoulders rising and falling with heavy breaths. My eyes lift to the mirror where I find Booker unabashedly staring at my arse. He flicks his gaze to mine, the storminess of his eyes causing knots to form in my belly. I assume he's going to look away. Blush. Something.

But he doesn't.

He simply returns his view to my arse. Sitting on the bench and drinking me all in. Every inch of me.

The cheeky bastard.

He's not even trying to hide it anymore. He's blatantly checking me out. I know that's what I wanted, but only because I thought it would make him sweat. Make him squirm. Make him regret what he did last night.

What I'm seeing before me is not a man living with regret.

It's a man who looks hungry.

What surprises me more than anything is that I *want* him to keep looking.

Happy Endings

I DON'T KNOW EXACTLY WHAT I'M DOING WITH POPPY, BUT I KNOW doing nothing isn't enough anymore. The day after the gym, Poppy tells me she's going to her parents' house instead of Dad's for our regular Sunday dinner, which I completely understand. They've missed her, too, and I get to come home to her every night.

Come home to her every night? Christ, Booker. Get a grip.

What I don't expect is the disappointment I feel when she texts me to say she's going to spend the night. I'm telling myself it has nothing to do with me, she's just catching up with her family. But there's an ominous fear in the back of my mind that she might be trying to avoid me again.

After a typical Sunday night dinner at Dad's, my space in my flat feels empty. Poppy's room is dark. The kitchen backsplash light is off. I leave it on for her every night so she doesn't get creeped out walking to the loo in the dark. Years of disturbing *Grimm's Fairy Tales* perpetuating her fear. I can't help but feel disappointed by how *quiet* it is. It's crazy how even with all the tension and awkward moments that have come and gone between us, I still want her here, no matter what.

I miss her.

Poppy is easy to miss.

Draped on my back on top of my big bed, my thoughts drift to her at the gym yesterday. I replay everything in my mind, wondering if I pushed too hard or too fast. Eye-fucking her probably wasn't the best idea, but I couldn't help it. The sheer cutouts on the sides of her leggings went all the way to her waistband, and I never saw a knicker line.

Fuck me.

That was a very different-looking Poppy. Not that she hasn't always looked great. But when someone returns after six years looking like *that*, you can't help but ogle. Her glutes never had that bounce. Her waist was never that defined. Her muscular thighs…Fuck me if I didn't picture them wrapped tightly around my hips as I drive balls deep into her.

Fuuuck. That night we had together feels like a lifetime ago. And I was merely inches away from slipping inside of her.

Working out with her yesterday was a bad idea. It just made me horny. Hornier than I've felt since I was a teenager.

My hand drifts down to my balls. I groan at the aching of my stiff shaft that shoots up just from thinking about her. I don't even need to see a picture of her to remember those large lush breasts pushing together as she did lat pulls.

I rub my cock through my shorts, flexing my fingers and hating that this need is so strong that I have to touch myself. Why can't I just go fuck someone else to get my mind off of Poppy? I'm not as man-whorish as Cam and Tan used to be, but I've gone out enough in London that I have plenty of phone numbers I can call. "Harris Hoes" is what Belle calls them.

The truth is, I've been tired of that game for a while and I don't want a Harris Ho.

I want Poppy.

I picture her here with me as I add pressure to my grip. A flash of her graceful neck on full display because of her short hair has me licking my lips, wishing I could taste the spot just below her ear.

Groaning, I slide my hand into my boxers and squeeze myself with my rough hands. Keeper's hands. I might wear gloves, but my palms take a beating.

My hard-on grows with every stroke. My grunts become louder, holding nothing back after three weeks of sexual oppression. Three weeks of denying what I want so fucking bad. I picture Poppy sprawled out naked on my sofa, that fucking nipple ring shining at me like a lighthouse calling in a ship. Her large green eyes blinking up at me like she's waited her whole life to feel me push inside of her.

"Fuck yes, Poppy." I husk out her name and, bloody hell, it feels good. It creates a frenzy of need in my lower stomach and spurs my climax to the very tip of my shaft. "God, fuck, Poppy. Yes!"

Repeating her name like a chant has me blowing like a fucking teenager all over my hand and boxers within minutes. Pathetic. I reach over and grab some tissues, wiping away the mess that I so carelessly blew all over myself. This is what the woman does to me.

Now I need a shower. And hell, maybe round two because I'm still semi hard.

After depositing the tissues in the trash, I rise from my bed and open my door, shocked to see the backsplash light on in the kitchen. Did I turn that on and not realise it?

I swerve my gaze to the left down the hallway. My heart explodes in my chest when I see the dim yellow light peeking out from under Poppy's pocket door.

"Fuck me" I whisper. "She's home."

Poppy

Oh my fucking God, oh my fucking God, oh my fucking God! I heave in big gulps of air as I stand out on the small balcony outside my room. Thank goodness fresh air exists for moments just like this. Moments when you overhear your best friend masturbating to your fucking name!

Unless he has a girl in his room who also has the name Poppy?

I scoff out loud. *No, not likely.*

I had planned to stay with my parents for the night to get in some good family time. However, Dad got called in for a vet emergency—some dog swallowed a pushpin—and Mum thought she should go with him. So they called me a cab and I dragged my arse back to Shoreditch.

To my flat.

That I share with my best friend.

Who apparently thinks of me while he masturbates.

What the fuck this all means, I have absolutely no idea. What I do know is that I paused in the hallway for much longer than was appropriate. Like a pervert, I stood there—my ear brushing the wood frame of his door—long enough to hear his happy ending. I cringe, a deep, hot flush of embarrassment running up my neck to my cheeks. But with that sensation, a pebbling happens over my nipples. I cup my treasonous breasts and my finger accidently catches on my nipple ring.

God, that feels good.

Not as good as Booker's hands and mouth felt, but it feels similar. Like if I close my eyes and tease it a little, I can imagine—

Jesus Christ, Poppy! What the bloody hell are you doing?

Was I actually going to start masturbating to thoughts of Booker? Tit for tat? The tingling sensation between my thighs is like a hot bolt of electricity pointing to YES! Good God, what is wrong with me?

Living with Booker was so much easier when he was consumed by football and travelling. Now that he's here, he's everywhere! I can even smell him on my shirt.

And God, it smells good. How does he smell so good?

This is madness. I need to get control of this situation. I need to remember what Booker did all those years ago. I need to remember that if he didn't see me romantically before, he won't now. He had a lifetime to develop feelings for me—real, genuine feelings—and he didn't.

I'll take a cold shower and put these raging hormones to bed. Without a happy ending. I simply need to keep being myself and let Booker Harris do whatever it is he needs to do.

There. Blocked that shot from a mile.

A Slip

Booker

Me: Hey, I keep missing you at the flat this week, but does 9:00 work to pick you up tonight for the party?

Poppy: Oh yes! I almost forgot. I finish at 8:30, so that'll be just enough time to run home and freshen up. Do you know what the attire is?

Me: Attire?

Poppy: Casual? Formal? Flirty?

Me: Flirty sounds good.

Poppy: <Side-Eye Emoji> Good for whom exactly?

Me: Depends where you're aiming it.

Poppy: …

Poppy: …

Poppy: …

Poppy: I think I have Belle's number in my phone from a few weeks ago. I'll text her to find out. I'll see you tonight. Are you sure I can't just take a cab?

Me: NO.

Poppy: There you go again, keepering me.

Me: Keepering you?

Poppy: I'll tell you tonight.
Me: Can't wait.
Poppy: XX

Two kisses. Is that a good sign? What does that mean? Are they two kisses like, "I heard you jerk off with my name on your lips, and I'm completely creeped out by you"? Or are they, "I heard you jerk off with my name on your lips, and I'm completely turned on by you"? Maybe they're just polite air-kisses that you'd give to European diplomats? If they are diplomat kisses, they are most definitely not a good sign. Not if you're thinking about your best friend naked…again.

I pull up in front of our flat in Tanner's big black truck that was relegated to me so he could get something even bigger. The wanker. I take our building steps two at a time until I reach our door. The smell of girlie perfume fills my nostrils as I enter. It always smells good in here. Growing up with brothers, it was common for our rooms to stink from month-old dirty socks stuffed in weird crevices. Living with a girl definitely has its perks.

Poppy strides out from the hallway, and I do a major double take. Triple take. Hell, quadruple take. She looks fucking fit.

Her short blonde hair is styled curlier than usual. It doesn't have the soft sweeping look it usually does. It has volume. Fluff. Sass. Like her personality. Her long lashes are thick and black, framing her round brilliant green eyes that remind me of the pitch. She swipes a shiny gloss over her lips that are stained a deep ruddy colour, making them look heavy and plump. My mind instantly pictures my dick in her mouth from our first night together.

But the dress. The dress is so characteristically Poppy. It's a sexy, nighttime version of a really short sundress. A shimmering black fabric with dainty pink and cream flowers printed all over. The straps on her shoulders are thin, holding up the dipping neckline that shows just enough cleavage to make me pant, but not enough to make me beg. She looks elegant. Like a woman.

"You look beautiful," I loll, hoping my tongue isn't hanging out of my mouth.

She looks up at me standing in the doorway. Her lower lip drops, parting from her upper as her gaze rakes over me. "You do, too. I erm…don't think I've seen you in anything but team tees since I've been back."

I self-consciously tug at my red and white checked button down that's untucked over my tight jeans. "My wardrobe is a bit limited."

She smiles. "I noticed."

I swallow as the image of her wearing my shirt at Tower Park slices back into my mind. "Are you all set?"

She nods and I gesture for her to walk out first, watching the sway of her hips under the floaty skirt as she exits. My eyes close in pain. *What the fuck are you doing, Booker?*

Old George is a favourite hangout of Camden and Tanner's. It's located in the heart of Bethnal Green, so it's nice and close to the stadium and pretty much all of our flats in East London. It's a bit more posh than our other hangout, Welly's, which is where we go every year to celebrate Vi and our mum's birthday because they share the same date. Vi has never loved her birthday because of that fact, but getting engaged to Hayden on it last year has surely helped.

"Who all is there?" Poppy asks as I drive the five minutes to the pub.

"It's pretty much just a Harris do," I laugh. "Indie's not the most social butterfly you'll ever meet."

"Really? I got on with her quite well at your dad's. How old is she, though? She looks too young to be a doctor."

"She turned twenty-six today, so she is young to be as advanced in her career as she is. Cam said she skipped a few years in school."

"That doesn't surprise me. She seems brilliant."

I look over at her. "So, you like her and Belle then?" I watch for her reaction.

She nods eagerly. "Those two are hilarious. Their banter had me laughing more than helping with the wedding plans. But I think they had it all covered to begin with. Indie's to-do list is meticulous."

I slide my hand down my jean clad thigh, wiping the sweat off my palm. "I was wondering if you'd want to come to that actually… Tanner and Belle's wedding." I can feel her head snap to look at me. "What?" I ask, squirming beneath her skeptical glower.

"You don't have anyone special you want to take instead?"

"Like who?"

She huffs, "Like a date."

Frowning, I reply, "Truthfully, I'd rather go with my best friend."

I can feel her eyeing me as I pull into a parking stall right in front of Old George. I cut the engine and turn to look at her. Her gaze sparkles in the darkness as she stares intently at me.

"What, Poppy?" I ask, tugging on my earlobe. "What aren't you saying?"

She fidgets with her hands on her lap. "Are we best friends again?" Her hoarse voice asking such a thoughtful question pulls me up short.

"Did we ever stop?"

"I guess not." She looks up at me again, staring at my face like she's trying to commit every millimetre to memory. A soft smile lightens her brow. "But I will tell you, Belle already beat you to the punch. She invited me to their wedding at your Dad's house. I think she likes me!"

That thought makes me smile as I exit the car and hold the door open for her. She has an extra bounce in her step as we enter the large bar and restaurant area. Old George is adorned with exposed brick, dim lighting, and quirky vintage décor. It's a cool place for a fun night out that's just a bit different that the dingier pubs we're used to.

We walk through two reception rooms full of diners and head to the back door that opens into the huge beer garden. It's a lattice and ivy ensconced oasis complete with twinkling Edison bulbs. A live indie rock band plays as we walk along the cobblestone footing toward the back where Camden reserved some rustic picnic tables for the night.

Everyone greets Poppy like she's one of the family. She's quick to wish Indie a happy birthday. I even see her slide a card over to her. Indie coos that she didn't need to, and they do that whole girlie bit where they argue who's the sweetest. Indie is all smiles, rocking her cheetah-print specs and eyeing Camden through all the chaos.

Tanner vacates his spot on the bench so Poppy can slide in next to the girls. Across from them is Dad, Gareth, Vi, and Hayden. They all fall into easy conversation, so I head over to the outdoor bar with Tanner and Camden to order Poppy a drink.

I can't help but notice Camden's fidgeting as he peels the label off his brown bottle of beer.

"Why are you acting so strange, Cam?" I ask and pat him on the back. "Have a bloody drink and try to relax. Indie looks like she's having a great time."

Tanner eyes Camden speculatively. "If I didn't know any better, I'd say you have something up your sleeve. But considering you tell me everything, that can't possibly be true, right?"

Camden looks at the two of us and throws his hands up in the air. "You guys caught me! The stripper is due to arrive any minute now."

Tanner chuckles. "Just what the doctor ordered."

"Nice pun, bro!" Cam high fives Tan.

I roll my eyes and grab Poppy's drink from the bartender. "You better be joking."

Camden scoffs, "So serious, baby bro. Don't worry about me. I think you need to turn your focus on your little flatmate situation. Just look at how easily Poppy seems to be fitting in with our ladies."

They follow me as I take Poppy's drink over to her. I can't help but observe her as she laughs at something Belle whispers in her ear. Poppy has always been charismatic and could talk easily with anyone. But seeing her slip in so effortlessly now that we're all grown up is…nice. My chest puffs up with pride.

She waves her drink glass at me in thanks, her eyes twinkling that familiar Poppy sparkle. "It's not tequila and cream soda, is it?"

Everyone at the table groans.

My eyes crinkle with mirth. "You'll have to taste it to find out."

The warning tone doesn't go unnoticed by her. Several layers of questions could be interpreted under that statement if she really wanted to dig. Regardless, she takes a sip of her drink and winks, the tiny gesture sending a jolt of electricity through my body.

She turns her smile to Vi and asks, "What did you do with Rocky for the night?"

Vi beams. "We got a proper sitter for the first time!" She raises her hands up in the air in mock celebration and then takes a drink of her beer.

"I wanted to babysit," Tanner bellows. "But Camden said I had to be here."

"We wanted to be here!" Belle defends, eyes wide and angry on Tanner. "It's my best mate's birthday. We wouldn't miss it, you knob."

"That's not what I meant! Indie knows I love her like a pig loves not being bacon," Tanner argues. "But I would have stayed in so you all could have a night out. I don't like the idea of leaving our Rock Star with some stranger off the street."

"She's not off the street!" Vi exclaims. "She was hired from an agency. She's been vetted. She's completely professional!"

Tanner scowls, scratching his beard. "I still don't like it."

"Well, we have to find someone we like before your wedding because I intend to pass off my little princess and party!"

Everyone laughs and then Hayden elbows Tanner with his mobile in his hands. "Two words. Nanny cam."

Tanner's eyes fly wide. "Oh, thank fuck for that!"

The two huddle over the phone like it's the next M. Night Shyamalan flick before Camden's stern voice interjects. "Are you all quite done?"

We look at him to see his stony expression. Very un-Camden like. Just then, a waitress walks toward us holding a flaming birthday cake with over twenty tall, skinny candles shooting off fiery sparkles. She sets it on the picnic table in front of everyone.

"Specs, can you come here?" Cam asks, his face bathed in golden light. He grips the back of his neck and looks away nervously. Truthfully, he looks how he does before a match. Like an edgy wreck.

Indie doesn't seem to notice, her eyes bright on the flaming cake as she stands and hurries over. Her hands clasp together with glee as she smiles at Camden. "Oh, Cam, I love it! What a surprise! Thank you!"

She leans forward for a kiss, but he pulls back, his face looking awkward. "This isn't your only surprise." He exhales heavily.

We all watch in silence as he digs inside the pocket of his jeans. He pulls out a black velvet box, and there's a collective gasp as he drops down on one knee. Indie's hands fly to her face, covering her glasses to hide her complete and total look of shock.

"No fucking way," she whispers breathily, dropping her hands. Clearly she did not suspect this.

Camden clears his throat. "Tanner and I have shared everything most of our lives, so I suppose it makes sense that we share our engagements, too."

Vi laughs inelegantly and croaks, "Oh my God! Is this real?"

My smile is a mix of shock and awe as I shake my head at the scene unfolding before me.

Camden smirks up at Tan and then steels himself to look at Indie. When their eyes connect, you can see it…The shift. The complete giving of himself to her. He opens up like a book for her to devour. "Specs, since the moment I was injured last year and thought my life was over, I've been proven wrong time and time again and shown that the best is yet to come. And all of those bests have been better because of you."

He opens the box, revealing a ring of diamonds around a platinum band. It's nontraditional. It's very Indie.

He takes a deep breath and exhales. "I am thine, and thou art mine, Specs. Marry me."

There's complete silence as he says the final two words. They don't come out as a demand. They come out as a plea. A raw, vulnerable plea for her to put him out of his misery. Suddenly, Indie starts laughing like a hyena. We all stare at her, completely gobsmacked and awaiting her reply.

Tanner flinches from Belle's tight grip on his arm as she shrieks, "Say yes!"

Indie looks at Belle with a big smile. "Yes," she whispers. Then she looks back down at Camden and shouts the three-letter word again. "Yes!" She launches herself into his arms. He stands up, lifting her off the ground and kissing her smile through his own. We all watch their embrace with cheesy grins of our own, happiness rolling off of them like the heat from the burning candles. It's intense.

Dad's voice cuts above the boisterous cheers. "Good grief. What other excitement is to come for this family?"

"I vote lots more babies!" Tanner cajoles and Belle elbows him in the ribs. He laughs and kisses her.

"Make a wish, Specs," Cam says, his arms wrapped tightly around Indie's waist as he stands behind her kissing her cheek.

She narrows her eyes and places a finger to her chin. "I wish… that Booker is next!" She blows out the candles, and I swear the whole world fades to black.

Poppy

Love is in the air. Heaping buckets of golden, sweet, melting, delicious love that you can't help but get drunk on. The Harrises are a family that was surrounded by so much darkness after the loss of their mother and the temporary loss of their father as he mourned. Booker was never one to talk much about his mum, but he spoke of how bad some days were with his dad. My heart aches for the children they were back then as they attempted to navigate adult problems.

Looking at them now, you can see that travesty created unshakeable bonds. And the universe is more than making up for those dark years. The Harris family is overflowing with love and happiness. On top of the stunning engagement ring Cam put on Indie's finger, Tanner keeps making proclamations about lots of babies, and Hayden and Vi keep smiling at Hayden's phone as they watch their daughter sleep on the nanny cam.

It's immense. It's breathtaking. Cake is eaten, drinks are shared, memories are told, laughs are had. The entire time, I think to myself, *This family couldn't be luckier.* They have their own network of love, friendship, and support, and I'm thrilled to be near it, even as just a friend.

Booker's eyes find mine all night long, starting with the moment Indie made her birthday wish. My knees nearly buckled when he looked straight at me with those eyes from the other night. Those eyes I wanted to see for so many years. His mouth may have been tipped into a half-smile as everyone erupted into laughter, but his eyes…*His eyes* didn't hold an ounce of humour in them. They watched me with purpose. His dark hair swept back showcased every emotion in his gaze, revealing the mysterious parts of his mind that I want to know. That I'm desperate to understand.

The rest of the evening, I feel the constant pull of energy wafting off of him. All directed at me. It's overwhelming. I'm not drunk on alcohol. I'm drunk on Booker Harris. On the possibility of what could be going through my best friend's mind.

After a million hugs goodbye, we make our way to the front of Old George. Booker opens the truck door for me and grips me around the waist, hoisting me up into the seat. His hands freeze for a moment, his gaze downcast, watching the hold he has on me as his thumbs stroke my sides. It feels like the way a boy touches a girl when he has feelings for her. Not the way a mate touches his friend.

He finally releases me and closes the door, allowing me to exhale heavy breaths and slow my heart rate as he walks around to his door and slides in.

We're completely silent the entire way home. It's a five minute drive, but it feels like hours. Hours of my mind racing over what's happening between us. What's happening to *me*. I've told myself that I'm not looking at Booker like that anymore. But right now, all I want is him. All I *feel* is him. I'm back to being that eighteen-year-old girl who was falling for Booker. But now I'm trapped in the body of a twenty-five-year-old woman who will demand satisfaction if I let myself continue to be so turned on.

Tension builds up inside of me like a rubber band ready to snap. Booker's chin turns, watching me out of the corner of his eye as I mindlessly rub my legs.

My. Aching. Bare. Legs.

I inhale a shaky breath and press my head against the headrest, trying to put a stop to this sexually charged torture. How is a silent car ride this fucking erotic? What universe have I fallen in to? I'm weak here. I have no power.

Finally, we reach our building. We climb the two floors to our flat, his footsteps close behind me when we reach the door. "Excuse me, Poppy." His voice is gruff and vibrates through every part of me as he slips past me with the key.

My eyes are downcast and my cheeks burn from the memory of my name on his lips as he reached his climax the other night. He pushes the door open and steps back for me to pass. I steal a glance at him and our eyes meet.—a million emotions roaring in his dark eyes.

I brush my arm along his firm chest and shiver at his sharp intake of air. He's feeling something, too. I'm not alone.

My heels clack down the hall to my room. Once inside, I look over my shoulder and watch him pause at the threshold of his own room. His forearms flex as he grips the doorframe, stopping himself from entering. He turns his neck and looks at me with narrowed eyes. It's then that I finally see it. I see everything clearly. Above all the other mixed emotions and confusions and unknowns, the one thing that shines over everything…

…is *want*.

He wants me. And I want him. So badly I can taste it. So badly I can remember the feeling of his hard dick in my mouth. I don't care that we shouldn't. I don't care how wrong it is because what I'm feeling inside my body can't be ignored any longer.

Booker drops his head back and looks at the ceiling, his Adam's apple sliding down his thick neck as he leans his back against the doorframe. His chin drops and he faces me full on.

It's a standoff. A dare. A game of chicken. Who's going to speak first? Who's going to break the silent tension that is wafting down the dim hallway?

Reaching up, his hands begin slowly unbuttoning his dress shirt. One tiny slip of a button at a time. A sliver of olive flesh showing on his chest with his descent.

My hands, too, develop a mind of their own. *More like a sexual organ of their own.*

I reach back and pull down the zipper of my dress, holding the bodice to my chest while the straps fall off my shoulders. My eyes remain downcast, basking in the heat of his gaze on me.

Watching. Waiting. Wondering.

Savouring the delicious build of him simply observing me.

Finally, I look up. And I want him. I want him more than I ever knew possible. I want his hands on me, his body pressed against mine. I want the weight of him on top of me as he morphs from my best friend to my lover.

My lover.

The heat in his eyes is a sexual promise and a command rolled into one. So I do what my body demands of me.

I drop my hands.

The dress slithers down to my hips, revealing my completely bare breasts and exposing so much more than my skin.

Fire explodes in his eyes. With strong, fierce strides, he eats up the floor in a second and I'm in his firm grasp in two. His lips collide with mine as one arm wraps tightly around my waist, grappling for my arse. The other slides along on my chest, stroking, rubbing, holding me in place while he drags his tongue down my neck, suckling a spot on my collarbone.

He twirls us, strong and fast into the nearby wall, pressing into me, his erection finding purchase between my thighs as I slide one leg up around his hip. My shriek is loud when he bends to suck my nipple ring into his mouth. He laps and laves the jewelry with his tongue, clanking the cold metal on his teeth. The bud is like a pressure line straight between my legs, my knickers dampening with need.

When my moans become cries, he moves his lips up to my neck, his hand skating up my bare thigh in a tight, claiming grip. When he pulls back to look into my eyes, his are blazing with lust. Then he steals my breath by fusing our mouths together again. It's a kiss that demands entry this time, not only connection. His tongue parts my lips as he imprints his against mine, massaging the flesh together in delicious erotic indecency.

A surge of warmth blooms between my thighs when his fingers snake inside my knickers. I pull away from his mouth and look down at his arm smashed between us. Like a crazed animal, I mewl as he sinks a long finger inside of me and then another. His exposed chest muscles contract and retract with each pump of his fingers. Over and over. Long, languid motions increasing in speed with each one of my laboured cries.

"Booker! I need…" I pause and gasp for breath as my hips gyrate into his touch. "I'm going to come."

"Good," he growls, his voice an aphrodisiac. "Come like I did the other night."

My hooded eyes can barely focus on him. "What?"

"Did you hear me, Poppy? Did you hear me call your name as I jerked myself off thinking of you?"

I swallow and can't bring myself to admit it out loud because I'm so embarrassed. But sickly, the mortification only turns me on even more. My head nods.

He half smiles, a naughty glint in his eyes I never knew existed inside of him. "Did you like it?"

"Yes," I pant, holding nothing back.

"Did you touch yourself?"

"No."

He frowns, disappointed. "Why not? Didn't you want to?"

My climax is building.

"Answer me, Poppy. Didn't you want to touch yourself?"

"No!" I exclaim.

His eyes narrow with determination. "Why not?"

"Because I wanted you to do it!" I snap.

And my orgasm tips.

Booker bites his lower lip as I spasm around his fingers. Roughly, he yanks out of my folds and pinches my clit so hard, all air is wrenched from my body. I go completely silent. The pressure with the orgasm and the pressure on my clit rendering me unable to release even a gasp as pinpoints of light blast off behind my closed lids. *Was that a double orgasm?*

After shuddering for what feels like hours, he releases his grip on me and my legs buckle. He deftly sweeps me up into his arms and murmurs into my hair, "Fuck, Poppy. I'm so fucking hard right now." His chest vibrates with a chuckle as my head lolls onto his shoulder.

The aftershocks of the climax are still sweeping through me as he walks me down the hall and lays me on his bed. My eyelids flutter open and I see him lean down to flick the lamp on. The yellow light casts warm shadows on his flexing pecs as he removes his shirt. His triceps bunching as he unbuckles his belt. His abs stacking on top of each other as he removes his jeans and boxers all in one shot.

My body squirms at the sight of him fully hard. So hard, I see pre-come seeping out the tip already. I thought I was spent. I thought that double orgasm or whatever it was might kill me on the spot. But seeing him there, naked, confident, and seeking entry *inside of me…* I've been awakened.

I want his cock to stretch the inside of me until I'm sore.

He taps my hips for me to lift them so he can shimmy my dress down the rest of the way. Now I'm laid before him wearing nothing but my sheer black knickers. Bending at the waist, he presses his face between my thighs, dragging his nose along my pubic bone as he inhales deeply.

"Oh my God," I moan as he hooks his fingers on the band of my knickers and pulls them down my legs. "Did you just smell me?"

"You smell so fucking good here." He kisses my belly and crawls up my body, holding himself off of me with his muscled arms. "And here." He kisses the divot between my breasts. "Here." He kisses the space below my ear. "Here." He kisses my lips. "Everywhere. And I'm going to fucking taste you again because you are making me lose my bloody mind, Poppy."

I nod because, quite honestly, when he says my name with those sex eyes, I can't think straight either. He spreads my legs and wastes no time swiping his tongue along my slit, groaning as he flicks over my swollen bundle of nerves. "I want to fuck you, Poppy. It's all I've thought of every night since you came back."

I moan and squirm, squeezing my thighs around his head and combing my fingers through his hair. "Me, too."

He chuckles against me and swipes a few more times before kissing his way up my belly, stopping at my breast to drop a soft, open-mouthed kiss around my nipple ring.

He positions his dick at my entrance and then pauses, looking down at me with a heady look in his eyes. "Should I…I mean, do you want me to get a condom?"

I shake my head because I don't want any type of barrier between us. I feel like we've been living with one for years and, for once, I want to feel him. All of him. I want to be as close to him as possible. And I trust Booker. I know he's a footballer and has been with other girls, but I know he'd never risk anything with me.

"Make lo—" I pause, my face flaming red as I nearly repeat the same words I said our first night together. The same words that scared him away from me like I was a hot torch. "I want you to fuck me, Booker," I croak. The words feel crass and cheap, but I need this to happen so badly, I feel like I could split in two.

"Poppy, you have no idea." He moulds his lips with mine as he positions his bare head at my entrance. Forehead-to-forehead, he looks down as he thrusts into me. My shoulders rise up off the bed as he fills me completely. His hand grips my arse, fingers biting into me as he shifts in deeper. He drags his lips along mine and murmurs, "God, you feel so good."

My hands grip his back muscles, my legs squeezing around his hips. "Fuck me, Booker," I husk because I can't say anything else. I just need to disappear into an orgasm as quickly as possible.

He kicks it up a notch once I've adjusted to his size and fucks me like the professional athlete he is, tipping me to orgasm within the first five minutes. Lithely, he rolls us over so I'm on top. He plays with my clit as I grind my hips on him and a second orgasm slices through me.

"God, you're fucking beautiful." His words speak straight to my heart. I feel it expand in my chest like a warm memory.

In the distance, I'm pretty sure I hear a neighbour yelling at us to quiet down. But we don't stop. We don't even hesitate. We continue on this wild ride because neither of us have a fucking clue where it will end up. Probably nowhere good. So I'm at least enjoying it while it lasts.

Booker

I just fucked my best friend.

After coming inside of Poppy, I realise without a shadow of a doubt that I have fucked up monumentally. And this time, it's so much worse because I didn't stop it when I knew we were going too far. I let it happen. Hoped it would happen. Did everything I could to make it happen. This is all my bloody fault.

I wasn't lying when I said Poppy makes me lose my senses. Why can't I get control of myself? All night around my family, I couldn't stop *feeling* her in my mind. Christ, that sounds stupid, but it's fitting. She encroached my headspace, and I couldn't get past the yearning I had for her. I wanted inside of her. Badly.

But I need to find that control. I'm not some fucking horny teen-ager who can do as he pleases. I'm an adult, and I need to find power over this feeling or I could lose her again. Maybe forever this time.

I need to fix this.

My head jerks when I hear the creak of the floorboards as Poppy scampers from the loo to her bedroom. Knowing I can't let her go to bed like this, I stand and pull on a pair of shorts. Her dress has a laugh at me from a heap on my floor, taunting me like the moron I am. Gathering it up, I slip out to see Poppy in her room, bent over and stepping into a pair of shorts. She quickly grabs a shirt up off the floor and yanks it over her head. Her short blonde hair is sticking up all over the place as she looks down and tugs the shirt into place.

She turns when she hears my approach.

"What are you doing?" I ask, my gaze drifting down her body to see she's in the Bethnal shirt she borrowed for the match. It's huge on her, but my chest feels funny at the sight of her swimming in something of mine.

She eyes my bare stomach and self-consciously swipes her hands through her hair to try to tame the fly-aways. "I was looking for some pyjamas."

I run my own hand through my hair, closing my eyes as I recall the feel of her fingers slicing through it as I tasted her. *Fuuuck, that is not what I should be thinking about right now.* Tugging on my earlobe, I ask, "Were you…erm…planning to come back into my room?"

Frowning like my question shocks her, she asks, "Did you want me to?"

I exhale heavily knowing that sleeping apart would be for the best, but sleeping together sounds like the more gentlemanly thing to do. But…it's Poppy. I can't do this with her. I can't *be* with her intimately. It's too much. We slept together as kids, but not like this. Not since I've seen her naked. "Well I don't expect you to sleep in here. I mean, not unless you want to."

Her face cringes with a look I can't quite distinguish. Annoyance maybe? She narrows her green eyes, her lashes covering nearly all the colour as she crosses her arms over her chest. "It sounds like you want me to sleep in here."

My face drops. "I never said that." *But like a big fucking prat, I am thinking it!*

"I know you, Booker," she snaps. "I can read you like a book. Otherwise, why else would you be standing in my doorway and saying awkward things?"

"Because I don't know what the fuck just happened, Poppy." I let out a harsh breath. "I mean, I know what happened, but I don't know what it means. Forgive me for not being up on the proper procedures for what happens after you fuck your best friend."

Her hands drop and ball into fists at her sides. "Well, maybe we can just go back to ignoring each other like the last time." Her voice rises a whole octave at the end.

"No! Fuck that," I growl and jam a hand through my hair. This is not going well. I'm feeling panicky on the inside, knowing I'm not getting this right. "That's not what I want. I just…guess…I want to know what this is. Was. What it means…to you."

This doesn't seem to calm her down. In fact, it seems to make things much worse. Maybe I shouldn't have said the last part, but I worry more about Poppy's feelings than my own. She's much less experienced than I am…At least I think she is. I don't know if sex means a lot to her or if she sees this as the mistake it was.

"Look, Booker. I don't want to go back to ignoring you either. I've been thinking about this, and I think for the sake of our friendship, I should move out and stay with my parents until my flat is ready like I originally planned."

My heart drops. Then leaps. Then drops again. Then runs around in circles like a distressed fucking dog. "What?" I croak, completely shocked by her suggestion and feeling a horrid ache erupt inside of me. The same ache I got the first time she left.

She looks determined. "I think if we want a chance at saving what remains of our friendship, it's best for us both to have some space."

"I disagree," I bark, my distress quickly switching to anger.

She huffs out an offended, bitter sort of laugh. "Why?"

Shoulders high, I walk toward her and close the distance between us. I reach out and put my hands on her arms, trying to project an air of confidence. I want her to feel assured in what I'm saying. I want her to believe in me. In us. *I need her to stay.* "I think if we want a chance at saving our friendship at all, you absolutely have to stay. It's the only way to work past it." My jaw clenches.

Her head snaps back and forth between my two hands as she shakes loose from my hold. "Don't you keeper me right now, Booker!" she sputters.

I pull back. "What's *keeper me*?"

She huffs indignantly. "Get all big and hot and overbearing"— she uses wild gesticulations as she demonstrates—"and try to bulldoze your way through this conversation."

Did she say hot?

I shake away the thought and purse my lips together, my eyes narrowing with frustration. "I'm not trying to keeper you. I'm trying to show you that we can get through this."

"Work past it!" She regurgitates my words in a mocking, sing-songy voice.

Arguing with Poppy is like arguing with a beagle. Just when they try to look tough and ominous, the opposite effect occurs. I try not to smirk as I step back and cross my arms, propping myself against the doorframe. "Yes, we can work past it, Poppy. Unless of course…" I eye her nervously, wondering for the first time if in fact this could mean more to her than I've considered. "Unless of course this does mean something."

"God, no," she shakes her head, hugging herself, my shirt wrinkling around her as she does. "It means nothing."

The words coming from her mouth don't bring me the comfort I'd hoped for. But nothing is better than something. Nothing is safe. Nothing is drama free. Nothing keeps Poppy here. A tightness forms in my throat as I parrot, "It means nothing."

"We simply…slipped," she states, pursing her lips with a nod, determination etched in her jaw. "Yes, that's what we'll call it. A slip."

"A slip," I repeat through clenched teeth.

"Yeah, you're right. I shouldn't overthink it. Moving out would be wildly dramatic. It was just a slip. We're not friends with benefits. We're not fuck buddies. We…slipped. Won't happen again." She seems relieved now that she's found a label for it.

I huff out a small laugh. "Whatever you want to call it."

"Yep." She nods, doe eyes wide and reassured.

"And you don't want to come back to bed with me?" I ask just to be sure we really are on the same page.

Her eyes turn to slits. "No, Booker. I think I've slipped enough for one night, thanks."

Tequila Sunrise

Poppy

I THINK *I MIGHT BE IN LOVE WITH MY BEST FRIEND…AGAIN.*

There's no question about it. Making love in his bed was the best night of my life. Feeling him in me, his hands on me, his breath in my ear, his weight on top of me. It was about as close to perfection as I could ever imagine. It made those six years I buggered off to Germany to reinvent myself a bloody fucking joke.

And then afterwards happened.

Horrible, awkward, soul-shattering afterwards.

Needless to say, things at the Harris Love Shack are fucking tense. Booker and I have been quiet the last couple of days, fumbling around and trying to avoid each other without appearing like we're trying to avoid each other. Just this morning he was making a protein shake in the kitchen and I did an accidental brush by. *It really was an accident this time.* He jumped backward like he'd been bitten. But then he realised how he overreacted and gave me his protein shake in apology.

Bloody hell.

I've been cycling through my mind, trying to figure out if our friendship is salvageable after what's happened. If I can get over my feelings and the hurt of Booker dismissing me so easily after what we shared together. Then when I threatened to leave and he got so worked up, I simply folded my cards. Cashed in. Because above all, I don't want to lose my best friend. I need to figure out how to make things suck less.

On my walk back from my Friday night class, I get a text from someone who actually might be able to help.

Belle: Poppy! What are you doing tonight?

Me: Massive amounts of cool and incredible things.

Belle: So…nothing? Like me?

Me: Bingo. You and Tanner aren't busy with wedding details?

Belle: Tanner is crap when it comes to wedding stuff. Indie and I are at my flat trying to pick out music for the wedding. We thought it might be fun to make a little impromptu hen night out of it. Have you ever drank Tequila Sunrises?

Me: No. Not a huge fan of tequila I'm afraid.

Belle: You haven't tried THESE! Can we come over?

Me: You want to come to my flat?

Belle: Yeah, my place is a bit destroyed with wedding stuff everywhere at the moment, and Indie's big ol' house is all the way over in Notting Hill.

Me: Okay, sure. Booker is babysitting Rocky at Hayden and Vi's flat tonight, so I'd love the company!

Belle: Lovely! See you soon! Xoxo

A flurry of excitement overcomes me as I hurry home to change and tidy up the flat. I've never had many girlfriends to speak of. Only a few from school, but we lost touch when I left for Uni. And since returning, I've been so engorged by…I mean entrenched by…I mean *distracted* by Booker that I haven't really tried branching out much.

Andrew from the gym doesn't really count, even though he is really sweet and fun when he spots me for my reps.

Belle and Indie seem like loads of fun, so maybe this is precisely what I need to get out of my Booker funk.

I open the door and find the duo standing before me with bags in their hands. Indie's wild red curls are in a messy top-knot, her signature eyewear a canary yellow this evening. Belle's silky dark strands are combed over to one side, and her dark eyes are heavily lined and stunning as usual. The two are fearsome sights to behold. It doesn't surprise me that they were able to tame the infamously wild Harris Twins.

Belle's eyes are serious as she says, "Indie has the booze. I have the chocolate. Please tell me you have crisps or we'll have to pop over to the shop."

"I have crisps!" I sing and then twirl into the kitchen to find them in the cupboard.

"Thank fuck." Belle exhales as the two drop their bags on the counter. "I love my chocolate, but drinking is so much easier with something salty."

"That's what she said." Indie giggles at her little joke.

Belle deadpans, "No fucking chocolate for you."

The two continue to jab at each other as they make themselves at home, grabbing glasses and mixing beverages like they've been here a hundred times. I eye them speculatively, grateful for my bottle of whiskey waiting in the wings when this tequila tasting goes sour.

Indie turns, handing me a tall glass with orange juice at the top and a red grenadine syrup floating at the bottom.

"It really does look like a sunrise," I say with a wistful sigh. I'm sure it'll taste awful, but at least it's pretty. Sometimes it's the little things.

Belle holds her glass out. "Tequila Sunrise, ladies."

Indie repeats, "Tequila Sunrise," and clinks her glass with ours.

"This a thing for you guys?" I murmur and sip mine gingerly.

They watch me with wide, expectant eyes.

My brows arch. "It's delicious!" I take another drink—a bigger, more satisfying gulp just to be sure. "You've cured me of my antipathy for tequila! I have to tell Booker about this drink."

The two eye me like I've revealed some gory secret. I ignore their looks and head over to the sofa where they join me, chocolate and crisps in hand.

Belle surveys the room. "Gorg flat. Booker has nice taste."

"Vi found it, I believe," Indie adds, dropping down beside me and pulling her feet up underneath her. "She wanted to be sure to keep precious Baby Booker nice and close."

The two giggle at the tiny, overprotective sister meddling in her four humongous brothers' lives like she always has. Vi may be small, but she is mighty and pulls no punches where those Harris Brothers are concerned.

"Well, it's all temporary for me I'm afraid." I exhale heavily. "I'll be moving at the end of July when my flat is open and, believe me, it can't come soon enough."

The two eye me seriously.

"Spill it," Belle states, nodding her head at me and taking a quick sip. "What's the real situation between you and Booker."

I frown and shift nervously. "Nothing. We're friends. Have been forever."

"That's not what he told Indie," Belle murmurs around the rim of her glass.

Indie's jaw drops and she slaps Belle on the thigh. "That's not how it went and you know it!"

"Ow, you twat!" Belle's mouth is dropped in pain. "I know he didn't say it in so many words, but you told me that he looked a bit… agitated or something at practice."

"Afflicted." She adjusts her glasses in a huff. "He looked afflicted. A very different word. Agitated puts blame on someone else. Afflicted puts blame on one's self."

"Okay, afflicted then. So…what gives?" Belle pins her dark eyes on me, awaiting my response.

I squirm in my seat. "Nothing gives. We're simply having trouble adjusting to friendship as adults. I was nineteen when I went off to Uni, and it had been six years since we'd seen each other. Going from BFFs to distant friends to flatmates would put stress on even the best of friends."

"And it doesn't help that you probably came back looking hotter than ever," Belle states, taking a big gulp.

I take a drink and look away.

"Roll your eyes all you want, Pop, but you're fucking tits hot. You have the neck of a swan. Hell, even I want to give it a lick."

I laugh and Indie smacks Belle on the thigh again. "You are beautiful, Poppy. But you're cool, too. Belle and I could tell right away. You have a really fun self-confidence about you that I greatly admire."

I stare at the two of them, gobsmacked. I'm sitting with two of the most beautiful women I've ever met—doctors to boot—and they are envious of *my* confidence?

"Well, I like you guys, too. But I think you might be a bit too good for those Harris Twins. You know that, right?"

They both look wistfully at the sparkling diamonds on their fingers, neither one put off by my jab.

Indie is the first to break the lovey trance. "I don't think we have to tell you that those Harris boys are some of the best ones out there."

I laugh awkwardly. "They're great and all, but I assure you, they're not perfect."

Belle toys with a lock of her hair, a look of astonishment etched on her face. "What on earth could sweet, sensitive, soulful Baby Booker have done? If you say he used to pull your pigtails in nursery school, I'm going to have to slap you."

I laugh, letting the happiness resonate through my pores for a moment before I dig into a part of my soul that I prefer to tap dance away from. "Booker is a great guy, but he's not immune to flaws. And even the good ones can let you down."

"This sounds juicy," Indie says, reaching out to the coffee table to grab some chocolates. She hands one off to Belle, who takes it without looking and begins unwrapping. Both their eyes glued on me.

"Oh, it's nothing." I try to wave them off. "It's all ancient history."

"So what?" Belle exclaims around a bite. "If it's a titillating tale of betrayal, then let me know and I'll pop some popcorn."

I sigh and can't help but smile at their wide, eager eyes. Maybe opening up to them some will help me get over it. And him. And if it brings us closer together, then all the better. I could use some more friends right now. "Very well then. Booker kind of…broke my heart when we were eighteen."

"He did?" Indie chirps and Belle whacks her on the arm to shush her.

"Were you two together?" Belle asks.

I shake my head. "No. It wasn't like that. We've never been anything other than friends. Never even kissed. But the older I got, the less friendly I saw him, if you know what I mean."

Belle nods. "You saw him naked"—she taps her temple—"in your mind."

Indie giggles. "I think of Cam naked all the time."

Belle rolls her eyes. "That's because he's the only man you've ever seen naked, my darling."

"I've seen lots of blokes naked. I was a surgeon and now I'm a doctor for a football team!" Her little put-out attitude is so bloody cute.

Belle swallows and replies, "Yes, but none of them deflowered you." She says it all so matter-of-factly, I'm left frozen.

Indie's cheeks heat. "I guess there is that."

They try to get me back on topic, but I can't get past what they revealed. I lean forward toward Indie. "Wait. Are you saying that Cam is the only man you've ever slept with?"

She nods.

"And now you're going to marry him?"

Her smile grows and she nods even harder.

I sit back, shocked. "I'm amazed."

"Why?"

I shrug my shoulders. "Because you're so confident in your decision. I went off to Uni thinking I needed my horizons widened. Growing up in Chigwell, I had such blinders on all the time. All I saw was my own little world. Then the moment something went wrong, it felt like the ground was ripped out from under me. I had to leave. I needed to experience other cultures. I wanted to meet men who made me feel less *fragile*."

Indie stares back at me thoughtfully. "Booker makes you feel fragile?"

I nod. "Like cracked glass."

Belle pries, "What did he do?"

My belly heaves with pain. An old pain. A pain I don't care to revisit and give life to, but a pain I can't ignore anymore. "God, you guys must think I'm pathetic opening up to you like this after one bloody drink. I just have nowhere to go for advice because the person I normally go to is whom I need advice about!" I sob internally over how wretched this entire thing is.

"Go ahead and let it out. We're here to listen," Indie says, reaching over and touching my forearm. It feels nice.

I groan and reply, "He took a place that meant a lot to me…to us…to our friendship, and he shared it with someone else."

"Another girl?" Indie asks, her voice quiet.

I nod and add, "It wrecked everything I thought I knew. It made me feel like I must have been delusional about things I thought were special between us. Surely I was off track. I didn't see the truth."

"Which was…" Belle prompts.

"That Booker didn't love me the way I loved him."

"He was eighteen," Belle says in his defense.

"So was I." My eyes begin to well, so I quickly slosh another drink in my mouth. "That only means it hurt that much more."

"But now you're both grown up," Indie says, a helpful gleam in her eyes. "Maybe this means things have changed. Girls mature faster than boys. Surely he's caught up and you see a maturity in Booker now."

I shrug. "It doesn't matter. I didn't come back to London hoping to see a difference in him. I came back for a great job. Regaining a friendship with Booker was just going to be a big bonus. I really did miss him, but I feel like I've bitten off more than I can chew." The image of his eyes on me at Old George flashes through my mind. Then the image of his eyes on me in my bedroom after we slept together and he flipped the switch. "Things are so complicated between us."

"Because you're not fucking kids anymore," Belle states pragmatically. "Because you're both shit hot and living under the same roof with plenty of free time. That's sexual tension for miles. Couple that with a history of friendship and heartache, and you're in the middle of a proverbial shit storm."

I groan and cover my face with my hands. "I know. So what do I do? I have to move out, don't I? I was foolish to think spending this much time with Booker would help us become Booker and Poppy again. I realise now that too much has happened. Too much has changed. I need to get out."

"Fuck that," Belle growls. "You need to take the power back."

Indie's eyes brighten. "Yes! I agree. Listen to Belle. She's the queen of crazy Jedi mind tricks."

Belle rolls her eyes. "I don't think you can move out without knowing the truth."

"What truth?" I ask.

"If he's in love with you, too."

I swallow hard and huff awkwardly. "I'm not in love with him. I thought I was when I was eighteen, but I was a child. I didn't know what love was."

"And now you do," Belle states. "And you still love him. It's written all over your face."

Belle's dark eyes pin me with a challenge. A heavy challenge. Indie's head snaps back and forth between the two of us, caught in the middle of a silent standoff of wills. Admitting the truth out loud is terrifying. It's one thing to think it in my head, but another to say it out loud to witnesses!

Do I love reminiscing with Booker? Yes. Do I love joking around with him? Yes. Do I love watching movies with him? Yes. Do I love drinking with him and dancing to music in the kitchen? Yes. Do I love being his flatmate? Yes, even in awkward moments.

Do I love the feeling of his hands on me as he pushes inside of me completely bare, nothing between us but flesh, vein, and muscle?

Fuck yes.

Do I love the feeling of his lips on mine? Do they give me life and make me feel like he's wrong and that we are more than friends?

A thousand times yes.

I used to confide my inner most secrets to Booker and that is what's missing. And it's missing because I've been harbouring this secret from him for years.

I'm in love with my best friend, maybe more than ever now.

I'm the first to blink. "What should I do? He seems intent on pushing me away every time things escalate between us."

Suddenly, the door opens and my heart leaps into my chest when I see Booker stroll in without a care in the world. He's kitted out with a sleeping Rocky strapped inside a cloth sling across his chest like she's part of his outfit. My cheeks heat as my eyes graze over his tight white, cotton T-shirt pulling at the biceps. One sleeve has a little bit of dried baby spit on the shoulder, but it doesn't detract from the rich olive tone of his thick neck. His jeans are tight around his thighs, and his hair has that soft unkempt wave on top. It's how he looks in the morning when he's just woken up.

Three pairs of eyes stare wide and wild on him as he twirls his keys around his finger. He looks up, noticing us for the first time and freezes.

"What?" he asks, wiping his mouth like we're staring at something smeared all over it.

"Nothing!" I sing.

"Yeah, nothing," Indie chimes in.

"What are you doing here?" Belle rushes out, her tone way too conspicuous to be normal.

He frowns at our peculiar faces. "I forgot my mobile. I figured I'd need it in case Rocky started choking or something." He reaches down and strokes her feathery blonde tresses as she slumbers beautifully. "I know what you're going to say. She only eats soft food. But hell if I know what can happen to a baby. This is the first time Vi's let me babysit, so I'm nervous. And my mind has certainly run wild. I came up with about eighteen different ways she could die all because I didn't have my mobile to call an ambulance. Then I walked back here to grab it because I haven't a clue how to run that car seat business to load her in my truck."

He picks up his mobile from the kitchen counter and then eyes the three of us once again. "What are you guys doing?"

"Nothing," I stammer.

"Drinking!" Indie flashes him her glass.

God, why can't we stop acting like morons.

Belle adds, "We were doing wedding stuff."

"Yes, that's right," I say, sounding a bit too impressed by her stellar response.

Booker tugs on his earlobe. "Oh? Everything going all right?" He looks at me.

"Yeah, lovely," Belle answers for me. "I have a question, though." She gets an evil look in her eyes as she gestures between me and Booker. "Are you two coming as each other's dates to the wedding?"

We both laugh awkwardly and sputter, "No."

"No?" she repeats, her voice rising at the end with suspicion.

Booker looks at me again, and I shake my head as he says, "No. Just mates. You know. Booker and Poppy." His hands hold onto Rocky for comfort as the skin on his neck turns red.

"Perfect! Then you can each bring dates. My parents aren't fucking coming, and I paid a bomb to have fresh lobster brought in."

"Erm…I'm not sure—" I stammer and Booker interrupts.

"What about the paparazzi—" he adds.

Belle cuts him off. "We've tipped the paparazzi off with a fake location and a fake date. Just don't tell your guests where you're taking them and we'll be fine. I need this, guys. My parents are pompous, egotistical prats, and I want my wedding to be a fun party. It's the anti-wedding basically. It would really mean a lot to me if you both brought dates so I don't have to stare their fucking lobsters in the eyeballs and have a *Bridesmaids* giant cookie freak-out moment, all right?"

She shoots us a crazy smile. A frightening smile. A smile that leaves no more room for argument.

We both nod.

"All right then, I'll just erm…leave you ladies to your evening." Booker wiggles Rocky's sleeping hand goodbye and strides out of the flat.

When the door clicks shut, all three of us exhale with relief. "Do you think he heard us?" I ask, my eyes wide and worried.

"Not a chance," Belle replies confidently.

"What the fuck are you trying to start with this date thing, Belle? I don't want to watch Booker with another girl," I state, crossing my arms over my chest and trying not to sulk too much.

"Oh, you'll see," she smirks and sits back, mirroring my stance and blowing on her nails like she just finished an epic bout. "Just get yourself a fucking date."

I nod and look at her and Indie. "So, do you guys want to talk about wedding music now?"

Belle laughs. "Fuck no. That was complete bullshit. We just

wanted to drill you about Booker."

Before the end of the night, I realise that Belle and Indie are master manipulators. Grade-A, psych ward level shit. Like maximum penitentiary prison type psychoses. Like Harley Quinn and The Joker from *Suicide Squad* are fuzzy puppies with good temperaments next to them.

After about four more Tequila Sunrises, we decide to map out my next two weeks leading up to the wedding. It's aimed at setting things up so that the wedding will be Booker's breaking point, so to speak.

Belle titled the list:

HOW TO GET BOOKER HARD by Dr. Love.

I might have side-eyed her concerning the title, but their suggestions are pretty spectacular.

Gloved Man

Booker

After the mess I walked into last night at my flat, I decided to crash at Vi and Hayden's. I needed some space to think. To clear my head. I wanted to stave off any more "slips" from happening with Poppy, but Belle's request for us to bring dates got right up my nose. Why the fuck does she think we need to bring dates to a small family wedding? It makes no fucking sense. I have half a mind to call Tanner and bend his ear about the whole bloody thing.

It's early when I hear Rocky stirring. Vi's flat is a massive penthouse on the eleventh floor, but it's only a one-bedroom. That means Rocky sleeps in their bedroom in a cot. I rise from the sofa in the living room and tiptoe over to their door, hoping to nip in and grab her before she wakes them. They had a special dinner with Hayden's family last night and were out pretty late.

I peer in through the door. Vi and Hayden are out cold in Vi's big gothic glamour bed. Bruce's head pops up off the floor from where he rests, watching me as I sneak in and grab Rocky. Her blonde hair is in wild sprays around her face, and her blue eyes are bright from a good twelve-hour night's rest.

"Hey, beautiful." I hold her to my bare chest and kiss her on the head. "Let's give Mummy and Daddy a lie in."

I walk out of the room and Bruce follows on my heels. I flinch at his loud clacking paws on the tile, but they don't seem to stir. I make quick work of changing Rocky's nappy and heating up a bottle. Then I take her and Bruce out onto the large balcony for a morning cuddle. Bruce can cuddle himself, the slobbering beast.

I stretch out on a lounge chair and inhale deeply as the bustling noise of a busy London Saturday morning buzz all around me. Rocky guzzles her bottle, watching me with her striking blue eyes the whole time. She looks so peaceful, so at ease with herself. She has nothing to trouble her yet.

"You're up early," Vi's voice calls from the doorway.

I turn to see her shuffle out in her pyjamas complete with bunny slippers. Bruce trots over to greet her with a slobbering nuzzle as she leans down and strokes Rocky on the head. "Morning, Adrienne. How was she last night?"

I smile. "Perfect. Bloody perfect. She's the best niece ever. I hope Tanner and Camden's little ones are half as good when they inevitably start procreating."

She flops down on the lounger next to me. Bruce rests his mug on her legs as she gives him a good fondle. "They will be little sods."

"Too right," I chuckle. "Did you guys have a nice time last night? All things considered I mean."

She half smiles, but it looks a little sad. "It's always an emotional night for Hayden's family. I think Rocky would have been a nice reprieve for everyone, but I didn't want to have to leave early if she decided she'd had enough. Plus, the anniversary of Hayden's sister's death is extra hard on him, so I wanted to be free to be there as his partner and not a scrambling new mummy."

I nod with understanding and readjust the bottle in Rocky's mouth. "How's he doing?"

Her smile is prideful this time. "He's good. He's My Hayden. He amazes me every day with how much he's overcome." She sighs and looks out at the London skyline, the pinks of early morning sun illuminating the city. "I think it helps that fatherhood really suits him. He already wants another."

She giggles at my dubious brow. "Marriage first maybe."

This makes her full on belly laugh. "Oh, look at you, Mr. Moral Compass over there."

I half smile. "Well, you've put off your wedding long enough. I'd just like to see you settled I guess."

She shifts so she's lying on her hip, facing me. "Putting it off is easier than change. Change scares me sometimes. We did so well adjusting together with Rocky, but I want to make sure we don't overwhelm ourselves with too much too fast."

I nod, my brow furrowed. "I can certainly sympathise." I pull the bottle from Rocky's mouth to sit her up for a burp.

"And what's new with you, my baby brother?" Vi's bunny foot kicks me in the knee as she tweaks her brows. "What's the latest chatter on the home front?"

I frown but feel a nervous energy creep up my neck. "Nothing."

"Bullshit," Vi deadpans. "Tell me. What's going on with you and Poppy? You were shooting her some serious heat at Indie's birthday."

I shrug, but I know there's no use keeping anything from Vi. She will always dig it out of me, using force if necessary. Shifting Rocky onto my shoulder, I reply, "It's been a bit of a complicated mess with Poppy actually. We've had a couple slips."

Her eyes narrow. "Slips?"

I really hope she's not going to make me say it. "Yeah, slips. But I put a stop to them. I'm done fuc—…messing things up with her. She tried to pull a runner on me, like she did when she buggered off to Germany. I can't let that happen."

Vi looks at me and shakes her head. "You and your bloody abandonment issues. I still remember how much of a nightmare you were when Poppy left."

"I wasn't that bad," I deny.

She scoffs. "Yes you were. Suddenly, you decided you wanted to hang with Camden and Tanner at the nightclubs and hook up with Harris Hoes like it was your job. That's never been you. You don't pull girls like them. You don't Bacon Sandwich Rule."

I roll my eyes at her reference to Camden and Tanner's ridiculous rule about "whomever licks the bacon sandwich first, gets it". Bacon sandwich being a euphemism for girls. Bloody pigs. "I didn't do all that because of Poppy leaving or fucking abandonment issues." I frown and then snuggle Rocky to me as a means of an apology for my coarse language.

Vi pins me with a sad look. "You've always been sensitive to change and people leaving. Don't you remember when Gareth signed with Man U?"

I scowl, immediately transported back to that awful day.

Booker

14 Years Old

"Over my dead body you'll go to fucking Manchester," Dad roars from the other side of the kitchen table.

I'm crouched down by the counter, hiding. Gareth and Dad came storming in so fast, my instinct was to duck and get the hell out of the line of fire. Fights between Dad and Gareth are common, but this one seems far more serious. The two are at a standoff, both on either side of our long kitchen table, clutching the edges like they could snap the thick wood in half. Both looking like a couple of bulls ready to charge each other.

Gareth's veins pop out on his neck as he screams, "I'm twenty-one years old. I've signed a contract. You don't have any say in where I live or who I play for!"

"I'm your God damned manager!" Dad exclaims.

"*Were* my manager." Gareth's upper lip curls with his words. "You're fired, Dad. Effective immediately."

Dad's face shakes with barely contained fury. "You'd actually go back to that place? The place that took her from me?" His voice cracks.

I grab onto both my earlobes, tormented between covering my ears so I don't have to listen but desperate to know what Gareth will say back.

"Manchester didn't kill Mum. And in case you've forgotten, I was the one with her when she died. Not you! And we sure as fuck weren't in Manchester. We were in this house. Upstairs. In the room no one can enter. I was the one wiping her tears when she cried. I was the one holding her hand. All you did was yell at her. I was a fucking child, but I was more of a man than you ever were!"

"You fucking ungrateful…" Dad shoots around the table, his hands outstretched like he's going to rip Gareth's head off.

Gareth doesn't run. He straightens and stands his ground, bracing for the hit. His dark eyes are full of determination as Dad grabs him by the shirt and slams him against the wall.

Where's Vi right now? She's the one who always puts a stop to them. When Dad slams Gareth against the wall again, I finally decide that I have to act. I stand up and scream, "Stop!"

The two freeze instantly, turning their heads to look at me, their breaths heavy like they've been running for miles. Dad's eyes blink like he just realised what he's done. He lets go of Gareth's shirt and steps away from him. His face contorts with pain. Agony. Defeat.

"I won't go back there," Dad croaks, his eyes staring down at the floor. "I won't go back to that place. I won't see you play. Not there. Not for that team." He covers his mouth to hide his trembling jaw. He looks old all of the sudden. Haggard. Completely broken. He looks up at Gareth. "I'll lose you like I lost her."

A strange guttural sound rips from his throat, and he turns and storms out of the kitchen. Gareth calls out to him, but he doesn't turn back.

Hearing that pain in Dad's voice breaks something inside of me. I've seen signs of his agony for years, but watching him lose it like that shakes me to my core. I don't want to lose Gareth like Dad lost Mum. I don't want to lose anyone in my family. This is bullshit!

My anger reaches a boiling point as I charge Gareth and shove him with all of my might. He doesn't move. "Of all the teams you can play for, you have to go there? To United?" My voice cracks. I clear my throat and sniff hard, swiping at the moisture on my cheeks.

"Booker." Gareth's deep voice is resigned. Sad. "There are many reasons I want to play for them."

"Why?" I scream. "So you can show Dad that you're better than him? A better footballer? Who gives a toss about that, Gareth? What about us?"

"What about you?" he scoffs.

"You're just going to bugger off to Manchester and never see any of us again."

"I'll still see you."

"When?" I yell and shove my hands through my hair. "Dad's right. We're going to lose you. We'll never see you anymore. Everything will go to shit like it did before."

I turn to run out the back door, but he hooks my arm, stopping me in my tracks. His hand is huge on me. He's so much bigger. Taller, thicker, stronger, older. He's everything I want to be and now he's leaving me behind.

"Booker." He says my name through clenched teeth, pinning me with a seriousness to his eyes that I cannot accept. "I'll always be here for you. I love you, kid."

"Fuck you," I spit and rip my arm out from his hand and run out the door without looking back.

What is love? Love means nothing if you still end up leaving.

Poppy's blonde hair is a welcome sight as I reach the depths of the wooded park behind our house. She's sitting on our tree. The tree where I first met her. She's got a ball of yarn on her lap, two needles, and the workings of a knitted blanket. She looks up when she hears me approach. "Booker, what's wrong?"

She drops the yarn and needles without a thought and rushes the rest of the way toward me. I turn, not wanting her to see my tears, but the softness of her touch on my back encourages them more.

"Gareth is leaving to play for Man U," I say, looking out into the trees instead of at her green eyes that always see right through me. "He's not going to live at home anymore." A sob rises in my throat as she hugs me from behind. Her thin, pale arms wrap around my waist, but I can't bring myself to touch her, even though every part of me wants to. "I hate this feeling, Poppy. It feels like after Mum died. Dad is going to be awful again. Losing Gareth will change him. It'll change my family. We won't be us anymore."

"Shhh, you're not losing Gareth."

"He's moving."

"He's Gareth. He'll never go far. You guys mean everything to him."

"We're Harrises. We're all supposed to be here for each other. Always. This feeling of losing someone…It hurts everything inside of me."

"I know," she murmurs into my back. "Loss is a pig of an emotion." She loosens her grip and peeks her head around so she can look up into my eyes. "But, Booker, nothing loved is ever lost. It's kept forever inside your heart."

I roll my eyes but reach down and hold her arms around me. "I don't ever want to lose you, Poppy."

She half smiles and sings, "I'll never leave you, Booker."

"You've been acting twitchy since the boys got engaged, too. Sofa-surfing and hanging about longer than usual. You're worried that everyone is going to move on with their lives and forget you."

"I am not!" I scoff as I continue to pat Rocky on the back for her burp. I'm avoiding Vi's eyes because, deep down, I know there's a sliver of truth to her words. I don't like change. And I don't like losing people close to me. I enjoy our family and how close we are. Losing any of that feels like a failure.

"Do you think Poppy going to Germany had something to do with you?" Vi's blue eyes pin me with a weighty look, like she's trying to figure out a puzzle.

"I don't know." I shrug. "I just know that when she told me on the doorstep of her parents' house, she was…not Poppy. Something had changed. Shifted."

"What do you think it was?" She bites her thumbnail.

"Whatever it was fucked up our friendship, and I've just finally started to get her back." Rocky burps, so I kiss her head and reposition her in my arms. "I don't want to do anything to risk pushing her away again."

Vi eyes me sternly for a minute. "You lost her before and survived. Why are you so much more afraid of losing her now?"

"Because it feels like she came back at exactly the right time." I rush out, realising that the answer has been sitting on the tip of my tongue all this time. "Everybody in our family is moving on with their lives but me. It's fucking unnerving. I guess it just feels nice to have my best friend by my side."

She sits back in her lounger, clutching her knees to her chest. "I guess I can understand that. But don't you think that means you love Poppy, too?"

Her words make my shoulders tense up and Rocky begins fussing. Vi's arms reach out for her, and she happily goes over for a mummy cuddle. I watch the two of them reconnect for a minute. A mother and her child. Such a closeness there. So much love. So much potential for complete and utter heartache.

I shake my head slowly. "I don't love Poppy. Not like that."

"I mean as a friend," she scoffs.

"No," I repeat. "I care for her. Deeply. I would be fucking devastated if something happened to her, but do I love her? No, Vi. I don't. I don't have the space to love her like that."

Vi throws her feet off the side of the lounger to stand so she can bounce Rocky in her arms. I watch her carefully because she seems to be so shocked, I'm worried for Rocky's welfare in her arms. "But you love me?" she asks.

I roll my eyes. "Family is different."

"What about your future wife?"

"That's a long ways away. And who knows if I'll ever get married?"

"You say that now, but that's only because you're not opening yourself up to love." A glossiness appears in her blue gaze.

"What's wrong?" I ask, leaning forward with concern.

"This makes me incredibly sad, Booker." Her voice wobbles as she begins to pace.

"Why?" I ask, feeling like I've stepped on some landmine I wasn't aware of.

"I had no idea you've never opened yourself up to love anyone outside our family." Her voice is a garbled mess of thick emotion. "You've loved us all so fiercely, it's shocking that you're that closed off."

"Love is not a word I mess around with, Vi," I argue, squeezing the back of my neck. "You saw better than I did what a mess Dad turned into because he lost Mum. He was a fucking nightmare for years. If it wasn't for Bethnal Green F.C., who knows how bad things would have been for us. Love has the potential to ruin a person's soul."

"Well, no shit," she snaps and shakes her head, shifting Rocky onto her hip. "But the rewards outweigh the risks. Surely you can see that, Booker, or I feel like I've failed you."

"Failed me how?" I exclaim.

"Because I didn't show you how to love! I was a shitty replacement Mum," she shrieks.

I stand and rush over to her, pulling her into my arms as she sobs against my chest. "Vi, it has nothing to do with you. You loved me better than any mum could. But I think the word love should be reserved for relationships like this. Family. I'll keep my keeper gloves on with everyone else."

"You're wrong, Booker." She pulls away and wipes the tears from her eyes. Rocky stares up at her with a confused expression, like she's connected to her mother's emotions. Vi looks at me with a severe glower and adds, "You're wrong and I'm disappointed in you."

My heart falls. Christ, this conversation has taken a turn for the worst. "You're what?"

"I'm gutted that you think love has to be so small. I love Rocky. I love Hayden. I love my future in-laws. I love my friends. My co-workers. I love you and the boys. I love Indie and Belle because they love Cam and Tan. I love my fucking gardener because he makes my Chrysanthemums look so bloody gorgeous, I'll never have to pay for a photography studio to take pictures of Adrienne!" She inhales a deep breath. "But I'm disappointed that you aren't letting yourself open up to love like that."

"I know what love feels like. I'm not fucking defective," I snap, anger coursing through my veins.

"Well, Booker," she huffs and makes her way to the sliding glass door. "When you decide it's time to open yourself up to loving someone who's not a Harris, I hope I'm still around to see it."

With that parting blow, my sister slams the door, leaving me on the balcony alone with her slobbering, useless dog that loves unconditionally.

Get Booker Hard

I HEAD BACK TO SHOREDITCH FEELING LIKE TEN TONS OF HORSESHIT after leaving an angry sister behind. I hate disappointing Vi. I hate seeing her cry even more. This is the kind of shit that keeps me up at night.

I walk into our flat to Poppy blasting music from her portable speaker. I drop my keys on the side table and frown at a strange setup in the middle of the living room. The closer I get, the more I realise what I'm looking at. It's a wooden rack with long dowels. Stretched over the wooden spindles are lacy, colourful knickers and bras. Red, black, print, pastel. You name it, Poppy has it. It looks like her entire drawer of unmentionables are spread out to dry on this rack in the middle of the bloody living room.

My dick twitches with awareness as I zero in on a sheer black pair of knickers that I recall from the other night.

"Fuckwit poppycox!" Poppy's voice exclaims from down the hallway. "No, please…God, no!"

She cries again and I rush to see what the commotion is. The bi-fold doors where the washer and dryer are located are open. When I peer around them, I see Poppy squatting down in front of the washing machine, shoving heaps of bubbles back inside the door.

One would think the oozing amounts of soap and water running out of the machine would catch my eye first, but nope. It's not. It's Poppy, down on the ground wearing nothing but a pair of pale blue knickers and a white cotton tank. It doesn't take a genius to know that the way she's trying to block the bubbles with her chest means she's going to turn around and—

"Booker!" Poppy states, as she catches me looking down on her from my high vantage point where I can see a clear hollow of cleavage peeking out. She moves to stand and shrieks loudly when her foot slips and she goes tumbling backwards onto her arse.

"Fuck, Poppy," I croak and bend down to grab her by the arms. She's stretched out on her back, soaked nearly head-to-toe with bubbles all over her.

The corner of my eye catches two dark spots on her white tank top that's drenched and completely fucking see through.

I'm totally not looking. I'm totally not looking.

Bloody hell, she's not wearing a bra.

I looked.

My dick presses against the back of my zipper as I move to help her stand. When I think I've got her stable, I reach over and press a button on the washer to stop it from running. The room falls silent aside from our heavy breathing.

"What's going on?" I ask, shoving a bubble-covered hand through my hair.

Poppy stands before me, tugging on the bottom of her tank top like it'll miraculously grow trousers and cover her bare legs that are on full display for my wandering eyes. Not that I'm looking.

"Laundry day?" she says with a shrug, her toes wiggling in the foam.

She glances down and her cheeks flame as she realises I can see her nipples through her tank. Her hands cover her breasts. "I wasn't expecting you home so early."

"Clearly," I murmur, my eyes warring with where to look that's not quite so bloody indecent.

"I had a little mishap with the soap powder." Her finger points to the washer.

I nod and turn my head so I'm looking at the wall. "I'll erm…get the mop. Maybe you should…get a shirt."

She nods awkwardly, and we brush against each other as we each make a move to go in opposite directions. *Fuck me, I think her hard nipples brushed my arm.*

I make my way to the kitchen until she calls out, "Hey, Booker." She stops at the doorway to her room and looks over her shoulder.

"What?" I turn my gaze, begging myself not to check out her supple arse barely covered by her blue knickers.

"I want you to know this wasn't done on purpose."

I pull my lip into my mouth and frown. "Why would I have thought otherwise?"

She gets a weird smile on her face. "No reason. Simply wanted to be sure you weren't thinking unfavourable thoughts about me."

I exhale. "Wouldn't dream of it."

Poppy

Sunday is Harris family dinner night. Booker invites me like he always does but is surprised when I accept this time. Since the first dinner, I've been visiting my own parents while he visits his family. But tonight, I have *goals*.

Belle and Indie's game plan for me to win Booker's heart is a bit half-cocked. Basically I have to sexually frustrate him in a million different ways until the wedding. It seems juvenile, but I enjoy treating life like a performance. If ever there was a way for me to find out if Booker Harris loves me, this would probably be it. The other option is to walk right up to him and tell him my feelings, but that plan went horribly wrong the last time. So I think this game plan is worth a shot. The one caveat Belle said was that I can't allow a slip before the wedding. She was very clear about that. I need to be "slip free" with Booker until D-Day.

Yesterday went a bit off script with the whole washing machine incident, but I think for once my clumsiness actually helped my cause. Bubbles on my tits…Fucking genius! I want to text Belle for a pat on the back, but I refrain because I'm not five.

Oh, fuck it, I'll text her anyway.

Me: Washing machine is knackered. Wet T-shirt contest for the win.

Belle: Bubbly tits? Fucking perfection! You're going to have him panting for it before the wedding at this rate!

The entire crew is present at the Harris house this evening because it's the off-season. Booker's oldest brother, Gareth, eyes me curiously when I come bounding in like an over-caffeinated child. Cam and Tan are wrapped around their fiancés, while Vaughn holds Rocky at the table.

I decide to help Vi prep for dinner, but I must have a crap poker face because she keeps giving me these looks like she knows I'm up to something with her brother. When Camden, Indie, Hayden, and Vaughn decide to take Rocky for a walk in the pram to see if she'll crash for a nap, I decide to activate day two of the GET BOOKER HARD scheme.

"So, Booker," I say as he sits at the counter chatting with Gareth about football as usual. "Have you found a date for Tanner's wedding yet?"

"Date?" Gareth and Vi both ask in unison.

"Yes," Belle pipes in, sliding over to stand at the end of the counter beside Gareth. Her face looks peculiar. "I told them they both need to bring dates so I have someone to eat those lobsters that my parents won't be welcome to."

Vi gives Belle a sympathetic glance. "Are you sure there's nothing that can be done about that?"

"I'm positive," Belle states, plucking a grape from the fruit bowl on the counter and popping it into her mouth. Tanner comes up behind her, giving her waist a cheeky squeeze.

"I offered to go over and have a chat with her dear old daddy, but she practically tied me to the bed." The two look at each other with naughty smiles on their faces, being about as subtle as a freight train.

Gareth's deep voice cuts into their emoji heart eyes. "Can you two please stop dropping details about your sex life into random conversations? Some secrets are better left kept."

"You're just jealous because you don't have sexy secrets to share," Tanner cajoles and smacks his hand on the counter. "Mr. Celibate over here."

Gareth's eyes narrow and he shakes his head. From the look in his glower, I have a feeling he's hiding loads of secrets. Quite honestly, I've always thought he'd be the type to have a Red Room of Pain—a kinky bugger through and through. Something about his beefy build and rogue face that's not classically handsome but oozing that dirty kind of masculinity has always made me a bit nervous around him.

I'll take dimpled face Booker any day.

"So, Booker? Date yet?" I ask again. He looks at me curiously, his dark, lash-framed eyes narrowing with speculation.

"In the one day I've had since Belle informed me I need to bring someone? No, Poppy. Not yet." He tilts his head, annoyance evident in all his features. "Why? Have you?"

Suddenly, Belle slides past me toward the refrigerator. "I'm grabbing an ice lolly. Anyone else want one?"

Tanner raises his hand, and Vi glares at all of us while Belle passes one to me and Tanner. She thinks we'll be spoiling our supper. Ever the mother hen.

Locking secret eyes with Belle, I quickly unwrap my purple ice treat and pop it in my mouth. I lean across the counter so I'm only a foot away from Booker, who's now watching my lips. "So, Booker"—I suck hard and then take a nibble, my tongue swiping out to catch the syrupy liquid on my lips—"Do you know anyone who might be good for me?"

"Good for you for what?" Booker asks, his face devoid of any humour as he stares at my mouth with heat in his eyes.

"For a date. I thought maybe a teammate of yours might be good because they are familiar with Tower Park. They could show me around the stadium after the wedding. Give me a tour." I wink.

His face turns red. "You're not taking one of my fucking teammates to my brother's wedding."

"Why not?" I ask innocently and then plunge the lolly back in my mouth, going deeper this time.

He frowns as he watches my lips. "Because if you want a bloody tour of Tower Park, I can give you one."

Rolling my eyes, I reply, "Fine, he doesn't have to give me a tour. But I'm out of touch with people since I left, and you have a gaggle of teammates, Book. Surely you know someone who wouldn't hate to spend the evening with me."

"Roan DeWalt would be fun for her!" Vi interjects, snapping everyone's attention to her as she whisks something in a bowl.

Tanner pipes up next. "Over my dead body he's coming to my wedding. I've finally stopped wishing dismemberment on the prat."

"It was only a suggestion!" Vi peals, looking perplexed. "It's just that I set him up with our cousin Alice and she loved him! Roan is a South African dreamboat." She waggles her eyebrows at me and I can't help but smile.

Suddenly, Booker stands, his stool screeching on the marble floor as he pushes it away. "Not Roan. Not any Bethnal players. None of them would work. You're not their type."

I hear Vi suck in a breath of air, and my cheeks heat with

embarrassment. "Why not?" My jaw is tight with anger as my ice lolly drips, forgotten between my two fingers.

His fists clench on the counter. "Because I know you, Poppy. You're not the kind of girl they'd go for."

The way he's acting gets right up my nose. I wanted to make him jealous, but that's not what's happening. He's insinuating I'm not good enough for his mates, as if they'd never go for anyone like me. He doesn't even know me as an adult. He's pigeonholing me into the Poppy he thought he used to know. It's complete and utter shit! "If you actually think I'm not good enough for your team—"

"They're not good enough for you!" he shouts, interrupting me as he leans over the counter to get in my face. Booker eyes me hard, clearly not amused by my request. "No teammates, Pop. Not Roan. Not anyone. Got it?" His shoulders rise and fall as he pins me with the most aggressive face I've ever seen on him.

I can tell the moment he snaps out of it because his neck turns red and he looks around at his family, who are all staring at us with their mouths open. He shoves two hands through his hair as he turns on his heel and strides out the back door and into the garden.

It's quiet in the kitchen as everyone sits there gobsmacked.

"Wrong button," Tanner quips and Belle elbows him in the ribs. I turn my red face to look at her and she nods with reassurance.

"I hope you girls know what you're doing," Vi says. Then she wipes her hands off and tosses the tea towel in front of me as she scurries out after Booker.

Poppy

The next morning, I wake to find Booker in the kitchen wearing nothing but his boxers as he brews a pot of coffee. Our ride home from Chigwell last night was quiet as he stewed over something he definitely wasn't interested in sharing with me.

But in the warm early light of day, watching him stand here in nothing but plaid, saggy-butt boxers, my chest contracts. He's my best friend right now. The boy whom I told all my secrets to. The one who held my hand during the scary parts of my favourite book. The one who told me he liked the mud on my dress.

The one who put a lamp in my room and toast and water at my door.

And for a moment, I want to be Booker and Poppy again.

I trudge out in my T-shirt and long socks. My strands of hair are strewn over my eyes, but I'm not awake enough to push them out of the way. He turns when I sidle up next to him at the counter.

"Is it done yet?" I croak, watching the droplets funnel down into the pot. As if on cue, the coffee pot hisses.

"Not quite," he replies, his voice deep and throaty. I really love his morning voice.

"I'm shattered," I say with a sigh and rest my head on his arm.

He tenses at first, but I feel him relax. Then he puts his arm around me, tucking me under him and pressing his lips to the top of my head. It's not sexy. It's not spine-shivering. It's simply…Booker.

"You should go back to bed," he drawls.

I groan. "I can't. I have my first meeting with the school today."

"For your German language job?"

I nod against his chest. "Just a standard meet-and-greet thing. I'm not used to getting up early like this."

He huffs out a laugh. "Well, why don't you go jump in the shower and I'll bring a cup to you?"

I nod and then close my eyes and press my lips to his arm before shuffling away. I pause halfway to the loo and turn to say something.

It could simply be that I'm not fully awake, but I'm about ninety percent sure Booker was watching me leave. And I'm about ninety-five percent sure he's pitching a tent in his boxers.

He realises a bit too late that I've caught him checking me out and shakes his head, the redness in his neck flaming as he turns to face the coffee pot again.

"Booker?" I croak.

He angles his head but keeps his hips facing the counter. He can barely meet my eyes. "Yeah?"

"The shower door is glass."

"Yeah," he deadpans.

"The see through kind."

"Riiight."

"So, erm…maybe just pour me a cuppa and I'll get it when I come out?"

"Of course," he replies quietly and turns back to the coffee.

I head off to shower, pondering that little coffee pot exchange more and more as my brain wakes up. Was Booker trying to set up a slip with the coffee offer? Am I really erection-worthy in a T-shirt and long socks? He's lady-boner-worthy, even in saggy boxers, so it's possible.

This is why I have a plan in place. I can't not think of him as more. And even though he's fighting it, I know he feels it, too. He feels more. He just won't let himself admit it yet. I have to stick to the plan.

Thirty minutes later, I leave my room and find Booker on the balcony. He's still shirtless, but now he's thrown on a pair of jeans that are popped open at the waist. His corded muscles are on full display, and I marvel at the smattering of hair that crawls down into his boxers. *Only a few more days, Poppy. You can do this.*

I step out onto the balcony with a coffee cup in hand. "Booker?" I say his name and he *huhs* me without looking. "Can I get your advice?"

He turns and instantly eyes my cleavage pouring out of my shirt. This is so not business appropriate attire. "Is this top too much for my initial meet-and-greet with my new coworkers?"

"Yes," he says without pause, his eyes trained on my chest.

"Really?" I ask, toying with the bow at the top. "I think it's stylish."

"It's too much," his voice is firm. "I can probably see your bloody nipple ring if I stand over you."

My face flames with embarrassment. Not over his comment, but that we're talking about his awareness of my nipple ring. Like a horrid film montage, I close my eyes and see snapshots of our passionate encounters. His hands on me. His fingers pinching my hardened bud. His dick thrusting in and out of me. I nearly let out a moan and quickly open my eyes to stop the images from flooding my psyche.

Booker's eyes are hot on mine. I swear he's thinking about all the same things. His arms are tense with a rigid stance as he watches me, looking like he's using every muscle in his body to not jump me right now.

Good God, I wouldn't mind being jumped.

I'm the first to look away, my voice shaky as I reply, "Fine, I'll go change."

I turn and pause at the doorway, willing myself not to look back. Begging the silly girl inside of me to be a strong woman.

I look back.

His lust-filled eyes now seem tormented. Disappointed. Like watching me walk away from him is as hard for him as it is for me. It makes the regret I feel come back full force. It's wrong to be playing him like this. I wish I could simply lay all my feelings bare. Put it all out there.

But if there's one thing I know, it's Booker Harris. The man is the most stubborn human. He requires a creative and delicate touch, both of which happen to be my specialty.

Booker

I spend most of the next day at Camden's new house in Notting Hill, grateful for the space from Poppy, who can't seem to stop turning me on at every corner. If it's not her breasts hanging out, it's her legs, or her arse, or her adorable bed-head that makes me want to pull her into my bed for a cuddle.

And I don't cuddle. I've never cuddled actually.

But bloody hell, she's confusing the fuck out of me. There's a constant argument going on inside my head between my dick and my mind. Dick wants a slip. Mind knows that it's a bad idea. If I keep slipping with her, she's going to try to bolt again. Move in with her parents or whatever nonsense she droned after the last time. I can't *just* slip with Poppy. She's going to need more and I don't want that.

So the mindless task of helping Camden build some furniture that he and Indie bought is a welcome reprieve. Tanner is here as well. Even Gareth showed up since he's been staying out at Dad's all week while his team is on break. This is the riveting life of a Tuesday for off-season footballers.

"Thanks for the help, my brothers. Indie is going to love this." Camden's voice is reverent as he strokes the top of the smooth mahogany desk we just finished. It's gigantic and sits as a focal point in the middle of an extensive library with floor-to-ceiling shelves that Cam already has half full of books. He's been an avid reader for quite some time, so it's kind of cool that he found a home with such a space for his collection.

"You mean you're going to love railing Indie on this," Tanner cajoles, lewdly hip thrusting the corner of the desk like an animal.

Gareth pops Tanner on the head. I fail to conceal a smirk at Tanner's pained frown as he rubs his man bun.

Camden smirks. "Don't talk about my fiancé like that, broseph." He lightly punches him in the shoulder. "But you are correct. I can't imagine a better place to bed my new fiancé than on top of a desk surrounded by books. Christ, I could get a stiffy just thinking about it."

Gareth wallops Camden next. I just roll my eyes and sit down on top of said desk. Camden's home is too nice for the likes of his dirty mind. He purchased a Victorian townhouse on an idyllic cobblestone street in Notting Hill. The neighbourhood looks like a movie set. The place is a stunning three floors and is very spacious for London. Arsenal certainly pays more than Bethnal Green.

Truthfully, I can't complain. Living with Dad so many years means that I was able to stash away the majority of my earnings. I should be able to retire from football around the age of thirty-five and not have to work if I don't want to. But I always fancied the thought of owning my own business someday. Just need to work out what that business would be. I should ask Poppy. She has such a creative mind, I'm sure she'd be great at brainstorming what I'd be good at outside of football.

"So, are you and Poppy at each other's throats after Sunday night dinner?" Gareth's deep voice asks as he sidles up next to me.

I frown. "No…We're fine." I think? Yesterday morning seemed fine. Until she asked my advice about that sorry excuse for a shirt, and I had to worry about concealing the bulge that formed inside of my jeans. Christ, if she really thought she could wear something like that to her new job, I'm seriously concerned about her idea of a professional workplace environment.

Tanner slides up on the other side of me, sandwiching me tightly between him and Gareth. He nudges me in the shoulder. "I think the girls are up to something."

"What do you mean?" I ask.

"Belle was looking at Poppy kind of funny," Tanner states, scratching his beard in contemplation. "I can usually tell when her crazy starts to show, and I definitely got a whiff of some crazy."

"The three of them did spend time together on Friday night,"

Camden adds, perching on the other side of Tanner.

"What could they be up to?" I ask, completely confused as I stare at all eight of our feet dangling in a row beside each other.

Tanner shakes his head. "I don't know. Has Poppy found a date for the wedding yet?"

I shrug. "I don't know." It's not really something I've wanted to ask her about. It's going to be weird watching her with another guy the way she is now…all *woman*. But deep down, I think maybe it's exactly what I need to get her out of my head. It's a miracle we got past the first two slips, so maybe seeing her with another man will be helpful in getting us back to the friend zone. The real friend zone.

"Have you lined up a date?" Camden asks.

"Not yet," I reply. "I am probably going to call Sidney."

"The one from our neighbourhood with the huge fake jubblies that you brought to Belle's charity event a while back?" Tanner asks, making a squeezing gesture over his pecs.

I nod and elbow him for being crass. He's not wrong, though. Sidney Carmichael does have massive boobs—something she apparently treated herself to after secondary school. Regardless, she's just a friend. We dated casually for a while when we were eighteen, but I had to end it. Her feelings were much stronger than mine and it became too much.

However, we've remained friends, and she's kind of turned into my go-to date for events. As a pro footballer, we're frequently invited to charities, formal galas, and award ceremonies. Sidney is easy and always available. And I don't have to worry about her latching on like a wannabe WAG because she knows how I feel.

Tanner tsks. "I think it's a mistake to bring Big Jubblies, baby bro."

"Why?"

"Because I don't think Poppy wants to see you with a date any more than you want to see her with a date."

"I don't care if she has a date," I bark defensively.

"Bullshit!" Gareth coughs into his fist.

"I don't!" I turn and look at him with accusing eyes. "I don't know how many times I have to tell you guys this. Poppy is just a friend. That's it. I couldn't give a toss whom she brings to the wedding."

"Well you acted like a jealous boyfriend Sunday night," Gareth prods.

I cut him a glare, his words causing a tightness in my shoulders. I wasn't trying to act jealous. I was trying to protect her. "Teammates are different. They're…off limits. You guys know why."

"Prove it," Tanner dares.

I swerve my head to look at him. "Prove what?"

"Prove that you don't care. Call Sidney to come with you," he challenges.

"You're a moron. I was going to do that anyway."

"Then there's no need to wait another day."

Rolling my eyes, I pull my mobile out of my pocket, find her number, and press CALL. They all watch me as it rings a few times.

"Hello?"

"Hiya, Sidney."

"Booker Harris! Hiii!" Her voice is loud in the quiet library, so I know my brothers can hear her as well.

I clear my throat. "Listen, I have an…erm…event to go to this Saturday night and was wondering if you are free."

"Bugger, I would have loved to go, but I'm in Cape Town for the week. I can look into booking an early flight home?"

"No, no. That's fine. Don't worry about it."

"Are you sure? It would be no trouble."

Actually, it would be a lot of trouble. "I'm sure. Don't worry about it."

"Okay, then." She sounds disappointed. "I'll give you a ring after I get back. Maybe we can grab a bite and catch up."

I nod. "Sounds fine. Have fun."

We say our goodbyes and I exhale.

"Now what?" Camden asks.

"I don't know. I don't really want to bring anyone else because they'll get the wrong idea."

"What idea is that?" Cam asks.

"That you're a free man?" Tanner adds, his brows tweaking.

I frown. "I *am* a free man. Sidney never expects more. Other girls do."

Gareth's voice loses all humour when he replies, "And you can't possibly be a free man because that would mean you'd have to close the door on Poppy."

I growl and jump off the desk to get some space from my pushy and annoying brothers. "You guys don't get it because you don't understand what friendship with a girl is like. If I were to be with her, she hops out of that friend box and into a much more complicated box. Poppy is my best friend and will be forever. End of. I'll find another bloody date."

I move past the desk and out the door, ignoring my brothers' calls to come back and stop being a baby. Stuff that. I'm tired of them thinking they know what's best for me all the time. I'm determined to show Poppy and everyone else that this isn't happening between her and me. We're just best friends, like always. She'll bring a date and I'll bring a date. What's the worst that could happen?

It's dark by the time I get home from Camden's. I enter our flat and all is quiet except for some strange noise coming from the loo. Frowning, I walk over and lean closer to the door where I hear shower water running.

Just when I decide that's all the noise was, a soft moan resonates through the door. Then the humming begins again. Actually, it's more of a buzzing. I press my ear against the door, stunned when

I hear the sound of what must be a vibrator because Poppy's hoarse groans echoing inside the loo can't be for no reason.

She moans again.

I clutch the doorframe with my hands and drop my chin to my chest. My dick instantly rises inside my jeans as I picture the scene happening in my shower. *This is wrong, Booker. This is so wrong.*

But fuck me, all I want to do is go in there and help her finish the job. Activate another slip by pressing myself inside of her and fucking her against the shower wall as her soapy breasts slide up and down my chest.

My thoughts are maddening.

I inhale sharply and turn away from the door, storming straight for the balcony. Cool air hits my face as I slide the glass door closed and breathe in the London night air. It would be melodramatic to scream out of sexual frustration, right?

Fuck me! Why do I keep wanting to fuck my best friend? This is bloody torture!

What man could resist someone like her pleasuring herself in the shower? *Christ, this is painful.*

My mind begins engaging my hormones. *Why can't you fuck your best friend?* Because she wouldn't be my best friend anymore. *Who cares? She'd be more.* She'd be more until she wasn't. Until it ended and then she'd want nothing to do with me. *Why does it have to end?* Because I'm not right for her. Poppy deserves love. True love. Like what Hayden and Vi have. I can't give that to her. I can barely give that to my family. *So what do you want?* I want her to stay. I want her to be my best friend. I want to trust that she won't leave again.

A noise snaps me out of my inner warzone. I hear something that sounds like her pocket door closing, so I steel myself to reenter the flat.

Curious, I stride down toward the bathroom door and look inside to see if the coast is clear. Steam billows out of the white, glossy loo. I step in and close the door, hoping that maybe taking a leak will help stave off my erection. When I lift the seat and pull myself out of my pants, I freeze, semi-hard cock in hand as my eyes catch sight of something shiny and silver on the bathroom counter.

Her fucking vibrator.

And now it's time for a cold bloody shower.

Poppy

My walk home from work tonight is riddled with thoughts of Booker. The past week and a half have been hell. The wedding is only four days away. I was supposed to be torturing Booker all this time, but all I've been doing is torturing myself. I'm running around like a sexually frustrated nutter.

Two nights ago, I was wearing boy shorts while playing PlayStation. I don't even like video games! You have the same results if you slide your fingers over all the buttons like a maniac as you do if you actually apply yourself. They're stupid and I don't understand the appeal. However, the agog expression on Booker's face was somewhat satisfying, if only he would have bloody acted on it! Instead, he mumbled something about meeting Cam and Tan for a drink and bolted.

Last week I was supposed to plant my vibrator somewhere Booker would find it, but I was so wound up, I had to use it first! I know that's not what Belle intended for me to do. Now, not only am I pathetic, but I've catapulted myself up to proper hussy level, leaving used vibrators out like I'm living in some sort of battery-operated brothel.

But I was desperate. Good God, I've never had such an active libido in all my life! This living with Booker Harris shit without having any slips is not my idea of a good time. Thank goodness the wedding is Saturday because I don't know how much more of this I can take. Above all, I *miss* my old friend, and I wish we could just go to the bloody wedding together.

It's too late now, though. I heard Booker on the phone with someone the other day, and it sounded like they were working out details for the big day. So when I saw Andrew at the gym yesterday, I secured him as my date for an "event," a.k.a. Tanner and Belle's wedding.

He was so excited, rambling on and on about what he should wear. Then he asked me what I will be wearing, what colour it might be, and how something form-fitted would be great for my body type. It was then that I realised Andrew likes boys. Really feminine boys. He told me so after informing me that he's a topper and then asked if there'd be any single, gay men at the event.

And since Andrew did such a top-notch job of over-sharing, I ended up confessing that I am in love with my best friend who's now my flatmate. I told him about our history and how I was planning to use him to make Booker jealous.

God, I'm a pathetic cow.

Amazingly, Andrew was delighted. He said Scots know better than anyone how to make lads jealous. So I think it's safe to say I found myself a devoted wingman. I'm thanking my lucky fucking stars for that because I don't have a clue who Booker is bringing. I can't bring myself to ask because I don't want to know. She'll probably be stunning and tall with legs up to her ears. I'll immediately regret this entire fucked-up plan that Dr. Love roped me in to.

It's almost ten o'clock when I return home from work. I walk in and find Booker scrounging around the kitchen. Before making my presence known, I take a moment to appreciate the simple beauty of him. He's reaching up to the top shelf of an open cupboard, and a sliver of smooth, olive skin shows between the gap of his dark green T-shirt and his faded jeans that are quickly becoming my favourite.

I want to run my hand along his skin so badly, I have to make a fist.

"Hello," I say with an exhale.

He pauses his stretch and looks over his shoulder at me. "Hiya."

"What are you doing?" I ask, dropping my keys on the kitchen table.

He turns and tugs on his earlobe. "I was looking for something to eat. We have nothing."

I nod. "Yeah, it's been a busy week. I was planning to go to the supermarket tomorrow."

"I can go with you," he says, looking hopeful.

"I'd like that," I reply.

His kind smile reveals his perfect dimples and it relaxes my troubled soul. It's been so strained between us. The sexual tension competing with our friendship has made it impossible to have any sort of relationship.

"Want to go for a walk and grab a bite?" I ask, gesturing toward the door. "I passed a food truck a few roads back that smelled divine. They had kcbabs."

He half smiles, the dimple on his cheek so cute I want to reach out and touch it. "Yeah, that sounds perfect. Let's go."

I run to change out of my work clothes, sliding on a pair of skinny jeans, some flats, and a T-shirt. I'm ruffling my hair when I stride out of my room and find Booker waiting at the door for me. We both smile and make our way downstairs.

As we walk, we discuss what it's like living in East London. It's such a slower pace over here than the more heavily toured west London. And it's diverse. From Americans to French, Bangladeshi to Eastern Europeans, you find all types of people walking the stunning mural-painted streets. The neighbourhood is built up with old industrial buildings teeming with a cool multicultural art scene. It's invigorating. I can see how perfect this area is for Booker. The tranquility allows him to live his life and focus on football without the hustle and bustle of proper London. He looks at home here.

We stride up to the Turkish kebab truck and argue over what we should order. We both want the same thing, but we want the other to get something different so we can sample each other's. Booker relents and gets the chicken while I get the lamb.

I do a little victory dance as we wait for our order. A homeless man sitting on the ground sees my moves and begins laughing at me.

"Don't encourage her," Booker groans with a rueful smile that he's doing a crap job at executing.

The man holds up a finger, so we watch him while he rustles around his pile of belongings. My jaw drops when he produces a golden trumpet. He presses the mouthpiece to his lips and begins playing some sort of bouncy jazz number.

My eyes are wide and my smile is huge as I turn to Booker like this is the best moment of my life. I thrust my hands in the air and wiggle my butt over to the talented musician, ready to get lost in the music for a bit.

Booker

Poppy's moves aren't sexy in the least bit. But her smile could light up all of London. She's like sunshine no matter what time of day it is. She wildly shakes her hair out over her face with her hands above her head as she dances along with the homeless gentleman. Even the passersby can't help but smile at the silly scene. She looks like a bouncing little girl trapped in the body of a beautiful woman.

I lean on a small tree and watch. Blue and red lights pour down on her from the busy pub next door. People inside are drinking and partying, using the pub to facilitate a fun night out, whereas all Poppy needs is a friendly face and a little music.

This is probably one of my favourite things about her. She's confident enough to start dancing anywhere she feels like, onlookers be damned.

The food truck worker hollers, "Hallo!" He's holding our two kebabs and frowning at Poppy. "She not very good dencer," he says in a thick Turkish accent.

I laugh and then laugh some more. "No…No, she's not. But she's something, isn't she?"

He shrugs and hands me the food. I stride over to her, meat-sticks in hand.

"Dance with me, Booker!" she sings.

"I've got the food." I shake them at her as if she can't see them plain as day.

"Who cares? Kebabs are street food, historically made for dancing. It's probably in some literature somewhere." She shimmies over to me and grabs one stick out of my hand. Then she takes my newly freed hand in hers and spins herself under my arm.

I stand there with a straight face as she continues using me to dance. "I'm just a prop to you, aren't I?"

She bites a chunk of pineapple off the stick. "Mmmhmm," she giggles and chews the food, wiping the bit that drizzles down her chin. "Because surely you can't dance. You never danced with me when we were kids even though I always begged you. Mr. Dull and Painfully Boring, this one." She sighs heavily, a naughty glint in her eyes that eggs me on.

I shake my head at her because I know exactly what she's doing. She's trying to goad me into performing for her like a puppet. And I don't fucking care.

Two can play at this game.

I hand her my kebab, and she jumps up and down with a squeal of delight over what she doesn't even know is coming. I bounce my head to the beat and the trumpeter gets louder. I inhale deeply before diving down on the ground to do the worm dance, repeating the smooth body roll over and over.

Poppy's shocked, gut-spitting laughter is so worth the bruises this will leave on my hip bones tomorrow. She's never seen me do this move before because I didn't learn how to do it until several years ago when Tanner wanted me in on a goal celebration. We had it all planned out. And when he scored a goal, he soared like a bird all the way across the field to me, where I was doing the worm. Then he did a dive-bomb on me, like a bird devouring a worm.

We looked ridiculous.

Naturally, it was replayed on sports networks for weeks.

I spring up to my feet and cross my arms over my chest for a brief b-boy pose before reaching out for my kebab like nothing happened. Poppy is buckled over laughing. Once she contains herself, she gives me a hearty round of applause with several whoops of cheering.

Smiling, I dig a note out of my pocket and toss a tenner in the man's trumpet case. His brows lift as he keeps playing, and Poppy pauses to look straight into the musician's eyes as she says, "Thank you for the music."

He nods a musical thank you and away we go with our street food.

We walk for a few minutes, silently eating before Poppy touches my arm. "Thank you as well," she says reverently, looking up at me as we head toward our flat. "For the food and the dancing and the music."

I look at her in wonder as she thoughtfully picks at her kebab. Poppy is quite possibly the most appreciative person I know. Even when we were younger, I remember her thanking me all the time. And it didn't matter if it was for something as simple as helping her up off the ground when she tripped, which she did a lot. She always made sure we connected eyes before she thanked me.

Here she is again, being so quintessentially Poppy and acting like truck food and a street musician is a night at the theatre.

I shrug. "See now, if you never lived with me, you never would have had the opportunity to dance on a London sidewalk at ten o'clock at night with a meat-stick in your hand."

She beams and pulls a piece off. "So true, Booker. I love it here. I hope I love Hoxton just as much."

The thought of her leaving in a month brings an uneasiness to my chest. "We can see if my building has any openings if you'd like."

"Sick of me already?" she exclaims in horror.

"No…Actually, I was thinking Hoxton seems a bit too far away." I can feel her eyes on me, so I grab a bite to avoid her penetrative gaze.

"Hoxton is only a mile away, you nutter!" I shrug, but she does a little twirl and continues. "You won't want me around in a month anyway. You'll be ready for some space."

I stop her from doing another spin and wrap my arm around her shoulders, pulling her to me. The fragrance of her perfume is faint this late at night but still present. "I'll never need space from you, Pop." I kiss the top of her head and let my arm rest on her shoulder as I pull a bite off my stick.

She nuzzles into me, probably because she's cold. But I can't stop myself from thinking how right this feels. How natural and normal. Safe and comfortable. I like having her with me again. I don't want to think about her leaving.

"The big wedding day will be here soon," she says, a sad tone to her voice.

I nod. "Yep."

"Are you excited?" she asks, her voice curious.

"Of course," I state noncommittally, pursing my lips off to the side, deep in thought. Truthfully, I'm really not excited. I'm happy for Tanner and Belle, but this whole having to bring a date thing is starting to bother me a lot more than I realised. I don't even know who Poppy's bringing. I can't bring myself to ask. And she's not asking me, so there's a big elephant in the room that neither of us is discussing.

I hate it.

I hate not knowing things about Poppy. It never bothered me when we were younger. I had girlfriends. She probably had some boyfriends. We never talked about it and it never got to me.

Now, things are different. Somehow, we've changed. Poppy is my oldest and dearest friend in the world, yet this is something I can't talk to her about. And I'm terrified of what that means.

Change Routes

Booker

T HERE ARE CERTAIN PEOPLE THAT CROSS YOUR PATH IN LIFE whom you will change your entire direction to follow. That was Poppy when I met her at seven years old, and that is Poppy this evening as she strides toward me on the night of my brother's wedding.

She's dressed in a short, bronze, sequin gown with long sleeves that reminds me of sparkling chocolate. My eyes drink in her curves beneath the fabric that looks like it's been painted on. The wide neckline shows off her delicate collarbone, courtesy of her short blonde hair that's swooped smoothly off to one side. A shimmering gold dust illuminates her skin, complimenting her thickly-lashed emerald eyes.

She's complete and total elegance.

I blink and my mind flashes back to the day I met her in that muddy yellow dress out in the park. She was a mess but still so confident. The history we've shared together makes this moment even more special. What she meant to me in my past is just as important as what she means to me in my present. These past few days we've spent together since we danced by the food truck have reminded me how wonderful our friendship can be. How easy and effortless. But it's her inner beauty I see through all the sparkles that makes me desperate to know what our future holds and how I can continue to be a part of her life…forever.

She looks me up and down, a soft smile tugging on the edges of her lips. "You look rather fetching." Her tone light and jovial—a far contrast to the intense feelings soaring through me at this second.

I clear my throat and adjust my thin black tie while staring at her glossy lips. "You're as pretty as always, Poppy."

My words are small and childish, but they feel like everything I never said as a boy or as a man. She's always been stunning. I just never allowed myself to really look.

Her smile falls as I step into her space. She looks up at me, still a few inches shorter, even in her wedge heels. Desperate to feel her, I reach out and cup her cheek. Her eyes close and I stroke my thumb along her soft, pale skin.

I caress her and she feels like mine. She feels like she fits. Like she should be with me, on my arm, going to this wedding by my side. Not with someone else. An urgency overcomes me as a crippling fear descends. What if she falls for this man? What if she kisses this man? What if she stops spending time with me because of this man? Can I really sit back and watch her leave tonight with someone else?

"Booker," she whispers. Her voice is thick with emotion, but she isn't opening her eyes. "What are you doing?"

The air feels heavy. The pressure of these feelings push my head down like an uphill ascent on a rollercoaster. Truthfully, I don't know what I'm doing. I'm touching her because I need to. I have to. It's not a conscious choice. My mind knows that this is wrong. That touching her leads to other things. Things that don't have a guarantee. Things that could make her leave me.

"I—" I'm interrupted by a sudden knock on the door.

Poppy's eyes crack open and she turns her head, pulling her face out of my hand. "That'll be Andrew."

I blink rapidly as my hand drops and I step away from her. The silkiness of her cheek still tingles my palm. "Andrew from the gym?" I ask, my fists clenching at my sides.

She nods and turns, her wedges thumping as she walks over to the door. I'm paralysed. Glued to my spot on the floor. My head aches as I listen to her greet him. He says something stupid in his thick Scottish accent I can barely understand. She laughs that familiar husky laugh and then they fall silent.

I force myself to look toward the door. Poppy is gazing over her shoulder at me nervously. Her hand clenched tightly on the knob, as if she's wisely shielding my view of the man on the other side. "Is your…erm…date coming here to meet you?"

I tug on my earlobe and reply, "I'm going to go pick her up."

She nods. "I'll see you at Tower Park then?"

I half smile and it hurts. The simple lift of the corner of my mouth pains me as I watch her wave and slip out the door without another look back.

Poppy

"If Booker Harris doesnae fall for ye after tonight, I'm turning straight and dating ye myself, Poppet. Ye look pure, dead brilliant. A proper bonny lass."

I smile politely as Andrew ushers me into his little yellow sports car. Glancing up before he closes the door, I say, "Can we maybe … not talk about Booker? Or my plan? Or my past? I'm feeling completely ridiculous about it all."

Andrew frowns and nods politely, shutting me in the car and walking around to his door. He slides in and the space practically expands with the scent of his cologne. He puts his hand on my balled-up fist. "Let's have some fun, shall we?"

I smile into his big brown eyes. "I'd love that." He winks and pulls out of the parking stall.

"So," Andrew asks after we've been driving a few minutes. "Where we headed?"

"Tower Park…for a wedding." He looks at me in silent question. "It's Tanner Harris and Belle Ryan's wedding. They're getting married on the pitch. Sorry I didn't tell you before. They were worried about the press finding out."

"Bloody hell!" Andrew exclaims, whacking the wheel with his palm as he hoots with excitement. "This is going tae be fantastic! I'm no a Bethnal Green fan, but ye'd have tae be deed tae no ken who the Harris Brothers are. Tanner and Belle had that big scandal in the papers earlier this year. Caught bollock naked in a car or something. By the sounds of it, Tanner Harris has turned shit around and is no quite the wild boy he once wis!"

He giggles naughtily and I can't help but giggle, too. Andrew's enthusiasm is cute. "Maybe don't mention that story tonight."

Andrew nods dutifully. "Of course. So, who else will be there?"

"Well, Camden will be there with his fiancé, Indie, who is Belle's best friend. Then their oldest brother, Gareth. I don't believe he's bringing a date, but I could be wrong. He's always a mystery. Their sister, Vi, will be there with her fiancé, Hayden, and their baby, Rocky. And a nanny, I believe, because Vi says she intends to party tonight. Then of course their dad, Vaughn. Oh, and Belle's older brother, Ronald, and his wife."

"Brill. No Belle's parents? Her dad's a judge or something, right?"

I nod. "Yes, but he won't be there. You're actually taking his place."

He lights up. "Does this mean I get tae walk her down the aisle?"

I shake my head and try to hide my laugh. God, Andrew is adorable. "Doubtful, Andrew. But fingers crossed for you."

A few minutes later, we pull up to Tower Park and are directed into a special parking area inside a fenced-in lot. All is quiet as we make our way to the door that's guarded by security. He checks our IDs and marks our names on a list and then directs us through a long, dimly lit hallway. The ceiling is low, so Andrew hunches a bit to avoid the fixtures. He reaches out for my hand when I nearly stumble on some cracked concrete. "Is now a bad time tae tell ye that I've got a fucking hard on?" he whispers in my ear as he helps me right myself.

My eyes widen. "Andrew!" I chastise.

"Big fucking football fan, Poppet." His voice is trembling as we approach some lights shining around the corner. "I'm a Heart's fan, but that's no matter. This is the stuff all footy fan dreams are made of."

I can't help but laugh. He looks like a kid in a candy store. "Well, try to tuck it into your waistband if you can."

He nods seriously. "Good thinking."

We turn the corner and the pitch is illuminated in bright stadium lights. A small number of white wooden chairs sit on a platform in front of a net that's covered in a sheet of white lights. From a distance, I see Vaughn and Gareth standing in their slim black suits, identical to Booker's. They appear to be talking to a female preacher. Beside them is a man and woman with acoustic guitars in hand, plugging into amps and adjusting their stools and microphones. Vi and Hayden are in the chairs, passing Rocky back and forth as they try to straighten the white, puffy dress she's kitted out in. Indie's red hair blows in the wind from beside them.

She sees me approach and scurries over to us in her floor-length silver gown. "Poppy, you look beautiful!" she beams and reaches her hand out to Andrew. "Hi, I'm Indie."

"Indie, this is Andrew," I say as they shake hands.

"I've got a wee hard on!" he blurts and then his face falls, his neck and cheeks flaming red as Indie covers her laughing mouth.

"I'm sorry, I didnae mean tae say that. I just mean I'm chuffed tae be here. Walking on this pitch is the most exciting thing that's happened tae me all year."

"No worries. It's pretty impressive. And we won't judge if you develop tumescence." She glances down at his package.

"If that means a Chubby Charlie, then cheers." He snorts out an awkward laugh and Indie and I can't help but join in. Andrew is a bit of a wanker, but a sweet wanker.

Indie points to the sideline. "There's a small bar over there with a few cocktail tables if you want to grab a drink before the ceremony begins."

Andrew looks at me.

"White wine?" I ask.

"I can handle that. I hope they have champagne!" He squeals and heads over.

"So, how's it going?" Indie asks, walking me toward the cluster of white chairs.

I roll my eyes. "Andrew's great. Gay as the day is long, but Booker has no idea, so he'll do for tonight." I exhale. "As for everything else, I have no bloody clue. I'm more confused now than ever."

Her face falls. "But why? Belle's plans always work."

I shrug. "At this point, I'm simply trying not to get my hopes up. He's acting different around me. For some reason, I feel a bit like he's trying to say goodbye or something." Indie's face looks sad, but I wave her off. "How's Belle? Is she freaking out? Trying to pull a runner?"

Indie laughs. "Her and Tanner are probably shagging in the bloody changing room as we speak."

"They've seen each other before the wedding?"

"They both refused to go in the visitor's locker room. They said it'd be worse luck than seeing each other before the wedding." Indie throws her hands up in the air. "And you know Belle's dress is red, right?"

I nod and smile. "She mentioned it."

"Nontraditional to the core." Indie beams. "I'm glad you're here. I hope you can still have fun with Andrew. We're doing a limo cruise around London after the ceremony. Then we're eating dinner at that gorgeous nightclub Belle mentioned."

I smile. "Can't wait."

The musicians begin waving Indie over, so she excuses herself to go see what they need. Just as I turn around to look for Andrew, my eyes collide with something that makes my heart hop up into my throat.

Booker Harris is strolling down the pitch looking fucking sexy as sin in his black suit, dimples, and broad keepery strides…

…with none other than Sidney Carmichael on his arm.

Booker

"I'm so glad I was able to catch an early flight back. It's not every day you get to see a wedding on a football field!" Sidney's voice seems an octave too high as we walk through the tunnel toward the pitch. Or maybe it's just because I've gotten so used to Poppy's deeper voice that now Sidney's seems too high in comparison.

"Well I guess it's good you saved me because I never did find a real date." I force out a laugh and adjust the cufflink on my left wrist. I was fully prepared to come alone when Sidney called me back a few days ago saying she changed her flight to come home early. I couldn't exactly take back my invitation, so here we are. Arm in arm. Painfully-forced grin to over-eager, toothy smile.

Sidney huffs. "Last I checked, I'm as real of a date as they get. Flesh and blood," she says with a flick of her tongue. "I can show you more flesh if you'd like."

She shimmies into me and I pull back. "Sorry, Sidney. You know what I mean." I look away, my jaw tense. If Sidney shows any more flesh, we're going to be seeing nipples. Her jubblies are on full display in her little black dress this evening. I can already hear the crass remarks Tanner will be making. That is if he looks away from his bride long enough to even notice.

We round the corner and I squint against the bright stadium lights. I do a cursory glance of the pitch and see Poppy staring right at us. Her face looks as if she's seen a ghost. I want to hurry over to see what's got her looking so upset, but Sidney's latched onto me as her *stiletto heels sink into the pitch.*

Sacrilege. At least Poppy had the sense to wear appropriate footwear.

Poppy scampers over to meet Andrew, who's walking toward her. She snatches a drink out of his hand and downs it in one gulp. He frowns and then looks around, his eyes finding me.

Then, he peacocks.

Hard.

His posture stiffens and he gives me a look like he could fuck me up if he wanted to. And I'm not one hundred percent sure he couldn't. I've got him in height, but he certainly has me in muscle mass. However, he doesn't realise that I'm walking with six years' worth of fucked-up best friend angst on my shoulders. I'm pretty sure I'd welcome a release on his jaw.

"Is that?" Sidney puts her hand up to shield her eyes from the lights. "Is that Poppy McAdams over there? With the short hair? It looks like her, but I haven't seen her since school."

"It's her." My tone is rueful as I realise I haven't mentioned to Sidney that I have a flatmate, or even a new flat.

All of the sudden, Poppy grabs Andrew's arm and hauls him in the opposite direction of us, clearly trying to avoid saying hello. My eyes narrow as I watch them leave, looking perfectly at ease with each other.

With a quizzical brow, I usher Sidney over to say hello to Vi and Hayden. My face lights up when Rocky reaches for me. Needing the comfort of her, I scoop her up out of Hayden's arms and hold her to my chest. She's all puffy in a white tulle dress, and a glittery head-band slices through her blonde wisps of hair. She instantly tries to pull my tie into her mouth. Sidney directs a pinched smile toward Rocky that has me turning away from her to sit down.

I'm half listening to the conversation Sidney is having with Vi and Hayden, more curious where Poppy's buggered off to with Andrew.

My focus is diverted when Gareth claps me on the shoulder and drops down on the chair beside me. "Hiya, Book." He stretches out his long legs as he gets comfortable and pins me with a curious look.

"Hiya," I mumble, looking past him.

He reaches out and gives his finger to Rocky, who immediately pulls it into her mouth. "Who you looking for?" he asks me.

My eyes narrow. "Poppy. I just…She doesn't know her date very well. I want to be sure we keep an eye on her."

"Suuure," Gareth drawls. "Nice to see Sidney could make it after all."

I shrug, glancing over at her. She's moved on to chat with the musicians. "She called me after changing her flight. It was too late to stop her. How's Tanner?"

"Cool as a cucumber. I just checked on him."

I shake my head and shift Rocky in my arms. "I can't believe Cam and Tan are actually getting married. It's unbelievable all the changes happening to our family."

Gareth retrieves his finger from Rocky's clutch and leans back in his chair. "I know. I thought for sure you'd be the first one of us to get hitched."

This makes me frown. "Me? Why would you think that?"

He shrugs like he didn't just drop a ridiculous comment on me.

"You seem the most emotionally stable out of all of us."

This makes me laugh. I don't feel emotionally stable. I feel like a fucking head case right now as I twitch all over looking for Poppy. I've never been more confused in all my life. Recently, something has shifted inside of me when I look at Poppy. Something that's making this whole bringing separate dates situation even harder than I expected. I'm having very un-best-friend-like feelings that I'm trying to work my way through.

"Vi wouldn't call me emotionally stable," I mumble through clenched teeth as I position Rocky on my shoulder. "She thinks I'm damaged."

Gareth exhales and replies in a weird saccharinely sweet voice as he addresses my comment to Rocky. "That's because you're lying to yourself and we can all bloody see it."

Rocky giggles from his attention, but I'm not amused. "I'm so tired of everyone saying that. I don't know what you guys expect from me."

Gareth cuts his severe hazel eyes on me. Where Tanner, Camden, and Vi took after our mum with blonde hair and blue eyes, Gareth and I got our dad's features, so looking at him is a lot like looking at Dad.

His jaw is tight as he speaks. "Booker, as a keeper, your instincts are spot-on. Your eyes are laser sharp, so you see every player on the pitch at all times. And you protect your net with everything you have, like it holds your most prized possessions. That's why you're so good. Being a keeper is who you bloody well are." His face softens. "But you are blind if you think Poppy hasn't made it into your net."

I exhale heavily. Just then, Vi breezes over, interrupting our tense discussion. "I need Rocky for a quick pic!" She grabs her from my hands and gives us a strange look. "You boys all right?"

We both nod and then she dashes away without a care in the world as she goes to join Hayden for a photograph by the net. I watch the happy family for a minute, wishing like hell I could switch places with them.

Gareth grips my arm and adds, "Fix this or you will lose your best friend, and I don't want that pain for you." His voice cracks, so I look over and I'm stunned to see his eyes become glassy. He looks at me with a severe expression that makes my heart pound. "I know what it's like to lose a best friend."

My breath catches. My single word response is a mere whisper. "Mum?"

He closes his eyes and nods. It's the most vulnerable I've ever seen him.

"Gareth, talk to me," I beg, witnessing a world full of emotional torment that he's never let free. Never given life to. He's got to be going mental inside that dark mind of his.

He shakes his head. "Another time perhaps. Today, I'm more concerned about you. Poppy's in your net, Booker. You just have to turn around and look at her."

My vision is distracted when I see Poppy re-emerge back onto the pitch, firmly clutching Andrew's arm. Her eyes look red like she's been crying. Without hesitation, I'm on my feet and marching straight at them in long, hacked-off strides, barely stopping myself from breaking into a run.

"Poppy," I bark. "What's happened? What's he done?" I turn a furious glower at Andrew, who looks shocked and dismayed by my accusation.

"Nothing, Booker," she says, stopping when we reach each other and avoiding my gaze as she dabs at her eyes.

"Bullshit. What's got you upset?" I thrust a finger into Andrew's chest. "If you've done something to her, I swear to fuck you'll be sorry. Harris Brothers come in quadruplets and we don't fight fair."

"Back the fuck off, lad!" Andrew exclaims, stepping into my space. "She's a grown arse woman. If she needs protecting, she'll ask for it. If anything, she needs protecting from ye!"

Andrew's words cut me as I look at Poppy. She eyes me with a sad look that hurts my insides. All of the sudden, this feels like the worst kind of betrayal. She doesn't belong with this prat. She doesn't need him for comfort and protecting. I should be Poppy's safe place. Her shoulder to cry on.

"Do you want to talk?" I ask, my voice shaky.

"No, Booker. I don't want to talk. I'm having a lovely time with Andrew, and I'd appreciate it if you'd go back to *Sidney* and leave us alone." Her voice is acerbic and flat. Nothing like how she usually talks to me.

"It's time!" Indie's voice calls as she hustles out onto the pitch with Tanner hot on her heels. "Everyone take your seats!"

My eyes reluctantly pull from Poppy as she walks away with Andrew. I turn to see Tanner striding toward me. He's dressed in a slim grey suit with a black tie. His long hair is down, nearly to his shoulders, and his beard is trim. He looks like a proper grown up.

His smile is beaming as he looks at me. "You look like shit."

I school myself to smile back at him. "It's nothing."

"Good because nothing can get me down today, baby bro. My future wife is fucking incredible." He wraps his arms around me and pats my back with a hearty hug.

I can't help but laugh. "Because she agreed to marry you?"

He shakes his head. "She went into the hospital early this morning, saved a twenty-nine-week-old foetus, and she's back there looking more fucking beautiful than the day I fell in love with her." His happiness is boiling over.

I clench my teeth and smile. "I'm happy for you."

"Let's get married," he says and gives me a shove toward the makeshift altar.

I rejoin Sidney while Poppy and Andrew sit on the other side of the aisle directly across from us. She continues to avoid my gaze as the preacher asks us all to rise.

The guitar duo's amp erupts into a stunning instrumental version of U2's, "With or Without You." The music swells, their rhythmic strumming echoing off the empty seats of Tower Park. Goosebumps crawl up the back of my neck.

When the male's voice begins crooning, Belle appears from the tunnel. She's dressed in a red floor-length gown, her long dark hair swept off to one side. She looks beautiful, but she's just standing there crying. Full on crying so hard that she's stuck in her tracks, trying to collect herself enough to move. Indie rushes toward her, and I glance back at Tanner, whose face is contorted with emotion. But he remains firmly in place at the altar, stoic as he can be with tears streaming down his face.

Indie reaches Belle and nods at her in encouragement. The two share a quiet word and then Belle grabs Indie's hand. They walk the rest of the way together. Strong. Loving. A friend giving away a friend.

When they pass by me, my eyes find Poppy, who's no longer avoiding my gaze. She's looking at me, her eyes pools of tears as she watches me with a sombre expression. Andrew whispers in her ear and then takes her hand in his, squeezing.

She shouldn't be with him.

She should be with me.

She should be in the chair beside me.

She should be holding my hand.

She should be *mine*.

And that thought terrifies me.

The preacher says some words. Belle cries some more. Tanner wipes her tears. They exchange vows. They make promises. They put rings on each other's fingers.

And then…they kiss.

Music erupts. Hugs are exchanged. Congratulations are given. And I'm just floating around all of it, trying not to get too close. If I give way to what I'm feeling, there's no telling what might happen.

After the service, the photographer takes clusters of people away for more photos while the rest of us congregate at the bar. Sidney is latched onto my arm, but I'm so far inside my head, I don't even know if I'm responding to her at this point.

A glass of red wine is shoved into my hand and then Sidney drags me over to the table where Poppy and Andrew are sitting. Poppy looks better now. No longer emotional. Her eyes are narrowed on Sidney as we approach.

"Poppy McAdams, how are you?" Sidney peals and reaches out to hug her. "Or do you have a new last name?" Sidney looks over at Andrew. "Are you Poppy's husband or…?"

Hearing the word husband attached to Poppy has me grinding my teeth.

"Friend," I bark out, though I'm not convinced he deserves that title.

Poppy eyes me. "Date," she deadpans and then turns to smile sweetly at Sidney. "This is Andrew William. Andrew, this is Sidney Carmichael."

Sidney's smile is tight. "Nice to meet you." She diverts her eyes back to Poppy. "It's been years, Poppy! I hardly recognised you with that interesting haircut. What brings you back to London? Last I heard, you were living in Germany."

"I got a job teaching German to Year 7's in Hoxton," Poppy answers, sipping her wine.

"Oh, how exciting!" Sidney exclaims, folding her hands on the table. "And where are you living?"

Poppy lets out a loud laugh and then looks at me with wide, blinking eyes. "Booker didn't mention that I'm his flatmate?" She continues to laugh like it's the funniest thing in the universe.

Sidney looks as though she's been slapped. Smiling around the rim of her wine glass, she replies, "No, it didn't come up. We've been busy catching up. It's been a few months since I saw him last."

"Nutty, Booker! Always so forgetful," Poppy sings, rolling her wine glass between her hands and eyeing Sidney speculatively. "You guys see a lot of each other then?"

Sidney leans her head on my shoulder and it makes me fidgety. "Booker likes to take me to his charity events and football functions. It's nice to have a *real friend* along for those obligations that can otherwise be rather dull."

Poppy sneers, "How lovely that you guys are so close that you can save him like that."

"Poppy—" I begin to explain, but Sidney cuts me off.

"How long have you two been together?" She points between Andrew and Poppy.

"It's new," Andrew answers in his dumb Scottish lilt, snaking a possessive arm around Poppy's waist. "But it seems promising. I get tae watch her gym sesh nearly every day, so there's no much of her I dinnae ken." He growls and playfully nips at Poppy's shoulder.

It makes Poppy giggle.

I hate him. I want him gone.

"You think ogling at her like a peeping Tom as she runs on a treadmill equates to knowing her?" My voice is deep and authoritative as my posture straightens.

"Booker—" Poppy snaps, but Andrew holds a hand up to her.

"Shhh," he says to Poppy. "I got this."

"Don't tell her to be quiet," I growl through clenched teeth.

"Dinnae worry aboot her, mate!" he exclaims, moving away from the table to come at me.

I step forward just as Camden barrels in between us and throws his arm around my shoulder. "Booker! We need you for a family photo!" His voice is jovial, but I'm still seeing fucking red.

Andrew huffs out a laugh as I am all but dragged away by my brother.

Keeper's Hands

Poppy

"Ow!" Andrew whines as I pull him into the tunnel out of the bright stadium lights. "Fuck me, ye got a lethal grip. Remind me tae have ye show me yer arm regimen at the gym next week."

"Andrew!" I snap. "You need to cool your tits, all right. What were you going to do there? Get in a fight with Booker?"

He smiles and shakes his head. "I wasnae going tae fight him. I just have tae alpha dog him a bit."

"What are you going on about?"

"It's simple. He's been a beta with ye yer entire lives. He wants ye, but he's too bloody soft tae dae anything aboot it. He needs something tae catapult him tae alpha dog status. Trust me, I ken how tae get a lad tae pee on yer leg."

I close my eyes and exhale heavily, pinching the bridge of my nose. "This cannot turn into a fist fight. These are good people. They don't deserve this kind of drama or the silly games I'm playing." My voice cracks at the end and tears fill my eyes. "I'm fucking spent over all of this."

Andrew's brown eyes morph from charged to soft as he steps

closer to me, rubbing his hands up and down my arms in slow, soothing strokes. "Poppet, stop feeling so guilty. Ye told me this wis all Belle's idea tae begin with. I'm sorry I went a little over the top. I guess I'm still a bit cross over what ye told me he did with that vile Sidney cunt by yer old fort."

I groan. "But you were right. I can't hold a grudge against him for something he did seven years ago!"

His face turns grave. "No, but ye can stop acting like the second choice lass because yer no. I'm no kidding. Yer no just beautiful. Yer special. Yer interesting. Ye inspire loyalty. And ye have killer glutes." He winks. "Sidney is all surface. Her arse is probably artificially plumped. Booker doesnae want her."

"He brought her!" I exclaim, thrusting my hand toward the pitch.

"That doesnae mean anything. Look, ye brought me and I'm certain yer no trying to shag me tonight." He looks off to the side, but I can't bring myself to turn toward what he's watching. The happy family of Harrises taking photos together is simply too much. This entire night is too much.

With a sneaky sort of smile, Andrew leans into me and whispers, "Dae ye trust me?"

"What?" I ask as his hands slide up to my face. "What are you doing?"

"Trust me and, for the love of God, dinnae fight me on this or those Harris Brothers will put my baws in a blender," he murmurs and then presses his mouth against mine.

I gasp in surprise, but my body relaxes when he begins reassuringly stroking my cheeks while he kisses me. Quite honestly, it feels nice. Affection. Warmth. It makes me feel wanted again after a week of insecurely trying to get Booker to want me. Andrew doesn't open his mouth to ravage me. He simply turns his head and moves his lips against mine like a sweet embrace.

"If you two can manage to peel yourselves off of each

other"—Booker's voice rips us apart, and I cover my mouth as if that will hide the evidence of what just happened—"they're loading up for the limo ride."

He's standing five feet from us, his face looking equal parts infuriated, hurt, and tired. His dark eyes are a storm of pain as he shoots daggers at my kissing partner.

"Erm…right," I stammer, moving Andrew's hands off my cheeks and nervously fidgeting with my dress. "We're ready."

"Poppy," Booker says my name with a sigh. "I need a word first."

Andrew barely hides his victorious smile as he says, "Maybe I'll nip off and keep Sidney company." He leans in to whisper in my ear, "Yer a first choice keeper, Poppet. Never forget that." With a parting wink, he walks past Booker, who stares him down the entire way.

Turning back to me, Booker's brows lift. "Glad to see you and Andrew are hitting it off." His tone is sharp as he unbuttons his jacket and steps into the darkness of the tunnel. The stadium lights cast shadows across his face, illuminating his beautiful features in an ominous way.

"Booker—" I start, ready to tell him everything.

"He's a wanker, Poppy. Anyone can see that." He slides his hands into his pockets, his eyes fierce on me.

"He's not a wanker," I argue, pushing myself off the tunnel wall and clenching my fists at my sides.

He lets out a haughty laugh. "Well he's not good enough for you, I can tell you that much."

I flinch. "And do you think you know who is?"

"I don't know, but certainly not Mr. Fucking Winkie Face Gym Junkie." He throws a hand in the general direction of the pitch.

"You're an athlete," I snap. "What do you have against guys who exercise a lot?"

"Nothing, all right! I just think you can do better. I think you deserve better."

"Then tell me who I deserve, Booker!" I exclaim, stepping into his space so he has to look down at me, tower over me, feel me beneath him like pesky dirt under his fingernails.

His eyes flick back and forth on mine, heavy with anger and frustration. He leans in, staring at my lips like he wants to kiss me but thinks better of it. "I don't know, but I can't watch you with him," he bites through clenched teeth.

"Why not?"

"Because he's all wrong for you."

"What makes you say that?" I ask, pulling my tone back so I don't sound like I'm begging.

"Because he is! His hands on you don't make sense."

"What's wrong with his hands?" I exclaim.

"The way they touch you is wrong…He doesn't handle you with…"

"Yes?"

"He doesn't touch you in the way that…"

"What the fuck is it, Booker?" I nearly sob.

"They're not my hands!" he roars, his loud voice echoing through the tunnel. "It makes me crazy to see another man's hands on you because they aren't mine and I want them to be!"

Chills. Immediate chills all over my body. The silence that follows is deafening as my heart sings from hearing the words I've wanted to hear since I was eighteen years old. Maybe even longer. Maybe even my entire bloody life. The words that he's been avoiding since the moment he touched me on night one.

His hands.

Keeper's hands.

There's nothing more valuable on his body.

But the pain on his face is all wrong. And the feeling in my gut over Sidney being here is still present. "What about your hands on Sidney?" My teeth are clenched. Simply voicing her name makes me nauseous.

"Sidney is nobody to me. She's just a friend," he answers, defeated.

"I'm just a friend."

"You haven't been a friend since the second you came back, Poppy, and you know it."

My breath shudders at his admission. He's said it now. He's practically laid it all out there, and now I need to do the same. *It's now or never, Poppy. No running away this time. You're a first choice keeper.*

My voice is timid when I utter the words I've been needing to say for far too long. "What if I told you I want your hands on me, Booker?"

I lift my gaze to him as a heaviness lifts from my shoulders. As scared as I am to finally put it out there, it feels as if the clouds over my entire life are parting.

He looks down at me, his jaw bone ticking viciously with unexpressed emotion. "You have a funny way of showing it," his voice cracks.

I exhale. "I've been trying to show you for weeks, you daft idiot." I shove him in the chest and he sways on his feet, looking at me in confusion. "Andrew is only a friend. He's actually gay and was probably picturing you when he kissed me."

His eyes turn to angry slits. "Is this a fucking joke to you?"

"No!" I cry, swiping a loose strand of hair out of my eyes. "Far from it. I've been tormented all week trying to get you to see that I'm more than just your old mate Poppy and a lot bloody more than a slip."

"You think I don't know that?" He spreads his shaking hands out in front of him, gesturing toward me. "You're a lot fucking more, and that's why this is so hard. I don't want to lose you."

"What does that even mean? Why would you lose me?" I close the space between us, gripping his face tightly in my hands. "Look at me! I'm right bloody here, and I'm telling you I have feelings for you!"

He holds my wrists and closes his eyes, refusing to look at me. His face looks so hurt and tortured I could cry. I slide my hands inside his jacket and wrap my arms around the warmth of his waist. I hate that this is so hard for him. I hate that this is so hard for us. I press my cheek to his hard chest. His pounding heart mirrors my own. He crushes me against him, his arms a heavy vice around me as I twine my fingers behind his back and squeeze. It's not a romantic hug. It's a hug of desperation. A nail-scraping grip of what we mean to each other. Like if we let go too soon, we could lose each other like we did that day on my doorstep six years ago.

"Hey, guys." Tanner's voice cuts into our bubble of emotion, and both our heads snap in his direction. "We're leaving now. Andrew is apparently taking Sidney home. She broke her heel, so they left. Everyone else is in the limo already."

"We're coming," I say, squirming out of Booker's grasp and wrapping my arms around myself.

"No worries, Poppy," Tanner says sweetly with a smile meant only for me. "Finish your talk. Just meet us at the club for dinner in an hour." Tanner flings a set of keys to Booker. He catches them swiftly. "Security is shutting everything down, so let yourself out the practice field door." He flicks his gaze between us and says seriously, "Booker, you've got Poppy, right?"

Booker's eyes find mine and he nods, a look of determination on his face as he grows taller before me. "I've got her."

"Great, we'll see you both soon. Don't do anything I wouldn't do!" He playfully taps the tunnel wall and is off, running toward the exit where a security guard waits.

When he's out of sight, Booker entwines his fingers with mine and pulls me down the long, dark tunnel. A friend in Germany once told me that you can tell a man's feelings for you by how he holds your hand. A clasp hold is friendship. A pinkie hold is just sex. A waffle hold…is love. I try not to read too much into his hold that's definitely waffling mine as he takes a left down another hallway illuminated by dim lights. He stops at what looks like a normal door and slides a key into the lock. When it opens, fluorescent lights automatically kick on overhead.

It's a mini turf football field, about a quarter of the size of an actual pitch. There's a regulation sized goalie net on one side and a rack of balls along the wall. Booker locks the door behind him and says, "This is where we practice manoeuvres and penalty kicks when the weather is shit or the pitch is under maintenance."

I assume he's going to walk to the other door on the opposite wall marked EXIT. Instead, he stops next to a medical bench and loosens his tie, pulling it off over his head. He leans back and runs a hand through his hair. "Let's talk."

"Here?" I look around nervously, like we're being watched.

He shrugs. "Why not?"

Slowly pacing the turf, my mind races with where we go from here as the rough texture of the fake grass scrapes on my wedges.

"I still don't know what I'm doing with you, Poppy." He shrugs his shoulders and shakes his head, clearly at a loss. "And I'm bloody terrified of that."

I chew my lip and nod thoughtfully. Even after everything that's been said, I can see there's still a chance that Booker could want to be just friends. And that might kill me. So, do I tell him I've loved him forever? Do I tell him why I left for Germany? Do I tell him that I can't even look at the woods behind our houses without feeling a million cuts all over my heart? If he's terrified now, all those truth-bombs are going to make him want to cut and run. I have to be creative about this. Explain that we could be great together in ways that he can better understand and without our old baggage weighing us down from the start.

I lick my lips and try to ignore his hunched shoulders and grave eyes. "Well I told you I have feelings for you. You said more of the same, but you're scared. Those are the facts we have in front of us." I pause, steeling myself to be brave before turning to face him. "We're on the practice pitch, so let's discuss the details in football terms. Maybe it'll help."

He laughs and shakes his head as I bend over and unbuckle my wedges. This is probably going to make me look absurd, but I don't care. Football has always been the part of his life that I avoided. I'm not a footy expert, but I know enough to be dangerous. Now I intend to go balls deep with him about it. *Maybe literally*, I think to myself with an immature snicker. I pad barefoot over to a bank of footballs on the wall and grab one, tossing it back and forth between my hands as I walk toward the goalie net.

"What are you doing?" He watches me with amusement as I position myself dead centre in the net.

"I'm playing your game. Are you going to make me play alone?"

He smirks and peels off his jacket, laying it on the bench before removing his cufflinks and rolling up the sleeves of his white dress shirt. His sinewy forearms make my knees weak as he strides over to me. When he reaches the goal line ten yards away, I toss him the football.

Staring at his large, strong hands digging into the stitching, I say, "For every answer you give me that I like, I'll remove a layer of clothing. Let's call it Strip Football."

"Answers that *you* like?" He laughs and shakes his head. "Everything is a performance to you, isn't it?"

"Don't act like you don't love my weird."

His face heats and his eyes blink rapidly for a moment. He clears his throat. "Need I remind you that you're wearing a dress?"

"I have undergarments on." I shrug a shoulder, attempting to be coy and probably coming off like I'm having a seizure. "Are there security cameras in here?"

"I don't think so," he replies.

"Kismet." I wink and then position myself between the poles, my legs spread as I clap my hands in front of me like I'm preparing to stop a ball. Thank goodness this dress is stretchy. "If you say something I don't like, you have to strip."

"I would have left my jacket on if I'd known that," he argues, propping the ball on his hip.

"Come on, Harris. You're not afraid to play with a girl, are you?"

His warm chuckle makes me feel like a million pounds. He drops the ball and holds it beneath his brown, wing-toed shoe.

"All right, so you're a keeper," I begin. "Balls fly at you all the time, correct?"

"Yes," he replies skeptically, softly kicking the ball at me.

I bend over and scoop it up with my hands. "Are you ever afraid of them?"

He huffs a laugh. "You can't be afraid of the ball as the keeper."

"Why not?"

"Because, literally, your only job is to put yourself between the ball and the net."

"So you sacrifice your own body for the save," I reply, pulling the ball up and holding it to my chest. "You put yourself in harm's way to protect the net. Why would you want that job?"

His brows lift. "The payoff of a great stop is worth it," he responds simply, like the answer is obvious.

"Are you telling me the benefits outweigh the risks?" My voice rises as I throw him the ball. "I quite like that answer."

Booker

Poppy straightens at my last comment, her smile warm, like I just touched her in a naughty place. My amused expression falls as she reaches over to her side and slides down the zipper of her dress along her ribs.

My hands tighten on the ball as she pulls her arms out of the top and shimmies the dress down her body. Now she stands before me in a black thong and a pink and teal polka-dot strapless bra. Mismatched. Quirky. Sexy.

Poppy.

She kicks her dress off to the side like a glittering football and then spreads her legs again, ready for round two. To keep my mind off of her body and the fact that I want to rush her and take her in my arms, lay her flat on this pitch and claim her, I turn my focus on the ball. I begin dribbling, my brown wingtips slippery on the turf.

"That's precisely how I feel about us if we give this a go," she says, gesturing between us. "We won't just be Booker and Poppy. We'll be more. And the rewards of that could outweigh the risks."

I sigh, nerves prickling my fingertips as Poppy regurgitates similar words I've heard from Vi. There could be so many rewards if I let myself be with her. If I just dove in and gave myself a chance at more with her. But my old fears are still there, and I can't make them go away. "But I'm not an offensive player, Poppy. I'm not used to glory moments on the pitch like Cam and Tan have as strikers. I'm a defensive player at my core, which means I'm constantly calculating risks and preparing for the worst case scenario. My knee-jerk reaction is to protect myself and what I hold most dear. In this case, it's our friendship."

"Take your shirt off!" she shouts, stopping my movement of the ball.

I snicker at her stern expression. "Don't like that answer?" I ask, my head tilted. She's so cute when her brow furrows like that.

"Nope. Strip, Harris." Her face is all business.

"I could take my shoes off," I goad, enjoying how wound up she is right now.

"I could put my dress back on," she challenges in return.

"All right, all right," I say, holding my hands up for a second before undoing the buttons and sliding my shirt off. I childishly enjoy the way she ogles me. Her green eyes raking up and down my chest. She doesn't even try to hide it, even though her cheekbones flush crimson beneath the fluorescents.

Clearing her throat, she continues, "All right, so what happens when a ball gets by you?" She shakes out her short blonde hair and then claps her hands together dramatically as she squats down into position. "Like, you see the striker coming right for you! It's Camden or Tanner, and you're certain you know what they're going to do. So in your sexy, overly-analytical brain, you work out precisely how to stop the ball, but they juke you out completely and you miss it."

"Did you just call my brain sexy?" I ask.

She bites her lip playfully, slipping out of character before shaking her head and snapping, "Focus, Harris! Now, what do you do when one gets by you? Do you quit?"

"No," I respond with a thoughtful frown, mulling over the image she's described and trying my hardest to ignore the way her breasts press together when she rolls her shoulders. I kick the ball to the far corner and it makes a cringe-worthy sound as it slaps back into the net. I hate that sound. I hate that feeling. "Of course I miss sometimes. No keeper is perfect. But it doesn't stop me from being gutted over the balls that get past me. No one is harder on me than myself."

"But can't you learn from missed saves?"

"Yes," I pause, deep in thought. "Actually, I learn more from misses than stops. Stops are predictable. You see them coming from a mile away. The surprising shots that sneak past you…Those are the ones that burn into your brain forever."

She nods subtly. "Are you afraid that I've snuck past you and made it into your net?"

"Yes," I answer, a thickness in my throat forming over her echoing the same words as Gareth. Everyone around me is convinced Poppy has breached my net, but why is it so hard for me to admit? "I thought I knew what it would be like when you came back and I was completely wrong. Now I'm terrified because I feel out of control. And if I mess this up, you'll leave again."

Her face falls, her round eyes sad. "I wouldn't leave, Booker."

"You've done it before." My voice is trembling, the humour of the game completely gone. The nakedness of our bodies forgotten. "And things are different already, Poppy. I hated Andrew holding your arm all night. I hated watching you leave with him. I hated not being the one you turned to when you had tears in your eyes. I hated all of that because things have changed between us, and if you leave again…"

"I won't leave." She sniffs. "I'm…different now. I know myself better. And I promise that if we try this and it doesn't work, you won't lose me. We will work our way back to being Booker and Poppy, no matter what."

"And you would be okay with that?" I ask, unsure if I would be okay with it myself.

She nods. "In time, I think I would, yes. Any Booker is better than no Booker." There's a fleeting pained look in her eyes, but she turns to grab the ball out of the net before I have a chance to confirm it. When she faces me again, there's a softness to her expression that hurts my heart. Her voice is raspy when she says, "And I know I can be a handful, but you're great with your hands."

Her words are exactly what I need to hear. I want every bit of the handful she is. And as terrified as I am, I can't just be friends with her anymore. Too much has happened. Too much has changed. I need her. I need *more*. I know it won't be easy, but neither is staying away from her.

A sudden desire sweeps through me as I husk, "Maybe I'll use a different catching technique with you."

She smiles and kicks the ball back at me with the side of her bare foot. Reaching behind her, she unclasps her bra. My dick hardens as she covers her chest with one hand and drops the fabric on the ground. Her two hands cup her breasts as she stands before me wearing nothing but her knickers with the net backdrop behind her and the light illuminating her body.

But I can't take my eyes off her face. She's stunning. She's open.

She's vulnerable. She's so much more than my best friend.

She's Poppy.

I eliminate the space between us in seconds. I reach for her hands, sliding my fingers through hers before placing them on my shoulders. Her fingers clasp behind my neck as her hard nipples brush along my abs. She feels so good pressed against me. So right. I look at her through lowered lashes, taking in the beauty of her as my fingers stroke along the sides of her ribs.

"You're in my net," I whisper, hunching down and caressing her lips with mine.

"Obviously," she murmurs in a bouncy tone. "I'm super athletic. I'm surprised you didn't realise—"

I smother her giggle with my lips, slowly rolling my tongue into her mouth, twining it with hers in smooth, languid movements. I reach down and grip her arse, hoisting her up so our faces are level and I can kiss her properly. Her legs wrap around my waist and squeeze. She's light in my arms as we devour each other.

This kiss feels different than the others. There's an awareness we both have now that brings it up a notch. It's not a sexy, lust-filled kiss. It's a new beginnings kiss, and I'm savouring every bit of it.

I want to curl my fingers beneath her knickers and see how wet she is. I want to feel the slick heat of her sex wrapped around me as I drive into her for hours, making her voice hoarse from exertion. But we don't have hours. We have minutes. And Poppy deserves a hell of a lot more than minutes.

"Poppy," I husk, pulling away from her swollen lips and trying to control the raging erection pressing against my trousers.

"Yes, Booker?" she moans. *God, I love her voice like that.* She peppers my jaw with kisses, panting and writhing in my arms, further stoking the painful desire shooting through my limbs.

I swallow hard and want to punch myself for what I'm about to say. "I don't want to do this here."

She pulls back and looks into my eyes. "Why not? I thought this would be a footballer's wet dream. Shag me on the pitch and get all tangled up in the net. Score a goal…All that jazz."

I press my forehead to hers and sigh. "I want to, believe me… And someday we are coming back here to do just that. But right now, I want you in my bed so I can hold you when we're done. No more separate beds."

She inhales, her tongue darting out to lick her pink lips. "You are so cheesy I could puke."

My face splits into a broad smile. "Well, get ready because I think there might be more where that came from, Pop." I drop a soft kiss on her agitated lips.

She begrudgingly slides down off of me. We silently get dressed, smirking at each other like horny teenagers the whole time.

When we're all put back together, I hold my hand out for her to take. "Let's go have dinner with my family."

She cringes. "Should I be scared? It seems kind of odd that we skipped out on the limo. I'm terrified Vi is going to come after me, guns blazing."

I laugh and drop a kiss on each of her palms. "Don't worry, you're in safe hands."

Spilled Marbles

Booker drives us over to the Mayfair-Soho area where the posh Cuckoo Club resides. It's an enormous nightclub spread over two floors kitted out in a rock chic motif, fusing a gritty glam with contemporary luxury. It's definitely a place you spot celebrities, but the over-the-top creative vibe is so fitting for Tanner and Belle's celebration, I can see why they selected it.

My belly is in knots as Booker waffles his hand with mine and leads me through the club to the upper level where they've reserved the VIP room for a private dinner. All eyes are on his tall, broad frame as he weaves through the crowd. It's an extremely eye-opening sight—a harsh reminder that Booker is not my childhood friend anymore. He's a professional footballer. A London-famous Harris with dimples and abs who girls throw their knickers at. I've never been the jealous or insecure type with other blokes I've dated, but this reaction is Booker-specific. I was insecure before he became a famous footballer. Now I have to accept that every girl here wants him to contend with as well. *What was I thinking?*

I don't look like the girls in this club who are eye-fucking him right now. These girls look like Sidney—the one he gave his heart to when he broke mine. What if I'm not enough after all? Why didn't I think this all through before stripping down and baring my soul to him in front of that fucking net an hour ago?

This is like that whole sharing a bathroom with a bloke incident that I didn't fully think through before I decided to simply hide my tampons in my bedroom. *God, I'm a mess.*

"Hey," Booker halts in the middle of a crowd and looks at me with a puzzled brow. "Are you all right?"

I shake my head. "No, Booker. I'm freaking the hell out. What are we?" I blurt out, unceremoniously. I was comforting him before on the pitch, but now it's my turn to have a mini breakdown.

He frowns at my pinched face. "What do you mean?"

"I mean, I'm about to be thrust in front of the infamously pushy Harris family and you're here…waffling my hand." I yank our hands up as proof. He just looks more confused. "We've talked through your fears, but not mine. And certainly not the rudimentary things, like labels. So before we go up there, what are we?"

I'm out of breath as he gazes down at me with an infuriatingly sexy smirk on his face that sets me off further.

"This is not the time to have a laugh," I snap. "My mind is imploding in on itself and you're looking at me like I'm a cute panda falling off a swing. It's a valid concern, Booker! I know we just talked through a lot of stuff, but I need more. Are we exclusive? Or are we seeing other people?" My lip curls as I take a moment to look around at the big-chested women moving in on us. Mumbling to myself but loud enough he can hear me, I add, "I'm sure there are a lot of girls here that would be more than happy to waffle hands with you."

"No," Booker growls, snapping me out of my insecure lady gazing. His face is stony serious as he presses up against me, cradling my cheeks in his large hands. His eyes are hard on mine as he says, "No, Poppy. We're not seeing other people. You belong to me. The rest, we'll figure out." He shrugs his shoulders like this current situation is no big deal and he didn't just say the most delicious thing ever.

I huff out an awkward laugh and try to calm the butterflies in my belly. "Well, that's good because, I'll have you know, there's quite a queue of blokes after my affections."

"Is that right?" he grins, his eyes dancing on my lips as he wraps his arms around me.

"Quite right. Once you get past the gay one from earlier, there are some legitimate prospects, so it's good you got here when you did."

His chest vibrates with laughter as he presses his lips to mine, sending a flurry of reassuring goosebumps up and down my spine. He pulls back and murmurs, "I'll always be first in line."

I can't hide my satisfied smirk as we enter the floor-to-ceiling, glassed-off room where the Harris family is congregating with champagne flutes in hand. The ceiling is bulb after bulb of purple shining down on the entire room, including the wall of purple, tufted velvet booths. On the other side of the booth tables are deep, plum armchairs. There are red roses and purple lilacs centred on each table and you can smell the beautiful fragrance instantly when you walk in the room. The scene is over the top colourful, and the glass barrier still allows the live rock music and nightclub ambience to pour in with the added benefit of privacy.

Vi is the first to see us enter, and her sharp eyes zero in on our hands. Frowning, she detaches herself from Hayden's arm and strides right for us.

"Incoming," Booker mumbles. I force a smile while squeezing the shit out of his hand.

"Booker, Poppy! You're here!" Vi's smile is a bit more toothy than normal as she grabs herself another champagne flute from the passing tray. Booker hands me one and I take a fortifying drink. "I was worried you two weren't going to make it. I tried to call you after I got Rocky squared away with the nanny, but you didn't pick up." She tears her eyes away from Booker and glances down at our interlocked hands again.

"We had some things to talk out," Booker states smoothly.

"On the night of your brother's wedding?" She tilts her head, her eyes scolding.

"Vi," Booker says softly. "We weren't gone long and Tanner was fine with it."

She squints speculatively and asks, "So, did you talk everything out then?"

Booker frowns at her and then turns to me, offering that tipped smile of his that I love. "We're starting to."

"Broseph!" Tanner's voice interrupts as he strides over with a blushing Belle tucked under his arm. "You missed an outrageous limo ride. Camden took his shirt off and stuck his head out of the sunroof, so Gareth closed the glass on him and it pinched his skin and drew blood!" He roars with laughter as Gareth walks over to join us with a smile, clearly amused by the scene he's replaying in his mind. "Best fucking wedding ever."

"If that was the best part of the night for you, we're going to have big problems!" Belle exclaims, pinching Tanner's side.

"Easy, wife! We have to get this fancy suit back to Gareth's lady in one piece."

Gareth's jaw clenches. "She's not my lady."

"Well, I venture to guess *Sloan* is a lot more than just your stylist." Tanner shoots a playful smirk at Gareth, who does not seem amused.

Everyone's eyes swerve to Gareth, Vi looking the most shocked. I can tell she wants to say something, but the scolding look he is shooting Tanner silences all of us. Without a word, Gareth turns and walks away, leaving us with a million unanswered questions.

Tanner—not the least bit put off by his brooding older brother—grins down at his new wife and says, "Also, I would have said the best part of my night was shagging you in the changing room before the wedding." Her jaw drops at his cheekiness, but he hurries his next sentence out, saving himself from a proper walloping. "But that was before you walked down the aisle and agreed to spend the rest of your life with me. Nothing tops that fucking moment."

He smiles a happy, dopey grin at her, and she reaches up and pulls his mouth to hers. They kiss and I feel Booker's hand tighten around mine. When Belle releases Tanner's bearded jaw, she waggles her brows excitedly at me, silently giving me a pat on the back for my position next to Booker.

But when Tanner jerks Booker out of my hand saying they need a manly drink, she goes shouting after them that they need to pace themselves. Now I'm left alone with Vi's piercing blue eyes watching my every move.

"What happened to your dates?" Vi asks, her tone crisper than I've ever heard it.

I smile ruefully. "Andrew and Sidney left together. I texted Andrew but haven't heard back from him."

Vi crosses her arms over her chest. "So, you arrived with one man and left with another?"

I frown, gripping my champagne flute tightly, trying to determine if I can take a drink without my shaking hands spilling it all over myself. "Not exactly…It's really not like that, Vi."

"Then enlighten me."

"Andrew is only a friend."

Her brows arch. "A kissing friend?"

"A gay friend." I look down, ashamed of the games I've been playing with Booker up until this point.

"So you were trying to force my brother into making a move by making him jealous?"

I mirror her crossed arms, attempting to put a protective barrier between the two of us. "No," I lie.

"That's what it looks like to me."

"Well I wasn't, all right? Mostly. Andrew took it too far. He acted on his own accord because he knows that…He knows how… He understands—"

"Understands what?" Vi prods.

"He knows that I am in love with Booker. He was trying to help I guess." I exhale heavily at the admission. Something I wish I had the guts to say to Booker instead of his big sister.

I look up to see Vi's face soften. "You're in love with Booker?" She looks shocked.

My eyes well for some reason unbeknownst to me. "Yes."

She doesn't look happy. She doesn't look mad. She looks…nervous. "For how long?"

I look down at my shoes. "Probably since the day I met him."

Her breath inhales sharply. "Poppy."

"Don't tell me you hadn't figured it out by now."

Her lips purse. "I'd suspected, but you and Booker always kept to yourselves. And he never really said…I just mean…Well—"

"I know his feelings are newer than mine," I interrupt, terrified of how she was going to finish her sentence. Whatever she's thinking, I don't want to hear it. She may know Booker, her brother, but I know Booker, my best friend. And he can do this. We can do this. Together.

Her eyes slant in sympathy. "Are you sure you know what you're getting in to?"

Her warning tone sends tingles up my spine. "I don't really have a choice."

She shakes her head, a look of fear casting over her gaze. "I understand that. I just don't want to see anyone get hurt."

Our eyes connect in a woman-to-woman silent exchange. The kind that says, "I'm watching you." It doesn't surprise me. Vi has the same protective look in her eyes I've seen my own sister give me when I was about to do something monumentally stupid.

"I'm sorry if I'm off the mark here, but I'm getting the impression that you're scared. If you think I'm going to hurt Booker, I can assure you—"

"It's not you I'm afraid of, Poppy," she interrupts.

My heart sinks, but we don't get a chance to finish because

Booker returns, sweeping me into his arms and planting a very public kiss on my lips. It's silly, but it feels like an important gesture. Like he's telling me he's not afraid of what anyone thinks and I should feel the same. Magically, it pushes Vi's ominous words to the back of my mind and allows me to enjoy the rest of the evening.

The Harris family makes it easy. As pushy and as opinionated and as nosey as they are, they are devoted to each other one hundred percent. The fierce loyalty they have for one another is admirable.

And Belle and Indie seem like the perfect addition to the group. Their teasing tones when they pin me in the corner for dirty details do nothing to temper their sublime happiness for the two of us. However, their smiles fall when I reveal that Booker and I didn't shag on the pitch after being left there alone for an hour. They make sure to tell me all the best times of day we can go back. Belle even tells me that the grounds manager, Sedgwick, found a lab coat of hers ditched in the stands once. *I'll make sure we avoid that area of Tower Park.*

Despite Gareth's mood earlier, he continually smiles warmly at me, like he's some kind of romance prophet who has known all along that this would happen. His reaction is much calmer than Tanner and Camden's, who take turns trying to teach Booker how to score because he apparently doesn't have a clue since he's only ever been a goalkeeper, not a goal maker.

Vaughn Harris seems too enraptured by his happy family to even notice that his youngest son is rubbing small circles on my inner thigh beneath the table throughout the entire meal. I'm putting on the performance of a lifetime because Booker has completely soaked my knickers using only the tips of his fingers on my leg. Quite honestly, I'm desperate to leave.

We both pause during dessert when our phones chirp within a minute of each other. It took both Sidney and Andrew nearly two hours to reply. I expected Sidney to scold Booker for ditching her, but he showed me her text that actually apologised profusely for leaving. Andrew's is similarly apologetic.

We end up having a blast the rest of the night, dancing with the group for several hours. Vaughn excuses himself after dinner and Gareth disappears at some point, too. Hayden and Vi are next, anxious to get back home to Rocky. Eventually, it's only the twins, their genius doctor partners, and me and my best mate, Booker. The six of us laugh well into the night and dance off all the champagne we drank. It's fun and carefree, and being wrapped up in Booker's arms feels so right, I start to imagine that maybe, in time, his feelings can grow like mine. If we take things slowly and enjoy each other like this with no big surprises and no sudden life changes, we can become as happy as Tanner and Belle and Camden and Indie. It can be the six of us taking London by storm. Happy. Relaxed. And in time, madly in love.

Booker

When we walk up the steps to our flat, I'm completely wired. The endorphins of the night push an energy through my bloodstream that has me so far inside my head, I don't hear Poppy when she asks me a question.

"What?" I say, sliding a key into the lock on the door.

"I asked if you feel as nervous as I do." Poppy's voice is soft and breathy.

"More," I reply, opening the door and feeling foolish. We've done this before, but for some reason, it feels like the first time.

I pause just inside our apartment and turn to face her, capturing her wrist as she steps inside behind me. I pull her against me, needing the physical touch of her body to serve as reassurance that what we're doing is going to be okay. That we're still us. She wraps her arms around me and we hug for a minute before the hug turns to a kiss and the kiss turns to a grope. Next thing I know, I'm walking her backwards toward my bedroom, kissing every bit of skin I can the whole way.

We pull apart at the foot of the bed, breathless and lust-filled. She watches me as I walk over to turn the lamp on. The dim light casts the perfect warm glow on her luminous dress. A heated blush crawls over her cheeks as I undo my tie and she begins to fumble with the zipper on her dress.

"I want to do that." My voice is guttural in the quiet of my room, revealing every bit of my desire.

Her hands drop and she nods woodenly as I toss my tie on the floor and walk to stand behind her. My hands rest on her hips as I lean over her shoulder and whisper in her ear, "I've wanted to bite this neck since the second I saw you horizontal on my doorstep with that new haircut."

She lets out a bark of a laugh, and I have to bite my lip to hold my own laughter back. Something about making her laugh always makes me laugh, too.

"You mean when I fell arse over tit and spilled all my stupid marbles?" she asks.

Smirking, I press my lips to her neck and murmur, "What did you have those marbles for anyway? I always meant to ask."

"Don't you remember?" Her voice catches when I touch my tongue to the spot below her ear. The tendons on her neck contract with a heavy swallow as she adds, "I fancy myself a top-notch Mancala aficionado."

My shoulders shake with a silent chuckle. "How could I forget? You made me play that bloody game during lunch period at school."

"Because it was the only game I could beat you at!" Her voice rises at the end defensively.

Her breath falters as I inhale deeply, devouring her scent before my tongue swipes out and licks, relishing in the taste of her salty skin. "Then you left me to eat with the girls."

She tilts her head to the side to give me better access. "I think you were the one to leave me first."

I ponder this for a second, knowing she's probably telling the truth. "We were getting older. It became harder to be around you," I murmur.

"How hard?" She reaches back and strokes me over my trousers. "This hard?"

I slam my eyes shut and attempt to clear my head enough to answer. "At times."

Her hand squeezes the length of me. "But you never looked at me like you did so many other girls."

I shake my head and croak out, "That's because you were just Poppy back then."

"Just Poppy," she parrots and her hand stills.

She begins pulling away, so I quickly turn her in my arms and crook my finger under her chin to look into her eyes. The hurt on her face is crushing.

"It's not like that," I say, rubbing the backs of my fingers along her cheek. "Saying 'just Poppy' was a compliment. You were my best mate. I couldn't see you any other way because I was young and stupid and I needed you as a friend more than anything else."

"It makes me sound dispensable." Her voice is sad.

"Never," I argue. "Hell, even after you quit eating lunch with me, I used to make sure our tables were near each other. Didn't you ever notice that?"

Her glassy eyes find mine. "No." Shock and disbelief are written all over her face.

I step in a little closer and slide my hands around her waist, anchoring them together on the small of her back. "I liked being near you because when you were truly happy, even if it wasn't directed at me, it made me happy, too."

"It did?" She tilts her head, an adorable crinkle between her brow that I have to lean in and kiss.

"Yes," I murmur against her forehead, letting my lips linger there for a minute. "And if you weren't happy, I'd do anything I could to make you happy."

I pull back and she smiles, earning herself another kiss.

"That smile." I smirk. "That's a beauty a fifteen-year-old boy cannot appreciate properly."

A softness fills her gaze that pierces me in the chest. All of the sudden, I can see us as children again. There was such simplicity to our lives back then. Such ease and clear boundaries. Those boundaries are gone now and, as terrified as I am, I can't turn back. I don't want to turn back.

My hand slides up to lower the zipper on her side. She bites her lip as I do and then shifts to pull her arms out. I squat and push the dress down over her hips, all the way to her bare feet. She must have kicked her heels off during our walk to my bedroom, but I sure as hell didn't notice.

She steps out of the offensive material as I drag my fingers up the backs of her legs, dropping soft kisses on her hips and stomach during my ascent. My fingers linger over the swells of her arse until I move to the back of her bra.

"I'm not a boy anymore," I husk, deftly undoing the clasp. The garment drops with a soft thud. I stare at her face for a long pause. It's a meaningful look. It's telling her this isn't just about sex. It's about *her*. I want to see and feel Poppy in a way that I never have before. "Now I'm a man."

Cupping the weight of her bare breasts in my hands, I slowly roll her nipples between my fingers. "I like this," I say, dragging my finger over her piercing reverently.

"Oh my God." Her eyes close and she whimpers. A thrill shoots through me when I realise she could likely come from nipple play alone if I teased it long enough.

"Do you like it when I touch it?" I pull on the bar softly.

She nods and rubs her thighs together, need evident all over her flushed, naked body. "God, yes."

"But only me," I state with an authoritative tone.

Her eyes open and lock on mine. "Only you."

A soft smile spreads across my face. "I like having this part of you all to myself."

She swallows and nods. "It's yours."

I bend over and suck the piercing, pulling the metal into my mouth. Her hands slice through my hair and her hips thrust toward me as she cries out uncontrollably. Christ, she's sensitive here tonight. Was she this sensitive before? Or is everything that much more intensified now that we can admit our feelings?

Desperate for more, she reaches out and rubs my erection again while tugging on my shirt with her other hand. Needing to see more of her, I turn and lay her on my bed, sliding her knickers off as I do.

My eyes revel in the sight of her, naked and spread out on my bed with her short blonde locks framing her stunning face. I can tell she's growing impatient, so I strip every bit of fabric off of my body for her hooded eyes to devour.

When I crawl onto the bed beside her, she pulls my hand to lay it flat over her stomach. "I like these."

I smile as her fingers slip between mine. "My hands?"

She nods. "They are always warm. I like how they feel on me."

This makes me smile. "They're yours." I repeat her words back to her.

"I also like this," she says, reaching down and gripping me in her hand, her shoulder rising off the bed as she pumps me.

I groan and my hips pulse into her. "You do?"

She bites her lip. "I like it inside of me. Bare. You're the only man I've ever done that with."

"You're the only woman I've ever done that with," I state, my tone serious as I gaze into her eyes. I've never even considered going without a condom with anyone else. But with Poppy, it was instinct. I think my body knew I wanted something different with her all along.

She stares at my mouth, an intensity in her eyes as she kisses my lips and whispers, "Fuck me, Booker."

Her desperate words send a jolt of need through me. Thick, hot need. But with it comes a strange sense of disappointment, like her words are not enough. They lack the meaning and depth I'm feeling right now. Before I can expand on that thought, she spreads her legs and pulls me to her. I position myself between her legs, holding my weight up with my forearms as the tip of my cock grazes along her inner thigh. She squirms and situates me along her slit, biting her lip and nodding for me to enter her. I press in just a little bit and it feels so good, so perfect, I ignore the voice in the back of my head that's confused about why her words disappointed me.

I flex my hips and thrust all the way into her. She throws her head back on the pillow, and the raspy cry she lets out has me nearly coming apart at the seams. She cups my face in her hands, quietly moaning "yes" over and over and over as I rock inside of her inch by incredible inch, taking in every part of her expressive face as she grips me.

"God, you feel good," I groan into her chest as I watch myself disappear inside of her over and over again.

Feeling her like this and letting myself embrace it is intense. When we fucked before, it was frenzied and rushed and fuelled by lust. This is more. So much more. It's slow and exploratory. There's an awareness about everything that wasn't there before. Allowing myself to give in to this feels extraordinary. Poppy is my best friend, and she knows me better than anyone. She meets my every thrust with perfect precision, like she was made for me.

Her body begins to grow tighter against mine. Her cries get louder. The words she utters push me into a passion I've never experienced. When her muscles begin to clamp down around me, I freeze, my face contorting with ecstasy. Her fingers dig into my sides. Her heels burrow into my thighs. Her voice croons out a sexy pitch as her orgasm detonates, squeezing me and pulling everything out of me and into her.

A possessiveness shudders over me as I fall down and hug her to my chest. I can't get her close enough. I've hugged Poppy a million times before, but never like this. Never with this sense of complete abandon. I want to feel her in my bones. Wrap around her like a blanket.

Swallowing the last of her sexy noises, I kiss her mouth and her neck and every part of her beautiful sweat-slickened body, relishing in the fact that it's utterly mental that being inside my best friend feels bloody perfect.

Maybe I'm the one who has lost my marbles.

Balls Deep

Poppy

WAKING UP NAKED ON TOP OF BOOKER HARRIS DEFINITELY has its perks. For one, I can admire his gloriously naked body. The morning light slicing in through the window casts the perfect glow on every inch of his bare chest and abs. His mouth is slack, still obviously in deep sleep. But the way he tightens his grip around me even in his REM cycle feels as if I'm in a delicious dream that I haven't woken up from yet.

But I am awake. So very awake. The soreness between my thighs is proof that this is not a dream. Booker and I did have sex, not once, but twice last night. The second time was by my prompting. I rolled over in the middle of the night and accidentally grazed the tip of his erection. He was out cold, yet he was still hard after going at it once already. The thought sent such a naughty thrill through me, I couldn't help myself. I dipped under the covers and pulled him into my mouth. I'd barely started sucking before I was yanked up by his strong arms, rolled onto my back, and pinned beneath him. It was dark in his room, a faint light streaming in from the hallway that he'd purposefully left on for me. But I didn't need to see much as he held my arms above my head and thrust inside of me so hard and so unapologetic, I nearly came on contact.

The complete trust and faith I have in him because of our history together makes sex so much *more*. Knowing that we know each other so well and that we are doing this together is completely liberating. It makes me brave and horny and excited and thrilled. He's looking at me differently and letting me into his heart, which means I can finally embrace this dark part of my soul that I've silenced for far too many years.

I can let myself fall for my best friend.

"You're awake," Booker's morning voice croaks as he stirs beneath me.

I smirk into his chest, biting my lip to stop myself from spewing out all the glorious thoughts raging through my mind. I feel them, but I sure as bloody hell can't say them yet. "Yep."

"What are you thinking about down there?" He reaches out to stroke a lazy thumb down my bare arm and I shiver into him.

"Just trying to figure out if dragging my tongue through the ridges of your abs would wake you or not." I silently give myself a pat on the back for my very clever cover.

His belly shakes with a silent laugh. "Dragging your tongue on pretty much any part of me would wake me."

I inhale deeply and look up at him. He props one hand behind his head and his bicep flexes a few times before relaxing. "Morning."

I smirk. "Morning."

"You look happy." His fingers push a strand of my hair away from my forehead.

"I feel happy." I nuzzle into his touch.

"I like seeing you happy," he states simply.

"Is this really how it's going to be?" I ask, resting my hands beneath my chin as I toss the serious question out there. I still can't believe this is actually real life.

"What do you mean?" His dark brows knit and then relax.

"You and me, naked lazy Sundays… All that jazz." I bite my

nail nervously.

The corners of his mouth turn down as he ponders that thought. "Naked lazy Sundays would be difficult to achieve at Harris Sunday dinners, but I'm willing to experiment if you are."

"You know what I mean."

I pinch his side and he chuckles while rolling me over and sliding down my body so he can drop soft kisses on my chest and belly. "I want as many naked lazy days with you as I can get. Not just Sundays."

"You're doing quite well with this so far," I state, combing my hands through his thick hair.

"Well, it's day two…Still plenty of time for me to disappoint you," he says to my belly.

This makes me frown. I pull his chin up so he has to look at me. "You're not going to disappoint me, Booker. You're my best friend, and this is already so much more than I had hoped for." His stunning eyes soften in a way that shows me he's thinking about something other than what we're discussing. "You know you can talk to me about anything, right?" I add, trying to break through whatever mental dilemma he's attacking right now.

He nods and kisses my palm. "I want to talk about that fucking vibrator you left out on the bathroom counter."

This makes me full on belly laugh. "I know, I'm horrid."

"You are the worst kind of tease." He shoots up and pins my wrists to the bed, straddling my naked body. His dick is hard and resting on my belly. "I think it's time for me to tease you the way you've been teasing me the last two weeks."

I bite my lip as he thrusts his hips upward so his cock glides between my breasts. I'm tormented between giggling like a teenager and moaning like a hornball. My voice is husky when I reply, "It was all Belle and Indie's idea. Most of it, I should say…Some of it was just dumb luck."

He stops his thrusts. "Bubbly tits?" he asks, his head tilting.

"Total accident. That must have been fate's way of giving me a helping hand."

He inhales deeply, shaking his head. "I couldn't stop staring at your chest for days."

"I noticed," I snicker and he drops down and attacks my neck with his morning-whiskered chin.

He pulls back and spoons me, his erection delectably stroking up and down my backside as he rolls his hips into me. Unable to stay still, I wiggle back against him, popping my butt out as far as I can.

I want him. Now. And always.

Without asking for permission, he slides one of his glorious fingers between my folds and finds me completely ready. I was ready the moment I woke up. I was ready all night in my sleep. I don't know if there'll ever be a day I'm around Booker Harris and not be ready.

Shifting slightly, he positions himself behind me and spreads my legs. I gasp as he pushes himself inside, hitting a spot that rockets through me like wildfire. He begins his slow, languid thrusts, and I turn my face into the pillow and bite the fabric to keep quiet because I don't want to break this soundless bubble we're in. It's not his fluid motions that are turning me on this much. It's the intimacy behind how he's taken me. Claimed me. Owned me. Like I'm his. I want to be his so bloody much, and that's precisely what's happening. This isn't a dream.

My heartbeat increases when he reaches around and begins playing with my nipples. Every touch he places clicks all the right buttons until we're both so frenzied, we can't help but cry out when we finally come at the same time.

After cleaning up in the loo, we're back in bed when Booker says, "Let's go do something today. Like a proper date. I haven't had a free Sunday in ages and I'd love to spend it with you."

This makes me want to squeal like a giddy girl, and it's not only because of the massive number of orgasms I've had in such a short amount of time. Instead, I nod. "That sounds cool."

"Maybe we can explore in the woods behind our houses like old times."

He looks at me hopefully and my face falls. I squirm out from his hold to turn away so he can't see the anxiety on my face. Pulling the sheet against my chest, I stammer, "You have a free Sunday. Why would you want to go out to Chigwell?"

He pulls me back to him so he can see my face. Frowning, he gives my protective sheet a yank like he's offended that I've tried to cover myself up. "That park is sort of special I thought. I haven't been back there in ages, so I'd like to see how it's holding up."

I force a smile and quickly heave myself off of the bed, busily picking up my clothes from last night. "I'd rather stay in London today. Let's go do something fun and different! Oh! There's this adult ball pit in Hackney that some students in my class were talking about. Apparently the balls glow in the dark. Doesn't that sound like fun?"

"A ball pit?" He arches a skeptical brow at me.

"Yeah, it's for adults. There are cocktails and everything. You can cop a feel when we're literally balls deep." I lean over on the bed and press a chaste kiss on his lips.

He laughs. "I'd never pass up a chance to go balls deep with you."

"Yay!" I peal a bit more loudly than I intended. Stopping at the doorway, I look back at the gloriously naked Booker and ask, "Shower first?"

Booker

Glowy McGlow, formerly known as Ballie Ballerson, is an immature adult's wet dream. A virtual playpen kitted out with two hundred fifty thousand clear balls set upon an LED dance floor that shifts into different colours.

It's bloody ridiculous.

Poppy's eyes alight with excitement over the setup as she all but drags me through the crowd on the second floor where the bar sits. Apparently Ballie Ballerson is the cool place to be on Sunday afternoons because it's packed with patrons sipping on planet-themed cocktails as they take breaks from the rigorous efforts of ball surfing.

Poppy adjusts her crop top that's displaying her perfect hourglass figure. I notice heads turn to check her out and wonder if this is always how it was for her, or if I'm just realising it now because we're together. I can't fault the blokes for noticing her. She's striking with her short blonde hair mussed high atop her head with some product. She's got an edgy yet classy look about her because of her angelic face and graceful neck. The combination is really fucking sexy, and it makes me feel like a lucky bastard.

When we make our way down the stairs to the pit, she looks over her shoulder and smiles brightly, her white teeth glowing in the black light. Hesitating before we step down into the balls, she yells over the loud music, "Come on, Booker! Stop looking so serious and go balls deep with me!"

"We could have stayed home for that," I yell back with a wink. She giggles, holding her hands out to me, fingers wiggling, body shaking with anticipation.

With a dramatic eye-roll, I plunge into the depths with her. The balls are waist deep on Poppy and hit high on my thighs. We move past a few groups of people until we're in a corner that's less congested. Laughing the whole time, we toss balls at each other. At one point, she tries to trip me with her foot and shove me backwards, failing miserably and managing to topple herself over instead.

I laugh and help her up out of the balls, snaking my arms around her bare waist and squeezing until she squirms. She feels so good in my arms. So right. I love that I can press my lips to her neck whenever I want. Being with her like this is surprisingly easy.

I catch her completely off guard when I wrap my arms around her and fall back, pulling her down on top of me. Her gleeful laughs are all I hear as the balls engulf us, sinking us lower to the colourful ground.

"This is fantastic!" she shrieks, face close to mine as the colours shift from pinks to purples, to blues, to greens, illuminating her happy smile.

"It's all right," I smirk from behind her neck.

She rolls over so we're face-to-face. "Shut up! You're loving this and you know it."

"It beats singing competitions in the woods," I exclaim.

Her eyes narrow and she begins wrestling with me in the balls, trying and failing to pin my arms beside my head. She wraps her legs around my hips, and I roll us so I'm the one on top. I hold her hands above her head and slowly thrust my pelvis into hers. The gasp she sucks in makes me smile.

"Yeah, I'm hard," I whisper in her ear.

"You're insatiable!" she giggles, looking around nervously.

"It's your fault for looking so bloody gorgeous all the time."

I stare down at her affectionately and she gives her own hips a little thrust. "You better get control of yourself, Harris, or we're going to end up in the papers like your brothers."

Shaking with laughter, I release my hold on her and we go back to playfully chucking balls at one another. Truthfully, it's the most I've laughed in ages. Playing with Poppy like we used to when we were kids but with the added benefits of being able to kiss her is a pretty fucking fantastic combination. It makes me wonder what life would have been like if we'd tried this when we were younger. Would it have worked out? Will it work out now? There are really no guarantees. I just have to trust that if it doesn't, she'll hold up her promise to not let it ruin our friendship because Poppy is not someone I'm willing to lose ever again.

After playing in the balls for almost an hour, we've both

worked up a sweat and decide to make our way back to the psychedelic bar for a drink. I order a beer and Poppy gets some sort of Saturn drink garnished with a floating balloon.

She looks so bloody happy as she sucks the red liquid through the straw. "This is so much fun! My mum and dad never let me play in ball pits growing up."

"Why is that?" I ask, taking a pull from my bottle of beer.

"They said children piddle in them." My nose crinkles and she giggles adorably.

Setting my beer down, I reply, "Until Vi had Rocky, I had no clue what that parental fear is like. But after watching her a couple weeks ago, I have a newfound respect for parents. There are a lot of scary things that could happen to her in the blink of an eye. It's a lot of pressure to be a parent full-time. Makes me content to just be an awesome uncle forever."

"Not forever, surely," Poppy scoffs.

I frown. "Probably forever."

She looks confused. "You're saying you don't think you'll want kids, Mr. 'I love my big family that I see every single week and can't go a day without texting or talking to one of them?'"

My eyes narrow. "Just because I'm close to my family doesn't mean I want to make a family of my own. I'm busy enough handling all their mania. Creating my own would be exhausting."

Her face falls and she huffs, "Well, only because you let your brothers push you around." Her tone is sharp.

"They don't push me around," I snap back.

She arches a skeptical brow. "Booker, they are nosey buggers and you fold whenever you're around them. And you drop everything to help them whenever they need you. Same with Vi."

"They do the same for me. And they're my family. That's what Harrises do for each other! What else would you have me do? Ignore them?"

"Of course not because you're a decent person. But I think you need to live your own life and create your own adventures. They still treat you like the baby brother all the time."

"They don't treat me like the baby," I bark, gripping my beer tightly in my hand.

Her eyes fly wide. "They do, Booker. Don't get me wrong, I love your family. But you are blind to how different you are with them than you are with me. I mean, bloody hell, you keeper me without hesitation and that's because I've always treated you like an equal."

Frustration and confusion envelope my anger. "Will you please explain this keeper me phrase again because I still don't know what you're going on about when you say those words to me."

She blurts out her words in a rush. "You just…fucking flourish." She shakes her hands out in front of her and gets a heated look in her eyes. "It's hard to describe, but I find it sexy as fuck. And I don't know if you even know when you're doing it, but it's like you get ultra-focused and commanding and you just…intensify every part of your body. It's…" She shakes her head with a shiver like the thought is turning her on, which then begins to turn me on. "It's *hot*, but it can also be intimidating. I think you need to apply that strength to your brothers sometimes and then you wouldn't feel so pushed over."

I want to argue with her, but deep down, I know there's validity to her claim. Before Poppy came back, I was feeling downright desperate around my family. Clinging to what we've always been and not giving them space to start their own lives without me. It wasn't that I didn't like Hayden or Indie or Belle. I just didn't want to lose sight of my connection to my siblings. It probably dates back to being younger and having Cam and Tan always running faster than I could keep up. It used to make me crazy that they'd take off knowing I wouldn't be able to follow.

I've always felt like I'm trying to hold onto them all a bit tighter than they've held on to me. Maybe it's because I lived with Dad for too long and became too codependent on that constant presence.

It's probably why I play for his team and have never considered going elsewhere like Gareth or Cam. It's also probably why Vi found me a flat near her, and why I let Cam and Tan push me into calling Sidney for the wedding. I always do what everyone tells me to do.

I look at Poppy through wide eyes and marvel at how insightful she is, even after all these years apart. She's always seen me as the man I want to be. Even as a child, she looked at me like I was Booker, not a Harris Brother. The idea of caring about someone enough to have children with them terrifies me, but maybe if I start seeing myself the way Poppy sees me, I will warm up to the idea someday.

My voice is soft when I utter, "Sometimes I wonder what I would be like if I never met you."

"What do you mean by that?" She looks offended, but it's only because she's not seeing herself through my eyes. She doesn't know how instrumental she is to my happiness. How utterly better my life is because she's in it.

"When we were kids, you just…showed up at the perfect time. You and Pink. You've always just…been there."

"That doesn't sound very attractive," she baulks and fiddles with the straw in her glass.

I reach out to cradle her face so she can focus on what I'm about to say. "When you spend a lifetime chasing after people who were always running away from you, having someone to sit still with can be really fucking attractive."

Her mouth falls open and her green eyes darken as she says, "There you go again." Her voice is like gravel. I tilt my head in silent question as she swallows and adds, "Keepering me."

The corner of my mouth lifts as I watch her lower lip pop out from between her teeth. I lean forward and connect us, parting her lips with my tongue, tasting her, encircling her, pulling her into my arms and clutching her to me like she's my most prized possession. I want to taste more than her mouth. I want her back in my flat, in my bed, between my sheets. *With me.*

I break our connection. Both of us are breathing heavily as I whisper against her lips, "Maybe I do it because you're a keeper."

She swallows slowly and whispers back, "Maybe I want to be kept."

Sunshine and Lamb Chops

Poppy

"**A**RE YOU READY FOR THIS?" BOOKER ASKS, PARKED OUTSIDE his dad's house in Chigwell. He pulls me across the bench of his truck to the middle and wraps his arm around my shoulder. Then he takes my hand and kisses the tips of each one of my fingers.

"Why are you acting like I haven't been here for Sunday dinner before, Booker?" I ask, half laughing and half turned on because he's moved onto my neck and ear.

"Because you haven't been to Sunday dinner as my girlfriend before, and the people in that house are vultures. I want to make sure you're mentally ready for the Harris Shakedown we'll probably get," he murmurs against the flesh of my neck.

I'm definitely ready for some kind of fucking with the way his whiskery chin is brushing my skin. Not to mention the glorious label he's tossed on me so easily. "Is that what you're calling me now? Your girlfriend?" I can't hide my smile. I don't want to.

"What else would I call you?" He pulls back and pins me with those hazel eyes, his dark lashes blinking curiously.

Looking away, I casually reply, "Oh, I don't know…Mistress, lover, main squeeze, the object of my erection."

His laughter vibrates right through me and it makes the warmth between my legs spread. "Those sound more like pet names. Is that where we are in our relationship? Should I come up with something a bit more intimate for you?"

"Obviously," I scoff. "I mean, we've been together an entire week. This is clearly the next logical step."

His dimple flashes as he brushes my cheek with his thumb. "Do you have one in mind for me?"

"Well, it's a tie between Lamb Chop and Keeper," I state without hesitation.

"Lamb Chop and Keeper," he repeats with a sexy chuckle. "Those are two very different options."

"I like variety." I shrug. "Depending on my mood and all."

"Whatever you'd like, Poppy." He kisses my lips, trying to distract me from the subject at hand.

I pull away. "Come out with it then. What do you have for me?"

He narrows his eyes and looks away, giving me his stunning profile as he ponders for a moment. When he looks back at me, he's lost all humour on his face. "Sunshine," he states confidently and then adds, "Because my whole life, you've always been the brightest part of my day."

His words go straight to my heart. They tell me so much and are nearly everything I've always wanted to hear from him. It's incredible. Is this really how it will be between us? Can it possibly be this natural? This easy? To go from best friends to content lovers without any awkward transitional period? *God, I really do love my Keeper.*

Quieting those words for now, I smile and reply, "That's a mouthful, but suit yourself." I press a chaste kiss on his lips. "Come on then. We better get in there, Lamb Chop."

Poppy

"So that's it? Yer boyfriend and girlfriend now?" Andrew asks as he spreads his legs wide on the bench and presses his elbow to his inner knee for a bicep curl.

"Yeah, I guess so," I reply, pressing my trainers together from my spot on the floor in front of him.

"Braw. So tell me, how's the sex?" he asks with a naughty wink that somehow perfectly matches his accent. "Although, I dinnae really need tae ask because I can hear yer cries of passion coming through the ceiling every night."

"Oh my God, you can?" My heart leaps up into my throat as I realise he is probably the neighbour who yelled at us the first time we had sex.

He smiles and winks. "Dinnae worry. I've learned tae put on my headphones."

"Good God," I mumble, deciding right then and there I'm going to bite a pillow from now on because this is mortifying. "Seriously, though. I thought after two weeks we'd be slowing down, but we're not. We go at it every bloody day, and it's the best I've ever had. I swear, he simply brushes my breast and I want to shag him."

"I'd shag constantly, too, if I had a man like him in my flat." Andrew gets a distant, dirty look in his eyes. "Just picturing those dimples wrapped around my cock would send me intae a raging orgasm."

"You dirty slut!" I snap. "Those are my dimples. Stop picturing them wrapped around anything but me."

"Possessive cunt," he murmurs. "Ye should learn tae share. Ye wouldnae even have those dimples if it wasnae for me."

I sigh heavily. "I'm not sure I ever told you what a good kisser you are."

His brows lift. "Cheers, Poppet. Nice ye noticed how fit my lips are. It's all that cock I suck."

We both giggle naughtily, and I bite my lip as my mind flashes to my shower sex with Booker this morning. Shower *oral sex*, I should say. Water isn't the best lubricant when you have a well-endowed footy player between your thighs, but our skilled mouths more than made up for it.

Quite honestly, though, it's not only about the sex. Not at all. It's all the intimate moments we've been sharing that are making my heart truly soar. The quiet nights we cuddle on the sofa while watching a film. The way he kisses my forehead every time I go to work. His husky morning voice when he says, "Good morning, Sunshine." It's all enough to make me fall even more in love with him than I already have. I had no clue that this is what embracing love could feel like. It's as if I'm living in a dream.

Normally, living together as a brand new couple is a disastrous idea, but Booker and I know each other so well. We know which buttons to avoid. It also helps that we don't have horrid sexual tension eating us alive anymore.

Even last week with his family was brilliant. They've accepted me as one of their own. Vi was a bit watchful at first because she's always been protective of her youngest brother, but she has softened toward me. We all had great fun. I couldn't help but join in on the laughter when Booker's brothers had a go at him for calling me Sunshine in front of them.

The only hiccup was when he wanted to go for a walk in the woods…again. I refused. I'm not ready to see that space. Not until I know that I'm different than Sidney. We're still so new. I don't want to mess things up by admitting to him the real reason I left for Germany was because of that horrid night I saw the two of them together. It's…embarrassing.

In a perfect world, Booker will love me the way I love him and that sad part of our past will be irrelevant. A nonissue. Not even worth mentioning.

"Well, I'm happy for ye, Poppet. And hey, I may no be the kind of neighbour tae help ye oot with a cup of sugar, but if ye ever have a late night condom emergency, I'm yer man. I'm sure footy players can rebound like no other."

His condom comment makes me wince. "Actually, we haven't been using them."

He gives me a hacked off look. "Poppet, riding withoot a saddle can be dangerous, even with someone ye ken really well."

I wave him off. "I know he's clean and I'm on the pill."

"Still, those footy lads have super stamina and super sperm. Havenae ye heard of all those illegitimate wee ones bringing in big money for their wannabe WAG mummies. There are articles in the papers weekly."

"I'm not one of them!" I nearly yell and then lower my voice when someone on a treadmill looks over at us.

"I ken, I'm just having a go at ye," he chides.

I force a laugh and then a peculiar heaviness that I've been ignoring presses down on my shoulders. I haven't had to sneak those tampons from my bedroom into the loo for quite some time. I had what was looking like the start of my period a couple days after Tanner and Belle's wedding, but it never amounted to anything tampon-worthy. I figured since I had all the normal cramps and aches of a period, it was simply one of those off cycles.

However, Andrew's concern awakens the little voice in the back of my head that I've been silencing because I don't want to stop enjoying all my time with Booker.

"Why dae ye look like a fucking ghost right now?" Andrew drops his weight and thrusts his water bottle in my face. "Dae ye need a drink?"

I shake my head like a lunatic. "I'm fine. It's nothing I'm sure."

"Oh my God, yer bloody pregnant." He drops down on his knees in front of me.

"Shut up!" I exclaim. "You don't know what you're saying."

"I dae. I have a sixth sense aboot these things." His brown eyes are grave. "I thought ye were pregnant at the wedding, but I didnae want tae say."

"I said shut up!" I shriek because I can't help it.

"Fuck me, ye *were* pregnant at the wedding." He thrusts a nervous hand through this hair and looks down at my belly.

"Would you quit? You are not some pregnancy whisperer. Just… stop saying so many words and let me think." I press my hands to my temples, resting my elbows on my knees. This can't be happening. I've been on the same pills since I came back from Germany. They are some German brand, but a pill is a pill, right? Some periods are lighter than others. It's nothing to worry about.

I cringe as I think back to how I struggled to communicate with the doctor in Germany. My German was not great and they'd said if I went back, there'd be an English-speaking doctor. But I didn't want to go back. I'd just met Nigel and was ready to let loose. I struggled through the communication barrier throughout the entire appointment, but "nein baby" is pretty much a universal phrase. I assumed the doctor knew what I was there for. I've never even looked that closely at the pill package, even after I became fluent, because I always used condoms.

Fuck me. Was that a period I had two weeks ago or not?

"Verfickte Scheiße!" I curse in German through clenched teeth because it feels like the language might be to blame if this all goes tits-up.

Andrew stands up with me, but my knees are wobbling so much, he has to steady me in his big arms. His voice is firm when he says, "Right. That's it. I'm nipping off tae the shop and we're figuring this oot right now. We need tae ken if yer with child."

"With child?" I bark. "What is this, *Game of Thrones*? We don't need to know if I'm *with child* because I'm not taking a test!" I snap. Taking a test would confirm what I feel in my core might be true. And if I don't take the test, we can keep doing what we're doing, being the new and improved Booker and Poppy. I force my hysteria down and smile. "I'll wait another week. My period will come. It's just peculiar this month."

Andrew side-eyes me. "Are yer cycles normally peculiar?"

I swallow hard. "Sometimes."

He sees right through me. "Yer taking a test."

Two hours later, tears prick the backs of my eyes as I sit on the bathroom floor in Andrew's flat staring at two positive pregnancy tests.

"Just as I suspected," Andrew states, his voice grim. "Yer up the duff. I could see it in yer breasts."

"This can't be happening." My voice feels like gravel in my throat.

"It's happening all right. These tests are highly accurate," Andrews says, looking at the back of the pamphlet that came in the box. "Especially considering how late ye are. The accuracy only goes up."

"But this isn't how it should be." I can't stop shaking my head. This will change everything. I finally got Booker to be with me. This will send him over the edge.

"Life doesnae always give a fuck aboot yer plans, Pop."

My eyes cut to him perched on the edge of the tub. "Can you please save the Pinterest inspirational quotes and tell me what I should do?"

He frowns like my statement is ridiculous. "Well, I'm all for a woman having options. But since ye love him, I cannae imagine ye daeing much else than having the baby and daeing the whole happy family bit. Yer already living together, so that's done."

"Temporarily!" I screech and shove the tests away from me. They slide on the floor and clack when they hit the tiled wall. "And I haven't told him I love him. God, he's going to want to go running for the hills when he finds out."

"Oh, weesht. He's yer best friend. And it takes two tae shag in yer birthday suits, so he's just as responsible as ye are. He wouldnae run."

"You don't understand," I whine and pinch the bridge of my nose as a massive migraine approaches that will certainly top all migraines.

"What's no tae understand? In the gay world, tons of lads have babies with their best friends. It can work oot."

"That's not what this is," I argue.

"Educate me then." He crosses his arms over his chest and awaits my reply.

"I had to push Booker just to consider being more than friends with me. I tricked him, and connived him, and convinced him, and made grand promises that we would always be friends until he had no choice but to go for it. I let you kiss me to make him jealous! He just told me the other day he doesn't even want kids. He's going to think I've trapped him!"

Anxiety grips my throat. I cover my face with my hands as Andrew leans forward and rubs my back. "He'd never think so little of ye tae say ye tried tae trap him. There's nothing tae trap anyhow. That boy is smitten with ye. Friends or lovers. This is going tae be okay."

I pull back and look up at him. "You really think so?"

He nods, his face sincere. "The question is, how dae ye feel aboot it?"

My brows lift. How odd is it that I get a positive pregnancy test and all I've thought about is what Booker is going to think? I haven't even let myself consider how I feel about it. "I guess I don't really know. I'm still…processing."

"Did ye fancy yerself a young mum aboot London? Yer a school teacher, so ye must like wee kids."

Horror overwhelms me. "God, I haven't even thought about my job yet! I'm going to have to tell them I'm pregnant before I start.

How ridiculous will that make me look?" I run my hands through my short tresses and attempt to calm the fuck down.

"Yer no ridiculous," Andrew states firmly. "Calm down, Poppet. Take some deep breaths." He breathes in and out a few times, and I straighten my posture and try to do the same. "Yer going tae figure this oot. And besides, happy accidents can sometimes bring aboot the best adventures."

I huff out a self-deprecating laugh. "Ye think this is a happy accident?"

"It's a baby," he shrugs. "What's more exciting than a wee baby?!"

I'm not able to accept those words just yet. I'm too busy worrying about how I'm going to tell Booker that he's going to be a daddy! Maybe I won't say it in those exact words, but more than anything, I need my best friend's support.

My stressed-out state is completely forgotten when my eyes drop to Andrew's knees that are currently eye level from my spot on the floor. Frowning, I look a little closer. "Andrew, is that your penis I see up your shorts?"

"It's certainly no a bratwurst," he deadpans.

I eye his clothing, noting he's still wearing his gym gear. "Do you not wear underwear when you exercise?"

"Christ no!" he baulks, clearly offended by my question. "My baws need tae breathe! And I've heard that if ye let the skin stretch, it increases yer penis size."

My face crumples. "Well, warn me next time before I prop myself in sniffer's row."

He waggles his brows. "Dinnae act like yer no impressed."

Brothers Grimm

Poppy

MY STOMACH IS ROLLING AS I WALK BACK FROM THE OUT-OF-hours clinic that's located four roads from Booker's flat. I rushed over straight from Andrew's in a fit, trying to convince myself the tests could be wrong. The on call doctor tried to give me another pregnancy test, but I demanded more proof. So here I am, with blood results in hand as if Booker might ask to see them. The doctor definitely spoke English and explained the birth control I was on is a low hormone kind, resulting in a lower effectiveness than others. That would have been a great side effect to be aware of in Germany. Luckily I never shagged anyone without a condom there.

I stride into Booker's flat and hear the shower running. I have to tell him. I can't wait. He'll see it on my face and dig it out of me. This secret would be so much harder to hide than the secret about being in love with him for years.

Maybe because there's another life involved..

I push the door open and hot steam billows out of the small space. Booker is standing in front of the shower wearing nothing but a pair of jeans that are unbuttoned at the top. My favourite look on him, especially now because the steam is clinging to his abs and drizzling down the divots all the way to his trim love arrow. He was helping his brothers haul some sort of flowers up to Vi's rooftop garden, so he's covered in dirt, some even smudged on his cheek. I glance down at his dirty shirt on the floor and it makes me sad. Like at any moment this will all be taken away.

"Hiya, Sunshine" Booker says, snapping me out of my reverie. "I thought I heard you come in."

I half smile and look up into his stunning eyes. "I just got back."

His brows lift. "Where were you?"

I swallow, my mind fogged over from the sight of his abs. "Just running some errands."

He grins at me, that perfect press of a dimple stamping into his face. 'Want to join me?"

Beads of steam cling to my face, and I want nothing more than to get in the shower and wrap my arms around him. For a few minutes, I want to forget that everything is about to change. I want to soak in another wonderful, blissful moment with Booker before I tell him our life-altering news.

We undress and step into the shower. He instantly wraps himself around me and pulls me under the water. His large hold on me makes me feel so safe and secure. It's warm and the damp smell of him is heavenly. I press my face to his chest, loving the feel of our naked bodies against each other as he rubs his magical hands up and down my spine.

"You okay?" he asks and I nod into his chest. "You sure?" I nod again. "Poppy, why aren't you talking? Something's up. You're usually singing by now."

Swallowing, I pull back and look up into his hazel eyes. Booker knows me better than anyone. He's attuned to my eccentricities in both personality and now in day-to-day needs, even leaving the cap off the shower gel because he knows I have trouble opening it.

We are still Booker and Poppy, but we are so much more now. He has to see that. He has to know that he's not just looking at me with lust anymore. His eyes are wide and full of…love. It's *love* he's looking down on me with. He's fallen for me, making it so mind-blowingly easy for us to become one. Surely this hurdle can be overcome as well.

Still holding back, I reply with a half-truth. "I have another migraine coming on."

His face softens. "Oh, bugger." He leans down and kisses all the way across my forehead, moving his hands so his fingers can make small circles on my temples. "Does that feel all right?"

"Mmm, that feels so good," I groan.

He massages for a while and drops a few more kisses before saying, "Wait until you see what I have planned for you after this. It should help you relax and take your mind off the pain."

I quirk a sardonic brow at him. "If you say I have to give you a blow job, I'll come up with some really creative ways to hurt your balls."

He shakes with laughter. "I'm sure you would." He presses his lips to my forehead again. "Come on, let me get you all bubbly and then I'll show you what I have in store."

After a gloriously romantic and sex-free shower with Booker, he tosses me one of his giant Bethnal Green T-shirts and tells me to crawl into his bed while he goes and gets something. When he returns shirtless and wearing only a pair of football shorts, my eyes zero in on what he has in his hands.

"Where did you find that?" I ask with a tired smile as he opens my Brothers Grimm collection of fairytales.

"In your wardrobe. I was looking for your earbuds and came across it." He strokes the leather bound book reverently.

"That thing is a relic," I reply as he sits down beside me, propping himself up against the large wooden headboard.

"I can read to you?" His smirk is adorable.

My eyes widen. "You always made me read to you when we were kids."

"That's because your voice is sexy and you did the character voices. But since you're not feeling well, we can change it up." He winks.

My smile is huge. "I'd love that."

"Let me see if I can find your favourite one," he says, thumbing through the book until he finds the story about Cinderella. The sky outside is beginning to darken, so he reaches over and flicks on his bedside lamp. When he's ready, he opens his arms to me and says, "Lie back. Let me hold you."

I turn and lean against him, pressing my back to his stomach so that my head rests right below his chin. He kisses my wet hair and holds the book with one hand while snaking his other under my arm so it's resting across my belly. His hold on me is so tender yet deliciously strong in his tan, sculpted arm. With this single embrace, he has the power to make me feel completely cherished.

His smooth voice fills the room with one of my favourite passages from the book. I let myself disappear in the story for a while, enjoying the respite from my mind over the last couple of days. This is why I ignored the oddness of my period. I wasn't ready to break this beautiful bubble that we're in right now. I didn't want to let the real world taint us. Everything is going so perfectly. The news will shake all that we've accomplished in a short amount of time.

After he turns the page, he readjusts his hold on me and begins playing with the hem of my shirt. The bottom has ridden up past my black knickers and hips. His fingers brush my lower belly with his small movements, like the universe is telling me there's more in the room than the two of us.

Suddenly, his hand flattens against my belly and the sensation feels so good, so wonderfully intimate, I can't help but wonder what if. What if I was happy about all of this? What if he was happy? What if we do this together? Be parents. Be a family. Be in love.

Booker and I have known each other our entire lives. Now we're sleeping together and becoming closer than ever before. The only thing missing is titles. The feelings are all there. I love him, he loves me. We haven't uttered the words, but I know we both feel the same.

For a moment, I allow myself to daydream about what the baby will be like. A boy or a girl? Will it be kind-hearted and protective like Booker? Or creative and flamboyant like me? Will our baby have Booker's passion? God, I'd love that. Booker is my favourite person, probably ever, and picturing any part of him on something we made together brings me complete joy.

Tears prick the backs of my eyes, and my voice surprises me when I croak, "I love you, Booker."

He tenses beneath me. His hand stills on my belly. I clam up, too, because I didn't mean to say those words out loud. I was so lost in the fantasy of being a happy family that they simply tumbled out.

"What did you just say?" he asks, his voice sounding completely different than it did when he was reading.

I swallow hard knowing that I can't turn back now. There's so much more coming, so I need to own this. "I said I love you." I turn to look at him, and my heart sinks at the horror in his eyes. "Why are you looking at me like I just slapped you?" I ask, my voice laughing at the end because surely this is some sort of joke.

"Because that is a lot to throw at me out of the blue." He jams his hand through his hair, pausing to grip the back of his neck.

"It's hardly out of the blue," I say with another awkward laugh, pushing my hair out of my eyes.

"We've been together for two weeks," he barks, pulling back from me and perching himself on the side of the bed so he's facing away from me.

I touch his back and he flinches like my hands are ice cold. My voice is hesitant as I say, "We've known each other our entire lives."

He looks over his shoulder at me. "And have you ever heard me say that to anyone who isn't family? Ever?" His voice is gruff.

"Wait a minute, what are you saying?" I'm completely baffled by what he's implying. My mind begins churning over the last two weeks together…Hell, the last two months together. Surely my instincts aren't that off the mark. "Are you saying you don't love me?"

"Love is a word I devote to family, Poppy." His words hit me like a blow to the chest. He turns and looks at me like his reply should explain everything.

It explains nothing.

"And I'm not considered family?" I bite back. "I thought I was *in your net*. I thought things between us have grown even deeper than ever before. This hasn't been casual for me, Booker."

"I never said it's casual." He stands up from the bed, his back muscles flexing as he rests his hands on his hips.

"So, what is this between us?" I ask, my mind reeling with what else this could be if it's more than friends but not love. "Is this just sex because I'm your flatmate and convenient?"

"No!" he snaps.

My chest heaves with a hysteric bubble of laughter as I prop myself on my knees and fist my hands in my lap, doing everything I can to contain the rage billowing up inside of me. "Then how can you look me in the eyes and tell me you don't love me? We're best fucking friends!"

"Because I still don't know if I can trust you, Poppy!" he roars, turning and dropping his hands on the bed so he's eye level with me. His face is mean and accusatory, staring at me like I've betrayed him all over again. "You buggered off to Germany without even thinking about me, like I was an inconvenient afterthought that showed up on your doorstep. You weren't even going to say goodbye!"

"Because I was heartbroken!" I scream back, scurrying away from his penetrative eyes and sliding off the bed so we're standing on opposite sides. I suck in big gulps of air as six years of pent-up history and hurt boil out of me like a hot tea kettle. How dare he look at me like I was the only one to do the hurting. How dare he act like I'm the one who can't be trusted. How dare he! "I was crushed because you took Sidney bloody Carmichael to the woods. Our woods! Our special place. The place where we grew up together. The place where…The place where…" I pause, nerves choking my voice box. "Sod it, the place where I fell in love with you! You sure as hell had no problem telling *her* you loved her right before you fucked her. Is she related to you, Booker? Is that why it's okay to love her but not me?"

"What the bloody hell are you talking about?" His voice booms in a manic outburst.

"I saw you guys that night after A-Levels before Giles Windsor's party. She said she loved you and you said it back." I feel like a child, but I can't help it. Speaking about it out loud makes it feel as real and as horrid as the day I witnessed it.

"That's not possible." He's shaking his head adamantly.

"It looked really bloody possible from where I was standing." My lips curl in disgust at the memory. "Those woods, Booker. That place. It's ours. Not hers. Why did you take her there of all the places?"

"I don't know!" he exclaims, shoving a hand through his hair as he racks his brain for some recollection of the evening that I can recall in perfect clarity. "I didn't think. She wouldn't shut up about wanting to see the woods, and I was fucking eighteen years old and wanted to get laid, Poppy. My brothers were probably home and I thought it would be some place private."

"A private place for you to tell Sidney Carmichael that you loved her," I state, voicing the real issue at hand.

"No!" he roars. "I never told her I loved her. I've never said that to anyone, Poppy. No one. Only my family."

I shake my head in disbelief. My voice silent as I think back to that night and what I think I saw. Maybe I didn't stick around long enough to hear the words, but he crushed everything I held most precious about our history. Our childhood. Our youth. My voice is softer as I reply, "It was still our spot, Booker. Did growing up there with me feel so utterly inconsequential that you didn't think twice before taking her out there to shag?"

"Jesus, fuck." He pins me with a serious glower. "I'm sorry, all right? I did a lot of stupid things when I was younger. And I had no idea you were in love with me!" he bites. The words look like they are difficult for him to say, even as a repeat.

"It shouldn't have mattered," I reply firmly. "That fallen tree was mine. I was there long before you ever were. And you took her there and broke my heart and ruined that fucking place for me forever."

He laughs, his eyes wide as he shakes his head back and forth, clearly at a loss. "So, you've kept this secret all this time? All these years? Is that why you left for Germany?"

"Yes," I swallow, not caring anymore how pathetic it makes me look.

"Because you developed feelings for me?" His jaw is tense with his denial.

"Because I loved you!" I scream, wanting to own up to all of it and not let him off easy. "Don't cheapen what I felt, Booker. I just unloaded a six-year burden and it feels bloody good to be shot of it, especially when I know it means nothing to you."

"It doesn't mean nothing. I just…I can't reciprocate it." He scrubs his hands over his face as he adds, "I've seen the havoc love can wreak and I don't want that, Poppy. The pleasure of love lasts a moment, but the pain of losing it lasts a lifetime."

"Then what are you doing with me?" I cry, my voice rising with thick emotion bubbling up inside of me.

"I don't know," he stammers. "I'm just trying I guess. I thought you were okay with that!"

"It's not enough," I croak.

"Why? Why the pressure so fast? Why do I have to feel a certain way right this second?" His voice is nearly begging.

"Because I'm fucking pregnant, Booker," I nearly sob.

He inhales sharply. "What?"

"I'm pregnant," I repeat, all emotion evaporating from my body.

"No," he whispers, his eyes searching all over the room for an escape.

"Yes."

"No."

"Yes!" I cry. "But don't worry. I won't expect anything from you."

"What does that mean?" he snaps.

I exhale heavily, the knowing words tumbling out of me with ease. "It means I'll do this on my own because I refuse to trap you in something you don't want, and I refuse to trap myself in another loveless life with you."

"You said we would never stop being friends." His eyes are wide and angry. "You said in time we'd be Booker and Poppy again, no matter what."

"I lied." I say simply with a shrug. "I lied because I've been in love with you most of my bloody life and I thought this was my dream coming true." I sniff back a sob that wants to escape, refusing to give myself over to it in front of him. "Now I see it's my worst nightmare. I've been teased with what we could have, and it's all for nothing because you can't love me. I wish I'd never had a taste of this at all."

When I move to leave, he slams his hand on the doorframe to stop me. The wood cracks from the force. "It's been two bloody weeks, Poppy. I need more…time. This is all happening so fast!" He grabs the top of his head, hysteria taking over.

The old me wants to comfort him and let him use me in whatever way he's emotionally capable of. But the new me knows I'm stronger than that. And I deserve better. They are simply words, but they are probably the most important words a person can ever hear.

"You've had a lifetime to fall in love with me. If it was going to happen, it would have by now." With those final words, my heart begins to break, splitting down the middle like a crack in pavement. Hardening with the exposure to the elements around me. "I have to go."

"You said you wouldn't leave!" he shouts, wrapping me up in a strong hold and binding my arms down.

His exquisite firmness sends treacherous shivers up my spine. Familiar shivers that know his touch and trust it so much that I want him even in this state. I look up at him for a moment, fire burning the backs of my eyes as I take in his face. It's likely the last time I'll ever be this close to him. His rapid heartbeat in his chest. His heavy breaths. His lust-filled eyes even in the throes of a fight. I'll never have any of this with him again.

I'm in love with my best friend…

…and this is where we end.

"I'm leaving, Booker, and you're going to let me because you know better than anyone how awful it feels to be second choice."

My words penetrate his frenzy and his arms drop, releasing me as he steps away from the doorway. I immediately dash into my room to throw on some pants and then storm down the hallway to leave. Without a look back, I walk out of his room, out of his flat, out of his building, and out of my best friend's life…again.

Loveless

22

Booker

POPPY MCADAMS IS A LIAR, I THINK AS I STARE AT MY FACE IN the bathroom mirror. It's been six days since she walked out of my flat. Six days since she went from being my favourite person in the world to the one that has the power to destroy me. She hasn't returned any of my texts or calls. There's no answer at her parents' home in Chigwell. Nothing. Complete and utter silence, similar to the time she buggered off to Germany.

This isn't how it was supposed to be. She promised me we would still be friends. The memory of her deceitful words on the Bethnal Green practice pitch haunt me.

"And I promise that if we try this and it doesn't work, you won't lose me. We will work our way back to being Booker and Poppy, no matter what."

I'm not even able to wrap my mind around the fact that she said she is pregnant because all I can focus on is the fact that she's fucking gone. I've lost my best friend. Again. This time feels worse than Germany because, even though I'm not able to love her the way that she wants, I know what it's like to feel her. Taste her. Desire her.

Miss her.

Her absence is a trigger, bringing back all the horrid memories of the first time this happened. In the two months she lived here, she became a part of my day-to-day life. I got used to her constant presence. Then the sex intensified our connection. Sped things up. Losing her feels like I've lost a limb.

When you get so close to someone and they disappear on you, you're not the same person anymore. Your voice doesn't sound the same. Your reactions aren't as natural because that person—whose affirmations you need to feel right in the world—is gone.

I miss my best friend.

I even miss all her nutty quirks. Like the way she lets out a sexy moan every time she crawls into bed, as if the feel of the sheets is a turn on. Or the ridiculous show tunes she blasts during her showers. Or all the girlie shit she stuffs into the bathroom cupboard. The hair products, the makeup, the lotions. So many lotions.

Doesn't she need her stuff? How has she gone through the last several days without it? There's no way she's been back to the flat. I would know. I've been holed up in here like an agoraphobic, terrified of the outside world and holding my breath every time I hear some-one climbing the steps.

Bloody hell, my flat feels empty without her. It makes me realise that I've never actually had to live alone. When my brothers and Vi moved out, I still had Dad. He was a quiet flatmate in a mansion of a house, so he wasn't much company. But there was another human around. Someone to talk football with. Someone to breathe the same air, share a meal with, and make sure I'm not dead.

Fuck me, what if something's happened to Poppy? It was getting dark when she left last week. I shouldn't have let her go. What was I thinking? What if she was taken? What if she's been drugged and sold into sex trafficking?

Before I know it, I'm dashing out of the loo and throwing on a dirty T-shirt from the floor. She's got to be at her parents' and is forcing them to screen my calls. Her dad never liked me. The second

Poppy and I became mates as children, he looked at me like he wanted to crush me with his bare hands. Considering he's six-foot-five and nearly as wide as he is tall, I'm sure he's man enough to do it. But I need to know she's okay.

I head for the door and pull her name up on my mobile, kicking myself for not going over there days ago.

When I open the door, Andrew is standing there with his fist held up in the air. His eyes narrow. "Booker."

"Andrew?" I say, my jaw slack as I look all around the hallway in hopes that Poppy might be with him. "What are you doing here?"

His eyes drop to the ground where a large wheelie suitcase sits. Avoiding my glower, he clears his throat and replies, "I'm here for some of Poppy's things."

His request surprises me. "Her things?"

Straightening his shoulders, he replies, "Yes. She asked me tae grab some items she needs for work…and some clothes and…toiletry thingies."

My hand slides up the doorframe and grips it tightly. "Is she staying with you?" If he says yes, there is nothing that will stop me from breaking down his door to talk to her.

"Nae," he replies and my shoulders drop.

"Is she at her parents'?" I ask knowingly, my voice tight with annoyance.

Andrew shakes his head and sighs. "She's no at her parents'."

My brows furrow. "Andrew. If she's at her parents' and commuting from Chigwell for work, I need to know. It's not bloody safe."

The corner of his mouth turns up as he huffs out a snide laugh. "I dinnae think she's yer concern anymore, *mate*."

His bravado gets right up my nose. "I'm not your fucking mate!" I bark as anger courses through my veins. How much does this prat even know? Why the fuck is Poppy sending him to my front door? "*I'm* Poppy's mate, and she will always be my concern. If you know where she is, you better bloody tell me."

"Fuck off," he scoffs, not the least bit intimidated. "Ye dinnae get tae sit here and make demands. No after ye get her knocked up and then break her fucking heart."

His loud voice echoes in the hallway and I see red. Blinding, angry, hot as fuck red as I lunge for him and clench my hands around the lapels of his prissy button-down. Shoving him up against the stairwell railing, I roar, "Tell me where the fuck she is!"

"Booker William Harris!" Vi's voice carries up the flight of stairs below us. I glance down and see her head peering up the foyer. "Let him go right the fuck now!"

I squeeze harder around the fabric in frustration and then yank him back into the hallway, nearly tossing him on the ground as I do. "You can get fucked," I state, pointing a finger at him and heaving big gulps of air back into my lungs. "You're not getting any of her shit."

"Booker," Andrew argues, straightening his collar. His face is beet red. "Ye have no right to keep her things."

"I have *every* right!" I seethe and walk toward the top of the stairs where Vi appears. "She's my best friend."

Vi's wide, accusing eyes find mine as she reaches the top step. She then swerves her murderous gaze at Andrew. "Andrew, I think you need to give me some time with my brother."

Andrew sniffs haughtily. "I'll be coming back." He grabs the suitcase and shoulders past me to the steps.

I watch him descend, fisting my hands at my sides the whole time. Out of the corner of my eye, I see Vi watching me with her familiar hands on her familiar hips. Mummy hat clearly on.

"What the bloody hell is going on?" she snaps.

I turn away from her, my jaw muscle ticking with anger. I can't find the words to begin telling her what's going on because I don't even know myself. I've never wanted to punch someone so hard in all my life. Gareth has the temper in our family. He's the one who rages and we all have to rip him off. There's never been a problem I couldn't talk myself out of.

This isn't me.

I look at Vi and her eyes soften when she takes in my changed expression.

"Booker," she says softly. "Come on, let's have some coffee."

She grabs my arm and pulls me inside, annoyingly rubbing my back as we enter. I sit down at the table while Vi makes herself at home in my kitchen. The smell of coffee brewing should bring me comfort. Instead, it makes me think about the time Poppy rested her head on my arm as we stood in perfect, blissful silence, enjoying the warmth of each other while awaiting the start of our day.

Vi sits down across from me and pushes a steaming mug into my hands. "Start talking."

I swallow the knot in my throat. "I don't know where to begin."

"Where's Poppy?"

I sniff once. "Gone."

"To where?"

"That's what I was trying to figure out when you showed up."

"Is that why you're not answering anyone's calls? And why you missed Sunday dinner last week?" she asks, tapping her hands on the side of the mug expectantly. "I came here today to make sure you don't miss this week's as well."

"I don't feel like Sunday dinner, Vi." I close my eyes as I take a tentative sip of the hot liquid. The burn feels good.

"Booker, what happened?" she asks, her voice pleading.

I shrug. "Everything I always expected to happen. Poppy told me she loved me and then she left."

Vi inhales sharply. "Why did she leave?"

"Because I couldn't fucking say it back!" I exclaim in frustration. Vi knows the answer to that question and I hate that she's making me say it. "Because you're exactly right! I'm fucking damaged goods and you should be ashamed of me."

Vi tsks and shakes her head, a sad look in her eyes making me feel like ten tons of dog shit. "What else did she say? Surely there's more to it than that."

I slam my eyes shut and drop my head into my hands, resisting the words I haven't even allowed myself to say out loud.

"Booker," she urges. "Is what Andrew said true?"

I look up at her knowing, glassy eyes and nod. She closes them and winces. "What are you going to do about it?"

"I haven't a fucking clue, Vi," I answer, emotion boiling over the top at admitting this out loud to the universe. "I can't even wrap my head around the fact that she's not still here, let alone the idea that she's growing my baby inside of her. She left again. Just like before. My best friend left and I couldn't do anything to stop her because she wants something I can't give her."

"Love?" Vi asks.

I nod. "I can barely say the word to you, never mind her. And the rest of you make it look so easy. You're playing happy family. Tanner is married. Camden is on his way. Now Gareth just needs to fall for someone and then I'll truly be completely alone."

"You're not alone!" she cries, an angry vein protruding on her temple. "Look at me, Booker. I'm right bloody here. We're Harrises! We don't give you enough space to consider the idea of loneliness. Tanner would probably come over here and spoon you right now if you gave him the green light."

"Oh sod off," I groan.

"It's true." She pauses and inhales a deep, shaky breath. "Look, we're all fucked up in our own way after losing Mum. There were some seriously dark years in that house we grew up in. I guess I thought since you were so young, you wouldn't be as affected by it, but I was wrong."

"I get it. I'm fucked," I moan, feeling more sorry for myself than ever.

"You're not fucked, Booker. But you need to understand that you sensed that loss with Mum when it happened, even though you were little. Because of that, I think you've clung to the family extra tight. So much so I think your inner child is afraid of losing anyone ever again."

"Did you just say inner child?" I ask, my brow furrowing in disbelief.

Vi straightens. "Yes I did. I've done some therapy sessions with Hayden, all right? I've learned a thing or two." She leans in again. "I also learned that no matter how motherly I tried to be when we were kids, I was still just a child playing make-believe and you deserved more."

The break in her voice makes my chest hurt. I reach over and clutch her fists. "You were great, Vi. You are great. You're the glue that holds us all together. If it wasn't for you, we'd never see each other. And I'd probably still be living at home, acting like an even bigger whore than Tanner."

Vi giggles and it brings a much needed smile to my face. "Hayden says I'm too controlling over you guys. That you need to figure out how to make your own mistakes."

"Oh, bollocks. Hayden just doesn't understand the Harris way. Your fuck-up is my fuck-up."

Vi laughs and swipes at a few stray tears that slip out. "He says you guys have a codependency on me to fix all your problems. Can you believe that?"

"That just sounds like psychobabble again." I wink and take another sip of my coffee.

"Exactly what I think." She smirks, but then her brows pinch in the middle as she watches me closely. "I'm sorry Poppy isn't the one for you, Booker."

Her words dig at a place in my chest, but I brush them off. "Yeah," I reply casually and set my mug down.

She clicks her cheeks and adds, "But you can't force love."

I nod, avoiding her penetrative gaze. "Right."

"And if you don't love her, you can't be with her." She brings her mug to her mouth and takes a sip.

Frowning at her repetition, I reply, "I know, Vi."

"Well, she deserves to find happiness, don't you think?"

"Yes." My spine straightens with annoyance. "But I don't think she was unhappy with me."

Her face scrunches as she ponders for a few seconds. "Even if she wasn't wanting love from you, it never would have lasted. These things happen for a reason, Booker," she states simply with a patronising head nod.

My eyes narrow on her. "Why do you think it wouldn't have lasted?"

Her brows lift. "Well, you're busy. And so young. And not even close to ready for that kind of responsibility."

"What responsibility are you referring to exactly?"

"Being a family man," she says, her voice rising in pitch like this is what she's been saying all evening. "We just talked about all the issues you have because of Mum's death. You're clearly not emotionally capable of being in love, let alone being a father. You need to have an open heart. And if you can't love Poppy, you won't be able to love the baby."

"What the hell are you going on about?" I snap, shoving back from the table. "You sound completely mental!"

"Well I'm just saying. Loving a baby is hard. They don't give you much to go on." Her casual tone is mind-boggling to me.

"I love Rocky," I state matter-of-factly.

"Well, *now* maybe. She's older and she smiles and giggles. That makes it easier. As newborns, they take and take and take."

"You've completely lost it, Vi. I loved Rocky the second she was born."

She rolls her eyes like I'm a fool. "Booker, I know you. And I know what's best for you. Take my advice here. You're better off this way. I'm sure Poppy will let you be a part of the baby's life in some small way."

"Fuck that!" I roar, standing up and thrusting a hand through my hair, a rising panic building in my chest. "I don't want some small way."

"But it's what's best," she states firmly.

"For whom exactly?" My voice booms.

She shrugs. "For everyone. If you're not terrified of losing Poppy every day of your life, she's not the one for you."

I huff out a laugh and begin pacing. My sister has completely lost it. She doesn't know me at all because fear is what's forced me to keep my distance from Poppy. Fear is what made me keep her at arm's-length our whole lives. Fear is all I've been living with the past two months with Poppy. Fear of her leaving. Fear of losing her. Fear of never seeing her again. And now, all my worst fears have come true.

"I'm not listening to this anymore, Vi." I pause and press my hands on the table, piercing Vi with a seriousness that she cannot ignore like she can a naïve baby brother. "You've helped me a lot and I appreciate it more than you know, but you're completely wrong about this. I'm going to love this baby *fiercely* because I've never been more terrified of losing someone than I am of losing Poppy. I'm so bloody afraid, I've never let myself admit that I'm in lov—" An intense pressure rises up in my chest as I realise what I was about say. I pull in shaky breaths as the words hang on the tip of my tongue, ready to fall out like lyrics to my favourite song. I look straight at Vi and say, "I love her."

I clench my jaw and wait for the doom to come, but it doesn't. Lightness comes instead. An airy, walking on water weightlessness that I feel all through my body.

"Bloody hell, Vi. I love Poppy." I exhale heavily. "Fuck me, it feels brilliant to say! I love her…I think I've loved her my whole life. Like it's always been there, but I've denied it." I hardly recognise my voice, but it feels fucking fantastic to hear.

Vi smiles and tilts her head. "You love Poppy?" She has a coy bounce to her voice.

"I…do. She's my world and I love her." I rake my hand through my hair and look around the room manically. "I need to tell her. Right now." I push my sleeves up and bound for the door, ready to break into Andrew's flat and choke him until he talks. "That frustrating Scot better sing like a canary."

"Booker!" Vi shouts, a weightiness to her tone that pulls me up short. I look back and she's standing at the table, a proud gleam in her eyes. "You can't just tell her and expect her to believe you. You need to do a lot bloody more than say the words."

I frown, pondering her words for a minute. She's right. Poppy has always had a flare for the theatrics. If she were in my shoes, she'd probably hire a marching band or a dance company. Hell, she'd probably write a song and sing it to me.

But I don't want to do something Poppy would do. I want to do something I would do. Something that reminds her of why she fell in love with me to begin with. "I think I have an idea."

Poppy

"I could really use my best friend right now," I croak into my pillow as I lie down for a nap in my childhood bed and beg myself not to start crying again.

Napping has become my new favourite thing. Napping means a break from the crying. Napping means a break from the panicking. A break from the moping.

Napping means remembering the feel of Booker's warmth pressed against my backside.

I guess even napping has its moments of treachery.

That's the crap part about your best friend being the man you love. When you lose him, it's a double punch in the gut. It's like retching and having diarrhea at the same time. As if getting sick isn't pathetic enough, now you have to sit on a toilet while doing it because you're pissing out your arse as well. Really, is there anything else that can make you feel so pitiful?

The doorbell rings downstairs, ripping me out of my colourfully descriptive pity party. My heart leaps into my throat as I slide out of bed and look out the window for Booker's truck. I've been waiting for him to show up since the moment I came to my parents' house last week. Hiding here has been easy since my parents are away on holiday for their thirtieth wedding anniversary—a blessing and a curse, really. A blessing because I'm alone, a curse because this house is full of Booker Harris memories. Even sleepover memories, back when things weren't so complicated between us.

I make my way down the long flight of stairs and tiptoe up to the front door. Peering through the peephole, I exhale with relief when I see Andrew standing on the other side.

"Oh good, it's only you," I say as the door swings open and I swipe the tear residue off my face.

"Nice tae see ye, too," he grumbles and strides in like he's been here a hundred times even though this is only his first. "Ye think I'd receive a more welcoming greeting considering I've driven all the way oot tae Chigwell." His nose wrinkles and he whispers, "I can actually smell the Botox in this neighbourhood. Is yer mum one of them?"

"No, she's not. And you don't have to whisper. She and my dad are in the Canary Islands for their anniversary. But you should still stop being so judgemental." I look down at his empty hands. "Where are my things?"

He lets out a haughty laugh. "Still at Booker's."

"He wasn't home?"

"Oh, he wis home all right." He looks around the house and says, "I need a drink."

Frowning, I follow him into the kitchen where he hoists himself up on the counter. "A nice red will do."

I roll my eyes and pull the cork out of the open bottle on the counter, giving it a sniff to make sure it hasn't gone bad since my parents have left because I sure as hell wasn't the one to open it. I pour the dark liquid into a wine glass and hand it over. "What happened?"

Andrew opens the collar of his shirt and rubs around the front of his neck. "Is it still red?"

I frown and look closer at the area he's touching. "No. It looks normal."

He huffs and takes a drink. "The wanker is lucky I dinnae press charges."

"For what?" I ask, my brow crinkling.

"Booker assaulted me!"

"Assaulted you?" I ask, disbelief in my voice.

Andrew's brown eyes widen. "He lunged at me and grabbed me around here." He yanks the collar of his shirt and demonstrates. "Practically held me over the stairwell, threatening tae drop me tae my death."

"Oh my God, Andrew!" I exclaim in horror. "I'm so sorr—"

"Okay, maybe no the death part," he interrupts before I have a chance to finish my apology for sending him there. "But he did put his bloody hands on me."

"Booker did?" I ask, still needing confirmation.

"Aye."

"Not one of his brothers?" I can't help but recall the time Gareth attacked one of Vi's ex-boyfriends in a Chigwell pub and had the police called on him. Paparazzi showed up and everything. It was a nightmare.

"It wis Booker and he wis by himself," Andrew confirms with a sip. "Who knows how violent he would have gotten if he had his pack of hot brothers there tae back him up."

I wrap my arms around my body. "I can hardly believe what I'm hearing. Booker is normally a pacifist. He's protective to be sure, but he's not violent. God, what's gotten into him?"

"You," Andrew grunts and downs the rest of his wine. "It's fine, though. I'm quite sure I could have battered him. I wis just being a gentlemen because the lad is clearly tormented."

"Tormented how?" I ask, my mind all over the place.

"For fuck's sake, Poppet, dae I need tae draw ye pictures? The man is in love with ye…Keep up!"

I lean back against the counter, shaking my head adamantly. "You're wrong. He is not in love with me. At all. And he's not a fighter. None of this sounds like the Booker I know."

"Well, he clearly cares aboot ye enough tae throw me oot of his flat and tell me tae get stuffed."

I shake my head again and deny everything Andrew is insinuating. "This changes nothing. Even if he is feeling something for me, it's not enough."

"No enough for what? No enough tae be the father of yer child? Poppy, I'm sorry tae tell ye this, but unless ye've been sleeping around, the jig is up." He pinches the bridge of his nose and exhales heavily. "I'm sorry tae be harsh, but what's yer plan here? Have me move ye oot of his flat entirely so ye never have tae see him again? Ye have tae talk tae him at some point. He's the father."

"You don't think I know that?" I snap. "I'm still figuring it all out," I stammer.

"Well it might be easier tae figure oot if ye quit hiding oot and start accepting his calls."

My eyes widen. "I can't possibly face him yet."

"Why no?"

"Because I love him too much!" I howl and cover my face with my hands, my voice rising to that nutter pitch that comes out when I want to cry. I shove my hands through my hair and look at Andrew accusingly. "Because Booker makes me feel anchored and right in the world. And if he comes to me and asks me to marry him, I will crumble and say yes."

"What's so wrong aboot that?" Andrew asks, his face screwed up in confusion.

"He doesn't love me. He's only my friend, so he cares enough to do the decent thing, but nothing more. Booker isn't tormented because he's in love with me. He's tormented because he doesn't want to lose me. But I'd rather lose him than go back to being friends."

"Surely being friends is better than nothing," Andrew argues.

"It's not," I sniff. "I've seen behind the curtain now. I know what we could be together. Anything less than all in will eat away at my soul and make me hurt in places I didn't even know I could hurt." I shrug my shoulders and add, "I want more. I want…real love. This baby deserves that." My voice cracks at the end because I realise I'm not only making this decision for myself anymore.

"So, what will ye dae?" Andrew's voice sounds grave. "Ye cannae avoid him forever."

"I know," I nod and swipe at a stray tear. "I'm just avoiding him until I'm strong enough to say no to him."

"Poppet," Andrew says, his brows knitting together as he watches me. "Are ye one hundred percent sure yer no just protecting yerself. I've seen the way Booker looks at ye."

I shake my head. "Don't give me a reason to hope, Andrew. I can't bear it."

Sporty Vs. Handy

Booker

"**W**HAT THE BLOODY HELL ARE WE DOING OUT HERE?" Gareth's deep voice echoes in the woods surrounding us.

I tear my eyes off the fallen tree and look up at my three brothers standing in front of me. They're all dressed in workout gear like we're going to football practice instead of attempting to build something from scratch.

"We're building a playhouse," I say, picking up one of the saws I found in the garden shed at Dad's house.

Camden's jaw drops. "Booker, are you serious?"

"Yes, dead serious," I reply, my tone firm.

Tanner strides over to the small amount of supplies I bought at a hardware store on my way over. It consists of a couple of tape measurers, hammers, nails, and extra timber. "You think we can build something with this sorry lot? We're professional athletes, not fucking craftsmen. This will take us weeks."

"Not weeks," I interject. "Days. We have until Sunday night dinner."

"Why the rush?" Gareth asks.

"Because I've made her wait far too long already."

Camden's eyes turn soft and he steps closer to me. "What's happened, Booker? Did you and Poppy have a row? Surely you can talk through it. I don't know what building a playhouse for a grown woman will achieve."

"It's not for her."

"Who's it for?" he asks, his brows crumpled.

I pause, tugging nervously on my earlobe but knowing that I have to tell my brothers. We don't keep secrets like this. "For our baby."

Tanner laughs. "Like a future baby you're dreaming about having with her or a real baby? 'Cause I think about future babies with Belle all the time. It's kind of an issue."

"A real baby," I state with a heavy sigh.

"Fuck me," Gareth states.

"Oh shiiit," Camden adds.

Tanner presses the heel of his hand to his forehead. "Baby Booker is having a baby. Jesus fuck."

"Look," I bark, my frustration with them reaching my limit. "I'm building this playhouse. Are you lot going to help me or not?"

"Booker," Gareth says, his voice softer than usual. "We want to help you, but we don't think this is the best way."

"It's my way and I'm doing it!" I exclaim, straightening up as tall as I can so my brothers stop seeing me as the little baby brother and start seeing me as the man I am. I'm about to be a father—a fact that would be a lot easier to wrap my head around if I can get Poppy to talk to me. And this is the only way I can think of to get Poppy's attention, so I'm done letting my brothers think they know what's best for me. I'm the one who knows what's best for me. And I know what's best for Poppy. She's not just in my net, she *is* my net. She's my home and I need to prove that to her.

I head over to the fallen tree that Poppy used as a makeshift stage when we were kids. I place the saw on the wood and look at my brothers one last time. "You guys still don't get it. Growing up,

Poppy was all I had when you guys were off doing whatever the fuck you got up to. Football. Girls. Tan and Cam, you always had each other. Gareth, you never seemed to need anyone. I needed Poppy. I still need her. She is everything to me, and I have to get her back. So if you guys aren't going to help me, you need to fuck off and let me do this."

Anger coursing through my veins, I begin working the saw into the brittle tree trunk. After one swipe, I know instantly that this is going to take a hell of a lot longer than two days.

Out of the corner of my eye, I see Gareth pick up another saw and head to the other end of the tree to begin work. "Fuuuck," I hear him murmur as I start to debate how we can get some power tools out here.

I look up as Tanner ties his hair up into a messy bun. He reaches down and picks up a piece of wood. "I seriously have no clue what the fuck to do with this."

"You build stuff with it, idiot," Camden snaps, snatching it out of his hand.

"Ouch, you prat! I think I got a splinter!" Tanner cradles his hand in his other hand and looks closely at his palm.

Just then, a loud crack comes from the east side of the woods. All our heads snap to the forklift driving straight toward us with a pile of timber and a large generator resting on the prongs. I can't see who's driving through the cab window, but I see a quad coming from farther in the distance with two blokes on it as well. One of them looks like Hayden.

The forklift comes to a stop twenty feet from us. The man who gets off is a huge, Jean Claude Van Dam sort of bloke wearing jeans and a plaid shirt. He has a worn tool belt around his waist, and his dark curly hair is sticking out from under a baseball cap.

"Which one of you is Booker Harris?" the man asks, his deep American accent smooth and confident.

I clear my throat and reply, "That's me."

He smiles. "My name's Brody. I'm a friend of Hayden's brother, Theo."

"Um…okay?" I stammer, confused. I've met Theo a few times, but I don't know him that well. What's his friend out here for?

I glance over as the quad finally pulls up beside Brody. Theo is driving while Hayden holds onto a bunch of equipment on the rack behind him. They both amble off, lifting the pile of building supplies down to the ground in one smooth motion.

Theo stands and straightens his thick, dark-rimmed glasses. "Booker. Guys." He head nods to all of us like it's any normal Friday afternoon.

"What's going on?" I ask as Hayden wipes his hands off and adjusts the thick leather cuffs around his wrists.

"Vi told me about your little project here. I thought you could use some help." Hayden looks over at his brother and then to Brody. "Brody is my brother's wife's best friend's husband."

"Say what?" Tanner croaks.

"My wife, Finley, and Theo's wife, Leslie, are best friends," Brody adds, trying to help.

My voice pipes in next. "Okay, yeah. I've met Leslie, but I don't think I've met Finley. But what does that have to do with anything?" I ask, unsure what the point of all this is.

"All you need to know is Brody's my friend," Theo states much more simply. "And since he moved to London a few years ago with his wife, he's opened a very successful contracting company."

"I renovate houses mostly," Brody adds.

Theo continues, "The point is, Hayden asked me to help, but I'm afraid my skills don't go much farther than custom furniture. This man here can frame houses." He claps a hand on Brody's back and smiles. "And I figured we can use all the help we can get."

"We?" I ask with a smile lifting my face. "You guys are going to help? Seriously, thank you. This is brilliant. We erm…have no fucking clue what we're doing."

Theo, Hayden, and Brody look down at the sad display of tools I have spread out and do a crap job of hiding their laughs. I can't say I blame them. To them, we look like complete knobs standing here in our footy gear trying to make sense of a hammer and nails.

I'm laughing when I say, "Maybe sometime after this we can play a little footy so we Harris Brothers aren't completely emasculated today?"

Theo smiles broadly and pushes his glasses up his nose. "Deal."

After thanking Hayden for saving the day, the seven of us get to work, with Brody taking the lead and directing us all on what to do. However, Tanner's request to operate the forklift is instantly rejected. He doesn't pout…too much.

A Place I Feel At Home

Sunday dinner will be starting any moment at the Harris house. If I squint hard enough through my bedroom window, I can see the top of their house through the wooded park. The thought of Booker being so close to me and operating business as usual guts me. If this was last week, I'd be going.

But it's not.

And the painful reminder that everything has changed is turning me into a big bloody crybaby. I guess that could be the hormones, too. Is it too early to have pregnancy hormones? I should get a pregnancy book and do some reading. The doctor said I was about six weeks along and needed to schedule an appointment with a midwife at eight weeks. Here I sit around seven weeks, so I guess I better figure this shit out soon.

God, this is really happening.

The doorbell rings, and my heart is in my throat as I walk over and gaze into the peephole. Relief casts over me when I see a redhead and a brunette whispering to each other on the other side.

I fluff my short tresses and swipe under my eyes. Thank goodness I got somewhat dressed today. My subconscious was terrified that Booker might stop by. If he did, I didn't want him to see me looking like Amy Winehouse after a bender, which is pretty much what my reflection has looked like all week, even though I haven't been drinking. So, today I slipped into a comfortable sundress that could double as pyjamas if I wanted it to. I even snuck a little of my mum's mascara to help myself feel more human. I may feel pathetic, but I'd rather not look it.

Smiling brightly, I open the door. "Fancy seeing you girls here. Have you been out drinking sangria with the masses of Chigwell WAGs around here?"

Belle's face sneers. "Don't be daft. I'd die before I'd go out in Chigwell."

Indie smiles awkwardly. "What Belle means is your parents' home is lovely."

Belle rolls her eyes. "You know what I mean."

Giving a polite laugh, I ask, "How did you guys know where to find me?"

Indie looks down and Belle tsks like she's annoyed. "Andrew snapped like a twig. For a hot Scotsman, he's not very strong."

I shudder to even imagine what they did to get Andrew talking. "Poor Andrew. So, what brings you here?"

Belle pushes her way past the doorway and steps into the foyer. "We know everything."

My eyes are wide as I look back at Indie and ask, "Everything, everything?"

They both frown at me. Indie is the one to reply. "We know you guys had a row and you're moving out."

I let out a breath I didn't even realise I was holding. I've not even told my parents I'm pregnant yet. The idea of Booker's family knowing already would be too much to handle.

Belle's voice snaps my attention to her. "Where are your parents?"

"The Canary Islands. I'm sorry. What all did Booker tell Vi?"

Indie replies simply, "That you left."

My brows lift and I feel like I could tip forward. "Is that all?"

"Yes," Belle states, her brow furrowing at me like I'm a mental patient.

I exhale with relief. "Do you guys have time for some tea? I'm extremely thirsty."

They follow me into the kitchen and sit up at the long counter island. I put on a kettle and then grab a few tea bags and mugs.

"So, how are you doing?" Belle asks like she's waiting for me to say something.

"I'm fine."

"Seriously?"

"No, but there's nothing that can be done. You were right. I wouldn't have been satisfied if I didn't try. And I tried."

"For two weeks," Belle scoffs. "I can't believe it all fell apart so quickly. What happened?"

I shrug, wishing I could tell them everything but knowing that it's not the right time. "I'm in love with him."

"I thought you were already in love with him?" Indie asks, her tone soft and sympathetic.

"I didn't even know what love was back then. The two weeks we spent together as a couple were some of the best days of my life. I drifted into a dream with him. Knowing that I can never have any of that back makes me hurt in places I didn't even know could hurt."

Belle and Indie are silent for a moment.

"But what if things were different?" Belle asks, glancing down at her watch and looking up at me.

I sigh, feeling like I'm reliving the same conversation I had with Andrew two days ago. "They won't be. I don't know if I'd ever be able to trust Booker with my heart again. Too much pain has happened." Belle looks at her watch again. "You guys need to get going, don't you? It's almost dark outside. Surely dinner is almost ready. Don't let me keep you."

Indie and Belle give each other a peculiar look. "Go for a walk with us," Indie says, her voice cheery.

"A walk?"

She nods. "Yeah, I want to see the wooded park behind your house."

This is getting stranger by the minute. "No thanks."

"Just a short one," Belle interjects. "I think it'd be good for you to go outside for a bit."

I huff, "I'm not going in the woods, guys. I…hate it back there. It holds my favourite and my most horrid memories."

"What if there was something out there that blasted out all of those memories? The good and the bad. What if there was something out there that made everything from the past disappear and all you could see are new memories to be made?"

"There is absolutely nothing out there that will help erase what's already been done. It's burned into my memory."

"Poppy," Indie states, her voice firmer than I've ever heard it. "I think you're incredible, but you're dead wrong."

"Dead wrong," Belle repeats.

Their serious faces have me completely curious now.

"Come with us, Poppy," Belle states one last time. "There's something you have to see."

"All right," I finally agree and follow them to the front door. I slip into my flats and guide them around to the back.

The sun is just beginning to set as we walk through the garden of my parents' estate. The golden tones saturate the green grass and manicured flowers in stunning light. We pass through the gate that leads into an open grassy knoll and then reach the edge of the woods where the park begins. It's a beautiful five minute walk amongst the mature pine, oak, and elm trees. Since it's the height of summer, everything's very green and lush. Idyllic really under normal circumstances.

It's been over six years since the last time I've been out here, so I'm surprised to find the path I wore down over time is still present.

Sadness creeps over me as I think about the lifetime of memories this wooded park holds. I keep my head down and try to steel myself for how I'll feel when we reach the area where Booker and I played the most.

When we draw closer, a white paper bag with a burning candle inside catches my eye. My head snaps up to find two rows of burning lanterns lighting a path to the place my fallen tree used to sit. The tree that once laid there with moss growing up the sides is gone. The place where I sang countless songs upon. A couple other trees that occupied the area are now cleared out as well. In their place is a bright yellow painted structure that looks like a children's play-house. But it's even more stunning because it's a bit of a ramshackle design—rickety and topsy-turvy, like a cartoon house. It even has a covered porch with thick, knotty tree branches for rails and an over-flowing flower box in the window. Whomever built this put loads of time into it.

"What's happened out here?" I ask, my voice breathy and awe-struck. "Do you know who did this?"

I turn and look over to Indie's water eyes as she answers, "Who do you think?"

My jaw drops. "When? Why? H-h-how?" I stammer.

Belle touches my arm and answers, "He made it for your baby."

My breath catches and my head snaps back and forth between them. I cover my mouth and mumble, "You guys know?"

Belle laughs and says, "The Harrises have no secrets, darling. You should know that better than anyone."

I laugh like a moron because she's totally right. Suddenly, I see movement out of the corner of my eye and look over to see Booker walking out from behind the house. He's dressed in a pair of filthy jeans with holes in the knees and a white T-shirt with yellow paint splattered all over it. His arms and face are caked in sweat and dirt.

He looks gorgeous.

And completely nervous as he tries to smooth back some of his wild dark locks spackled with paint. "I planned on cleaning up before you got here, but it turns out I'm not very handy. At all," he laughs. "And I greatly underestimated how long this would take."

We laugh awkwardly as Belle and Indie begin to back away. I hear their retreating footsteps behind me, but my eyes are zeroed in on Booker. He's covered in dirt, but with the golden sunlight slicing in behind him, I'm not sure he's ever looked more handsome.

I walk a little closer and stand in front of the mini porch to get a better look. It's truly exquisite, right down to the adorably crooked front door. "What is all of this?"

"It's a playhouse," he replies and stuffs his hands in his pockets. The manly scent wafting off of him is so familiar, I have to stop myself from moving closer to him.

Smiling, I reply, "I can see that. But why did you build it?"

"Because I want a place to create new memories with you, Poppy."

My heart sinks. "Booker, this doesn't change—"

He cuts me off. "Because I'm an arse and I screwed up when we were kids, but I swear on my life, Poppy, I never slept with Sidney out here. She told me she loved me and tried to use sex to manipulate me into saying things I didn't feel. The second she did, I knew we were over. I never slept with her that night or any night. And I certainly never loved her. I've never said those words to her or anyone who isn't family. Ever."

I purse my lips together and beg my chin to stop quivering. Hearing him say all of this soothes a dark part of my anxious, troubled soul. But not all of it. There's still a huge segment that needs more. "I'd be lying if I said I'm not thrilled to hear that, Booker. But it's only part of the problem between us."

"I know," he replies in a hurry. "But I needed you to know that before I tell you the rest."

"What's the rest?" I ask, crossing my arms over my chest for protection. This is so painful. Every moment of my insecure childhood is looking me right in the face. I feel like I could crawl out of my own skin.

"Sidney asked me to bring her out here because I would never shut up about *you*. About how special *you* were. About how I wished more girls were like *you*. I took her to that hospital charity last year because you weren't here, and Sidney feels safe because I feel nothing for her. The whole time you were in Germany, I never settled down with anyone because they weren't *you*. Poppy, I've never discussed pet names with a girl before. Or invited them to my matches. I've certainly never brought them to Harris Sunday dinners. I need you to know that you're different."

His words do nothing to alleviate the ache in my chest. "I believe I'm different, Booker, but only because we're best friends and that's all."

"Rubbish," he growls, stepping into my space so close that I could easily touch him. His hard eyes pin me to my spot as he says, "I know you think I'm not all in with you, or that you think you know what I'm feeling. But you don't, Poppy. You can't possibly. This right here"—he touches the beam on the overhead porch—"This little house I made with about six other blokes because I'm a shit carpenter…I made this because I want to bring our child here to play. I want to tell her…or him everything you and I did here together as best friends. All the adventures we created. All the fun we had. And I don't want to do that by myself. I want to do that with you."

"Booker," I say with a sigh. "This playhouse is extraordinary, but I want more than a friend. I want love."

"You can have that with me, Poppy!" he growls and shoves a raw, callused hand through his hair, exhaling heavily and moving closer to me. The smell of sweat and dirt radiate off of him, and my traitorous body wants to move in and rub his scent all over me.

"Poppy, you are everything I want as a man and everything I took for granted as a boy."

Shaking my head in frustration, I reply "I don't even know what that means!"

"That's why I brought you here," he growls. "We missed so many kisses growing up. Kisses I should have given you, but I was too stupid to understand what real love was at the time."

My breath inhales sharply at the word love coming out of his mouth so easily. "What did you just say?" I stammer. Surely he didn't mean to say it.

"I'm going to show you every single kiss we missed." He leans in, his breath warm on my neck as he whispers in my ear, "Like the first time we met kiss, when you were in that dirty yellow dress and made me smile because of the way you talked to your dog, Pink, like he was a real person." He kisses me on the cheek.

I swallow hard as he pulls back and looks at me with so much affection in his eyes, it makes my legs wobble.

He licks his lips, clearly just getting started. "First cheeky kiss, when I slept over at your house and I wondered what your lips tasted like, so I snuck one while you were asleep." He leans in again and murmurs, "Close your eyes, Poppy." I do and he brushes his lips on mine so softly, it's like a feather stroke. Then he pulls away, and my eyes flutter open just in time to catch a rueful smile tugging on the corners of his mouth.

"A first date kiss, when I finally manned up and asked you out on a proper date. But I was too nervous to kiss you the way I wanted to, so I did this instead." He cups my face in his hands and then plants an awkward, chaste peck on me. I can't help but giggle.

His dimples crease into his cheeks as he watches me laugh. "A horny teenager kiss."

My mouth tightens with excitement, but then he surprises me completely when he dips his head to my neck and sucks so hard, I yelp in pain. "Booker!"

He pulls back and fails to conceal his cocky smile as I rub the love bite that I'm sure he's left there. "What?" he asks, laughing.

"You're a cheeky sod," I grumble in a scolding tone.

He watches me fuss for a moment. Then his smile slowly fades, revealing that his mind has moved on to the next kiss. He exhales a shaky breath and whispers, "A first *real* kiss."

Looking nervously into my eyes, he moves his hands down to my waist and pulls me flush against him. My hands land on his chest as he finds my expectant lips and swiftly parts them with his tongue. A soft whimper slips out of my throat as he deepens the kiss, his tongue urgent and coaxing. My body melts into his as he tightens his grip around me, commanding me in his tight hold.

Without warning, he breaks the kiss. I'm breathing heavily as our eyes find each other, half closed and half turned on until his face grows serious. He suddenly looks sad. Greif evident in the pupils of his eyes.

"A goodbye kiss," he states, his voice raw. His eyes slam shut as he bends my head back and kisses me so hard and so passionately, I think there might be bruises left in his wake. His lips beg for something heady. They beg me to be his. They beg me to stay. To let go and forget about leaving. I'm instantly transported to the day I left for Germany. He was so tortured, so surprised. And I was so determined at the time, I thought nothing could change my mind. Quite honestly, though, if he would have kissed me like this, I would have stayed forever.

When he pulls away, his eyes are glassy and it breaks my heart. He sniffs and says, "A new beginnings kiss." He strokes the backs of his fingers down my cheeks and kisses me softly. Timid and gentle at first, but then he strengthens it like he did our first night together.

We separate after a moment, both panting. But he's not done. He reaches forward and strokes my belly. The sensation causes a knot to form in my throat as he says, "The mother of my child kiss." I brace myself for a kiss on my lips again, but instead, he bends over and presses his lips to my small belly.

A sob bubbles from my throat. I can't help it. It's the realest this entire thing has ever felt, and hearing him recognise the baby is more emotional than I could've ever imagined.

When he rises, tears are streaming down his face. A face that I've loved for so long, I can't remember a time I didn't love it. Can I really let myself go with him after a lifetime of love not being reciprocated?

"Booker—"

"These are all the kisses I owed you throughout our friendship. But the most important kiss of all…The one I've been denying since the day we met, Poppy McAdams, is the I love you kiss. The real, soul-ruining kind of love. The kind where you feel like you're free-falling and it's thrilling but scary as hell. Or maybe that's just how it is for me.

This is where I first felt it for you, Poppy. Not the day you moved back to London., and not the day you told me two weeks ago. I've felt it for most of my life. I'm only sorry it took me until now to realise it."

He steps closer and cups my cheeks, saying the words I've been aching to hear. "I am completely in love with you, Sunshine."

Those words. Never have I known how powerful words are until this moment.

My breath.

My heart.

My soul.

My entire world shifts as he erases the distance between us and presses his lips to mine, causing me to crumble inside. Every brick that I built up against my feelings for Booker turn to dust and create a swirling storm of complete love and devotion for this man. No longer a boy. No longer a best friend.

Booker Harris is the man I love and the man who loves me back.

Like Old Times

Booker

Fuck me, I think kisses taste better with love because Poppy's lips have never tasted so bloody good. I want to pull her into the playhouse and kiss her all night long, but it's not all up to me.

I hurt her. A lot. And I hurt her when she was the most vulnerable she's ever been. She needed me and, like a sod, I let her walk away. For a bloke who's terrified of losing people, I've sure seen more of Poppy's back than I ever care to again.

Needing to hear how she feels, I regretfully break our kiss. Her lips are raw and parted as she sucks in huge gulps of air. I take a minute to appreciate her in front of me. She's as beautiful as ever. Maybe even more so with her flushed cheeks and the red mark forming on her neck. Her dress hangs on by two thin straps, revealing her delicate neck and shoulders. I want to press my lips to every inch of her skin, but I need to know that we're okay first.

"Poppy, will you say something?" I croak, swallowing nervously. "I've kind of laid it all out there, but you have yet to say much of anything. I hope after all this you see that I'm serious about us because I really do love you. I love you so much that if you try to walk away again, I'm going to have to follow you and embarrass you wherever you go."

Poppy's giggle brings comfort to my heart, but like the greedy sod I am, I need more.

"Please, Sunshine," I beg. "Say something."

Her smile fades and she tilts her head, her eyes sweeping over every part of my face, like she's seeing me in a whole new light. "I can see you mean it. And I'm relieved, Booker, because there is seriously no one else in this world I could love more than you."

I close my eyes and let her words soar through me. For a keeper who's not used to shooting, I feel like I just scored the best goal of my life. I want to throw her over my shoulder and cheer so loudly that my family can hear it from our house. Hell, I even consider dropping down and doing the worm in a victory dance if only Tanner were nearby.

Instead, I wrap my arms around her waist and lift her up above my head. I spin her in a circle and the sound of her raspy laugh makes me feel like I've won the World Cup for my team. Her short blonde locks fan over her face like a halo as she looks down and kisses me.

"I love you, Booker," she murmurs against my lips.

I set her down so I can kiss her back and reply, "I love you, too." It feels good to say. Easier than I ever expected. The feelings have always been there. I just denied myself the words.

"Thank you for this." She looks at the playhouse with tears in her eyes. "I can hardly believe you managed all of this."

"I had a lot of help," I state, threading her hand in mine and leading her over to the covered porch. "Come on, let me show you more."

I open the tiny, crooked door to show her what's been set up inside. While we were working, Vi brought out a stack of thick, cosy blankets, some throw pillows, a lantern, and a picnic basket. She gave me a hug and said we could skip Sunday dinner just this once. The proud look on her face was all I needed to continue with this crazy plan.

And it all worked. Poppy's face as she steps inside and drops down on the floor is awestruck. She touches the walls—a natural knotty cedar plank provided by Brody and Theo. The tipped over tree ended up on the roof as quaint, half-circle shingles. It turned out to be bloody perfect. I never could have done it without them.

Poppy's eyes are teary as she rubs her finger over the carving I put on one of the walls. It reads: BOOKER LOVES POPPY. A bit cheesy to be sure, but fitting, considering our history together as children.

We sit on top of the plush blankets. The inside is just long enough for me to stretch out on my side as I prop myself on a pillow. Poppy sits crisscross and continues to marvel at the small space. The sun slips behind the horizon, so I flick on the lantern and the tiny room is bathed in a soft yellow light.

"You really fancy seeing our child play in here?" she asks, soft shadows darkening half of her face.

Hearing her say "our child" sends a rush of adrenaline through my body. "I hope so."

Her face looks nervous. "So, does this mean you're excited to have a baby?"

Frowning, I reply, "Of course I am. Aren't you?"

She fiddles with the seam of a throw pillow on her lap. "This isn't precisely the way I wanted it to happen. I haven't even started my proper job yet. We're both so young. You said before you didn't even want children."

The anxiety on her face has me pulling her down on the ground next to me. We both lie on our sides facing each other with our hands fisted between our chests. It reminds me of all the sleepovers we had growing up. All the times we fell asleep staring at one another. I really have loved her forever.

"Poppy," I state, tucking a loose piece of hair behind her ear. "When I said I didn't want children, it was because I was scared."

"Scared of what exactly?" she asks, her voice timid.

I pull her to me, my hand resting on the dip of her waist, our legs tangling around each other. "Do you remember that match you came to of mine? The one where you held Rocky in the stands next to Vi?"

She frowns and nods, so I clear my throat to continue. "When I saw you up there with my family that day, I thought you looked like the most beautiful mum I'd ever seen. You looked so at ease and so happy. It came naturally to you. All of the sudden, I saw your whole future having marriage, kids, parks, play dates, holidays. Everything. And it terrified me because I didn't think I was capable of that life. You need a lot of love to have a family, and I've always felt a bit… broken in that regard."

Her green eyes gaze into mine, fear etched in the crinkle between her brows. "And now?"

"Now that I realise how in love with you I am, having a baby feels like the best way to share that love. I want kids with you, Poppy. Hell, I want loads of 'em. Enough to make a footy team maybe."

"Oh God!" she shrieks and giggles, tears slipping out of her eyes. "I think we should start with one and see how we do."

"Fair enough," I reply and watch her laughter die down. "Does that mean you're happy about the baby? I haven't asked how you feel about everything. What's been going through your mind since you left my flat?"

She exhales, her full lower lip pulled back in between her teeth for a minute before she replies, "Well, I'm terrified to tell my parents, mostly because I think my dad might try to murder you."

My whole body tenses at the way she says the last bit so matter-of-factly. "Surely your dad wouldn't kill the father of his future grandchild." I swallow slowly, hoping Poppy will put my mind at ease.

"Well, I would hope not." Her nose wrinkles and it brings me no comfort. She continues, "But aside from that, I want this baby. It's been quite easy to dream about how wonderful it could be. No matter how hard I tried to be mad at you this week, I couldn't help but envision the baby with your dimples and intense passion. And maybe my green eyes and imagination. I even thought about what a great playmate Rocky will be. You know how my mind gets carried away sometimes…I don't know…I can see us being a happy family together."

"Of course we can," I state, wrapping my hand around her side and pulling her closer so our bodies are flush with each other. "I want exactly that. I know this all came as a shock, but you're my best friend, Poppy. I feel like, together, there's nothing we can't do."

She smiles and cups my cheek. "I agree."

I stroke her cheek and move in to press my lips to hers when an errant thought pops in my mind. I murmur, "I'm going to need you to cancel the lease on your flat, though."

She stops kissing me and pulls back with a frown. "Why mine? Why not yours?"

I chuckle and kiss her forehead. "Fine, I'll cancel mine and live in yours if you'd like."

She huffs with indignation, clearly not happy with my reply. "So we're going to move in together all in one go? We've barely dated!"

I give her a quizzical look. "Poppy, we've known each other our whole lives, we're already living together, and we're having a baby. I'm pretty sure we've covered all the steps."

She growls another little noise of frustration. It's adorable. "Well, you could bloody try to work for it and woo me a bit first!"

My jaw drops and I gesture animatedly to the space we're lying in. "I just built you a playhouse!"

Undeterred, she replies, "And I love it, but you're talking about living together like it's a bloody bill you have to pay."

With a growl, I grab her face and kiss her hard, my lips pulling into a smile as I do because I love her even when she's mad. When she finally relaxes and wraps a leg around my hip, I pull back and look deeply into her eyes as I say, "I want to live with the woman I love so I can wake up next to her every day and touch the baby we've created together." My hand finds her flat stomach. "So, Poppy McAdams, my Sunshine, my best friend, will you please move in with me?"

"That's the ticket!" she sings and rolls herself on top of me, peppering my face with giggles and happy kisses. "Was it so hard to put a bit of effort into it?"

"No," I reply with a laugh. "And I'll give you a lifetime of effort if that's what it takes."

Clearly pleased with my answer, she spreads her legs to straddle me. Her dress rides up her thighs as she begins wiggling her hips. Smiling the whole time, she turns our happy moment into a sexy one. She throws her head back and runs her hands through her hair, mussing it up in a way that gives my dick a jolt of awareness.

Dropping her chin to lock eyes with me, her palms slide slowly down her neck and over her chest. She places her hands on my abs to use me for balance as she gyrates her hot centre on top of me. My dick presses against the back of my zipper with every roll of her hips. Reaching up, she hooks each of her spaghetti straps with her thumbs and pulls them down over her shoulders. When she slides the dress down lower and reveals her gorgeous bare chest, I can't sit and watch a second longer.

My hands glide up her stomach, over her ribs, and cup the exquisite weight of her breasts. She bites her lip and swivels her hips over my rock-hard cock.

"Booker," she groans holding my hands against her chest. "Make love to me."

I sit up and band my arms around her waist, devouring her neck with my lips. "I'd love nothing more, Poppy."

Just as my hand slips into the back of her thong, a loud knock blasts through the tiny playhouse.

"Oi, you two! Get your arses decent and get out of there right now," an unfamiliar male voice bellows from outside.

Poppy's wide, terrified eyes find mine as she grapples with the straps of her dress. Trying not to smile, I look out the window to see the man walking away from the playhouse.

"Fuck me," I whisper, noticing his uniform. "It's the park warden."

"No!" Poppy exclaims, her hand covering her mouth.

Squinting out again, I reply, "Christ, I think it's the same one from when we were kids."

"How is that possible?" Poppy shrieks in a whisper. "He was old even then!"

The two of us giggle and fumble to get ourselves decent. Poppy fixing her dress, me fixing my erection. We make our way out, and I see all the lanterns have already burned out. I assume the old man must have seen the light from the playhouse.

When we walk over to stand in front of him, we must look the picture of guilty because the short, chubby old man blasts his torch in our faces and barks out, "Where the hell did this building come from?"

I squint against the light and hold up my lantern to get a proper look at him. It really is him. The same short, paunchy old git who busted us in the park after hours when we were kids. His hair is white now instead of grey, but he looks as grumpy as he did back then.

"I built it," I reply, holding my hand up to block his light.

"This park is owned by the council. You don't have the clearance to build anything out here." I wince at that little tidbit I never considered, but he's not done. "Who are you and where do you live?"

Scrunching up my face in shame, I reply, "I'm Booker Harris. My dad is Vaughn Harris. He's one of the homeowners whose property backs up to this park.

"Oh, bollocks," he growls. "You're not a Harris."

Frowning, I reply, "I assure you, I am."

"All right, take me to the Harris house then. We'll see whom you belong to." He makes a gross throat clearing noise as he flicks his light away from us.

Shaking my head, I reach over and wrap my arm around Poppy. This is certainly not the way I expected our night to end. I lead us on the path toward the back of my dad's property. The park warden shines his torch on our backs as we trudge through the trees.

Poppy whispers in my ear, "I feel like I'm twelve all over again."

Smiling, I whisper back, "Me, too. Blue balls and all."

She pokes me in the ribs as we reach the back gate. I open it and we make our way through the garden toward the kitchen entrance. I can see my family sitting down at the table, preparing to eat. Vi is the first to notice us and gestures for everyone to look. *God, we must look like naughty children.*

I open the door and Poppy scampers in, avoiding everyone's eyes on us. She crosses her arms over her chest and looks as awkward as I feel as she stands by the wall.

My father stands abruptly, his grey eyes narrowing on the sight before him. "Dad, you may remember the park warden," I grimace. "He, erm…doesn't believe I'm a Harris."

Dad scoffs, "This is my youngest, Booker Harris, and I'm Vaughn Harris, owner of this home. What's going on here?"

The warden's cheeks flame red with embarrassment, but he maintains his stance as he replies, "Well, I caught these two being indecent in the woods after hours, inside some sort of structure. The park is owned by the council. Unless he had a permit to build, which I'm certain he didn't, that structure has to be taken down."

Dad lets out a haughty laugh. "Are you referring to the playhouse my boys spent the last two days building around the clock?"

"That's the one," the warden nods. "It's an unapproved structure and it must be disposed of."

"Well, we'll call it a donation to the park," Dad retorts.

The warden shakes his head. "That's not how it works, Mr. Harris. The council has rules about unapproved structures. There will be a fine, and it's going to have to be taken down immediately."

My heart sinks, but Dad doesn't seem the least bit put off. "I'll talk to the council myself."

The growly man looks around the room at everyone and huffs,

"You Harrises still have absolutely no respect for the law."

"We have the utmost respect for that park," Tanner dejects. "That dead tree had been out there for years and the council never once saw it fit to remove it."

"Yeah," Camden adds. "It was a safety hazard, and we took care of it and beautified the area with it."

"We'll handle the fees and then some," Gareth's voice booms. "Surely the council wouldn't resist a monetary donation."

Hearing my brothers stand up for me has me finding my voice as well. "And surely other families that frequent the park would enjoy that playhouse."

"Exactly!" Vi adds, lifting Rocky out of her high chair. "My daughter for one."

The warden's head snaps all around as my family chirps out their arguments. He stammers, "I'm not sure this is the kind of problem you can throw money at."

"We'll be sure to find out," Dad replies, narrowing his eyes at the man. "Now if you'll excuse us, Sunday is family day. And as you've said, the park is closed, so nothing can be done about it tonight. We'll address it first thing tomorrow."

Tanner strides over to the door and opens it, gesturing with his hand for the warden to exit. From the doorway, the old man looks back over his shoulder and scoffs, "You Harrises. Thick as thieves and dirty as 'em, too."

Tanner chortles. "Yeah, we're wicked villains building adorable playhouses for children. Be sure to write that up in your report."

When the door closes, everyone bursts into laughter.

"I can't believe that old man is still alive and kicking," Dad states, trying to cover his laugh with his hand.

"His temperament certainly hasn't improved with time," Vi adds with a snicker.

Tanner is the next to speak. "What were you guys doing out there that got him all hot and bothered anyway?"

I look over at Poppy, who's laughing so hard with everyone, she has tears streaming down her face. Eating up the space between us, I wrap her in my arms and kiss her forehead. "Nothing you dirty thieves wouldn't have done."

Everyone continues laughing and cracking jokes as they begin to clean up their dinner mess. Poppy is pulled away to chat with Belle and Indie. As I watch her with affection, Dad's eyes find mine. He head nods for me to join him outside.

We make our way through the door, the back patio area dark, illuminated only by the light from inside. Still able to hear the muted laughter of everyone, Dads asks, "Are you ready to tell me what's going on?" He looks at me curiously. "All I know is that you had to build a playhouse for Poppy. Your brothers and sister have been pretty tight-lipped about the rest, which is completely unusual for them, so I figure it must be big."

I tug on my earlobe and wince, trying to find the right words but knowing there are no right words when you tell your dad you're going to have a baby that wasn't planned. "Well, Dad, remember how you said the other day that you want more grandchildren?"

His eyes fly wide. "Poppy isn't—"

"She's pregnant." I finish his question with a statement and grip the back of my neck. There's so much more I need to tell him. So much I need him to understand. But Dad and I don't really talk like this, so it all feels a bit weird. "I'm sure this isn't the way you wanted grandbabies, considering we're not married and all that, but it's happening. And believe it or not, I'm chuffed to bits over it. Dad, Poppy is…my best friend. She's family and I love her. I'm quite sure I've loved her forever, but that isn't an emotion I embrace easily. Now that I have, I can't help but feel excited about this adventure with her. We'll figure out—"

My words are cut off when my dad wraps me up into a huge bear hug. Shock and confusion are my first reactions because my dad is not a hugger. He's not affectionate. He's usually stoic and stiff and…

not a hugger! He squeezes me so hard, my surprised laughter is muffled by his shoulder.

He claps my back heartily and pulls back, looking at me with his glassy, grey eyes. "I'm chuffed to bits, too, son."

"You are?" I ask, struggling to believe his reaction.

He nods and I swear I see real tears forming in his eyes. "Another grandbaby for me, a cousin for Rocky…Yeah, Booker, I'm happy."

"But I'm not doing it the proper way," I stammer, thinking maybe he doesn't understand what's going on. "You were angry when you first found out Vi was pregnant."

His face tightens. "Well, she's my only daughter. And that was before I held that little baby in my arms." He looks back toward the house, his eyes finding Rocky who's currently in Gareth's arms. "I had forgotten how much little babies light me up inside, Book. I had forgotten that's why your mum and I had so many together. Every baby she had brought another smile crease to her face. I loved those creases, son."

His voice catches and my eyes well with tears. Hearing him speak so openly about Mum is such a rarity. And while I don't have any memories of her myself, she's still a huge part of my life that I mourn.

Dad wraps one arm around me and says, "She'd be proud of you, and she'd love Poppy." His smile turns down as a tear slips out and falls over his crease-covered face. "This isn't a cause for tears. This is a cause for celebration."

He turns and drags me back inside, surprising everyone when he shouts, "I'm going to be a granddad again!" We all laugh nervously at his outburst because it is so uncharacteristic for him. "Vi, do we have champagne?"

Vi beams. "I think there is a bottle in the fridge."

"Well, get it out. We have some celebrating to do." His eyes scan the room and land on Poppy, who has a timid smile on her face. He walks over to her, grabs her by the shoulders, and kisses her on the temple. "Pour some milk for the new mummy-to-be."

He hugs her and I think my heart explodes inside of my chest at the sight. My three brothers all wrap her up into a group hug next. Even grumpy Gareth cracks a smile. As Poppy is passed off to Vi, who gives her an affectionate squeeze, Hayden comes over and pats me on the back. We look at each other and have a silent conversation of understanding because they went through the same thing. He's not looking at me like the youngest Harris Brother who's in way over his head. He's looking at me like a man who's about to become a father. And what a wild adventure that will be.

When Poppy first emailed me about coming home, I said it was destiny's way of bringing us back together to rekindle our friendship. However, I think destiny must be laughing at us because she had a much grander plan all along.

I guess things work out for a reason. For most of my life, I thought I had to close my net off to others because the fear of letting too many in and losing control was overwhelming. But what I've realised is that opening my heart and allowing myself to love Poppy is like being caught by a beautiful safety net.

And that's a goal I'm willing to let slip by.

Safe Hands

Booker
Seven Months Later

ANY GOALIE WILL TELL YOU THAT IT'S NOT THE HIGH SHOT THAT is the hardest to save, but the knee-high blast to a corner, where quickness and explosiveness really come into play. My coach always said I had great hands, but my explosiveness was only good. And good can be the enemy of great.

I guess that's how I was with Poppy. I had the hands to be a great friend, but I needed the explosiveness to go all in with her. To love her fully. To give her my everything.

And now that I have, everything seems easy.

Lying on her back beside me, Poppy is out cold. Her breaths heavy, her lips parted. A soft snore exhales through her teeth every once in a while that makes me stifle a laugh. Her hair is longer now, growing crazy fast due to all the pregnancy hormones. But she says she doesn't intend to let it get much longer, which is fine by me. She's growing in other ways that I appreciate as well.

I stare down at her protruding stomach that I've been watching for the last ten minutes because our little future footy star in there is kicking up a storm. Poppy's skin pulls and stretches with every move our little boy makes. I can't believe she can sleep through the acrobatics going on in there.

God, she's beautiful.

And not just because her breasts have grown two cup sizes over the last several months. Because she's holding a piece of our love inside of her. A piece of our friendship. A mini Booker and Poppy.

Not a mini Andrew like our nosey neighbour downstairs likes to jest.

The excitement I feel over meeting our little boy is unlike anything I ever imagined. I didn't fully realise how incredible this experience would be. The scan when I first saw him was fantastic, but it paled in comparison to the first time I felt him move inside of Poppy. Then it all became real. I couldn't get the baby room finished fast enough.

I'm going to be a dad.

Poppy and I are going to be parents.

This baby isn't even born yet, and it's already given me the best gift of all. It's completely opened my heart.

It didn't take me long to realise that I loved Poppy even before we found out about the baby. But the fact that she's the one giving this experience to me has brought us even closer than I thought possible.

Exhaling heavily, I whisper to her stomach, "I love you. I love you. I love you. I love you."

"What are you doing?" Poppy groans with a sleepy giggle, her raspy voice deep from lack of use.

I cringe for waking her and answer, "I thought you were asleep."

"I'm a top-notch performer, Lamb Chop. I can fool even the best of them."

I chuckle against her stomach. "I'm just practicing." I drop a kiss to our future keeper and move up to do the same to Poppy's lips.

"Practicing for what?" she asks, reaching up to run her hands through my hair.

My lips pull into a smirk. "Practicing the words while it's still just the two of us and I have the time. I think I'm getting quite good at saying them."

Her long lashes fan her face as she blinks. "Well, don't be practicing when I'm not awake to hear them. I'll never tire of how they sound."

I look into her eyes and tuck a piece of hair behind her ear. "I'm pretty much crazy in love with you. And I'm going to marry you, you know."

She inhales sharply. "Steady on. You've just gotten the hang of loving me and we're due to have a baby in a couple of weeks. I think we have plenty of time for marriage."

"That's perfectly fine," I reply with ease. "I'll wait as long as you need me to, but I'm certain about what I want and it won't change. I want to marry you, Sunshine. And it has nothing to do with the fact that we're going to have a baby together."

"Are you sure about that?" she teases and pokes my lips with her finger.

"Completely." I kiss her fingertip and stare into her green eyes. "It's quite logical because I haven't forgotten that we're supposed to make sure each other gets to Heaven."

Her jaw drops, the precious words from our youth turning her into a statue. Smiling, I move up, drop a kiss on her lips, and add, "The way I see it, it's easier to keep track of each other with rings on our fingers."

Tears slip down her temples as she slides her hands through my hair. Looking up at me with glassy eyes, her voice trembles when she utters, "I'm so in love with you, Booker Harris."

"I'm so in love with you, Poppy McAdams." I kiss her palm and then move down to kiss her stomach. "And I love you, too, little one. You're going to hear that a lot growing up, so get used to it."

She laughs and then laughs some more. Then she stops laughing because I kiss the laugh off her face. As our lips fuse together, a smile of complete happiness tugs on the corners of my mouth.

I get to kiss these lips forever…

…because my best friend is a keeper.

THE END

Gareth Harris is finally coming next!

Be sure to sign up for my newsletter to be notified of the release date:
www.AmyDawsAuthor.com

Keeper is part of my Harris Brothers novels and a spin-off of the London Lovers Series.
Hayden & Vi, Tanner & Belle, and Camden & Indie all have stories available! *Even Brody and Theo have stories too!* Read on for the full reading order of my series standalones and get lost in my wonderful world of London.

MORE BOOKS BY AMY DAWS

The London Lovers Serie:
Becoming Us: Finley's Story Part 1
A Broken Us: Finley's Story Part 2
London Bound: Leslie's Story
Not the One: Reyna's Story

A London Lovers/Harris Brothers Crossover Novel:
Strength: Vi Harris & Hayden's Story

The Harris Brothers Series:
Challenge: Camden's Story
Endurance: Tanner's Story
Keeper: Booker's Story
Surrender & Dominate: Gareth's Duet

Payback: A Harris Brother Spin-off Standalone
Blindsided: A Harris Brother Spin-off Standalone
Replay: A Harris Brother Spin-off Standalone
Sweeper: A Secret Harris Brother Standalone

The Wait With Me Series:
Wait With Me: A Tire Shop Rom-Com
Next in Line: A Bait Shop Rom-Com
One Moment Please: A Hospital Cafeteria Rom-Com
Take A Number: A Bakery Rom-Com

Pointe of Breaking: A College Dance Standalone by Amy Daws &
Sarah J. Pepper

Chasing Hope: A Mother's *True* Story of Loss, Heartbreak,
and the Miracle of Hope

For all retailer purchase links, visit:
www.amydawsauthor.com

Acknowledgements

I am so crazy lucky to have such an amazing support system that allows me to write these books! These people make my books better, and this is my time to thank all those beautiful souls.

For starters, my alpha readers! Every book-writing process is different, and I needed a lot of hand-holding on this one. Writing a best friends to lovers story is a lot of pressure. There's so much history between a couple. It's not the simple boy meets girl story idea that I'm used to. It's a lot of depth and backstory, and I needed to get it right for Booker and Poppy. So big, big thanks to Jaci, Julia, Bethy, Jen, and Karla for early reading and chatting with me about these characters like they were real!

To my beta readers, Megan and Franci! Thank you guys for giving me awesomely insightful feedback!

To Lynsey, my special British sounding board. Bruv, you so Britty!

Nana Malone. Thank you for all the mad cool craft talk. With every book, I need to up my game and you help me do that. Next time I see you, I'm coming in for a big hug. You can't stop me.

To my proofers, Lydia and Kirsty and anyone else who agreed to lay eyeballs on it last minute (Dawn and Gemma). Thank you!

My editor extraordinaire, Stephanie. Thank you for knowing my characters and my series inside and out. Thank you for keeping track of the way everyone says hello. Thank you for keeping notebooks of my Harris Brothers and London Lovers. And thank you for continuing to push me.

Thanks to my formatter, Stacey at Champagne Book Designs, who is literally the easiest money I ever spend on a book!

To my husband, a.k.a Brother Joseph when his beard is looking extra Amishy. Thank you, my love. Thanks for taking Lolo to the lake so I could write. Thanks for working around my writing schedule.

And thanks for not patronizing me when I think my book belongs in the bottom of a burn barrel. We get better with every book, don't we, babe?

To my Lolo Hope. My kid. I can't believe you're five now. Your fun imagination inspired parts of Poppy's personality because you are my favorite person in the whole entire world. Never stop telling the teachers at school that Mommy says you can pee in the lake because you totally can. It's fine.

To my special six. My sky babies. Being a mom was my ultimate dream and losing six babies could have ruined me. But you six were the reason I started writing to begin with. Thank you for giving me my words. I've written close to a million words now, and it's all because of my angels.

MORE ABOUT THE AUTHOR

Number 1 Amazon Bestselling author Amy Daws writes spicy love stories that take place in America, as well as across the pond. She's most known for her footy-playing Harris Brothers and writing in a tire shop waiting room. When Amy is not writing, she's likely making charcuterie boards from her home in South Dakota where she lives with her daughter and husband.

Follow Amy on all social media channels, including Tik Tok under @amydawsauthor

For more of Amy's work, visit: www.amydawsauthor.com

www.ingramcontent.com/pod-product-compliance
Lightning Source LLC
Chambersburg PA
CBHW051253210726
48287CB00002B/482